"A FANTASY DONE WITH
COMMENDABLE RESTRAINT . . .
ECOTOPIA
SHOULD BECOME THE WORD FOR
ENVIRONMENTALISTS."

—San Francisco Examiner

"Nearly every sentence offers yet another sensible proposal, giving the book substantial density . . . As a first primer for how to get it together as a stable-state, humanitarian society, it is the best book I've seen yet."

—Not Man Apart (Friends of the Earth)

"Freakish and daring fiction."

—San Francisco Chronicle

BANTAM NEW AGE BOOKS

This important imprint includes books in a variety of fields and disciplines and deals with the search for meaning, growth and change. They are books that circumscribe our times and our future.

Ask your bookseller for the books you have missed.

THE ART OF BREATHING by Nancy Zi
THE CASE OF REINCARNATION by Joe Fisher
THE COSMIC CODE by Heinz R. Pagels
CREATIVE VISUALIZATION by Shakli Gawain
THE DANCING WU LI MASTERS by Gary Zukav
DON'T SHOOT THE DOG: HOW TO IMPROVE YOURSELF AND OTHERS THROUGH BEHAVIORAL TRAINING by Karen Pryor
ECOTOPIA by Ernest Callenbach
AN END TO INNOCENCE by Sheldon Kopp
ENTROPY by Jeremy Rifkin with Ted Howard
FOCUSING by Dr. Eugene T. Gendlin
THE HEART OF HEALING by Bruce Davis and Genny Wright Davis
HERE I AM, WASN'T I!: THE INEVITABLE DISRUPTION OF EASY TIMES by Sheldon Kopp
HOW TO IMAGINE: A NARRATIVE ON ART AND AGRICULTURE by Gianfranco Baruchello and Henry Martin
I CHING: A NEW INTERPRETATION FOR MODERN TIMES by Sam Reifler
IF YOU MEET THE BUDDHA ON THE ROAD, KILL HIM! by Sheldon Kopp
IN SEARCH OF SCHRODINGER'S CAT by John Gribbin
IN SEARCH OF THE BIG BANG: QUANTUM PHYSICS AND COSMOLOGY by John Gribbin
INFINITY AND THE MIND by Rudy Rucker
KISS SLEEPING BEAUTY GOODBYE by Madonna Kolbenschlag
THE LIVES OF A CELL by Lewis Thomas
LIVING WITH NUCLEAR WEAPONS by Carnesale/Doty/Hoffman/Huntington/Nye and Sagan
MAGICAL CHILD by Joseph Chilton Pearce
MAGICAL CHILD MATURES by Joseph Chilton Pearce
THE MEDUSA AND THE SNAIL by Lewis Thomas
METAMAGICAL THEMAS: QUESTING FOR THE ESSENCE OF MIND AND PATTERN by Douglas R. Hofstadter
MIND AND NATURE by Gregory Bateson
THE MIND'S I by Douglas R. Hofstadter and Daniel C. Dennett
MISSILE ENVY by Dr. Helen Caldicott
NEPTUNE'S REVENGE: THE OCEAN OF TOMORROW by Anne W. Simon
NEW RULES by Daniel Yankelovich
ON HUMAN NATURE by Edward O. Wilson
THE ONE-STRAW REVOLUTION by Masanobu Fukuoka
ORDER OUT OF CHAOS by Ilya Prigogine and Isabelle Stengers
PROSPERING WOMAN by Ruth Ross
REENCHANTMENT OF THE WORLD by Morris Berman
SILICO SAPIENS by Joseph Deken
STRESS AND THE ART OF BIOFEEDBACK by Barbara B. Brown
SUPERMIND by Barbara B. Brown
SYMPATHETIC VIBRATIONS: REFLECTIONS ON PHYSICS AS A WAY OF LIFE by K. C. Cole
THE TAO OF LEADERSHIP by John Heider
THE TAO OF PHYSICS, Revised Edition, by Fritjof Capra
TO HAVE OR TO BE? by Eric Fromm
THE TURNING POINT by Fritjof Capra
THE WAY OF THE SHAMAN: A GUIDE TO POWER AND HEALING by Michael Harner
ZEN AND THE ART OF MOTORCYCLE MAINTENANCE by Robert M. Pirsig

Ernest Callenbach

ECOTOPIA

The Notebooks and Reports of WILLIAM WESTON

A BANTAM NEW AGE BOOK

BANTAM BOOKS
TORONTO • NEW YORK • LONDON • SYDNEY • AUCKLAND

RL 10, IL age 14 and up

ECOTOPIA
A Bantam Book / published by arrangement with Banyan Tree Books

PRINTING HISTORY
Banyan Tree Books edition published January 1975
2nd printing ...... May 1975
3rd printing ..... April 1976
4th printing ...... July 1976
5th printing .. December 1976
6th printing ... April 1977

Condensations in OREGON TIMES *published October 1975 and November 1975*

Condensations in HARPER'S WEEKLY *Published May 1976*

Bantam edition / October 1977
2nd printing ... January 1978
3rd printing .. December 1978
4th printing .. November 1979
5th printing .. November 1980
6th printing .... August 1981
7th printing ...... May 1982
8th printing ... December 1982

ISBN 0-553-23471-4

Published simultaneously in the United States and Canada

Bantam Books are published by Bantam Books, Inc. Its trademark, consisting of the words "Bantam Books" and the portrayal of a rooster, is Registered in U.S. Patent and Trademark Office and in other countries. Marca Registrada. Bantam Books, Inc., 666 Fifth Avenue, New York, New York 10103.

PRINTED IN THE UNITED STATES OF AMERICA

H 17 16 15 14 13 12 11

ECO-	from the Greek *oikos* (household or home)
-TOPIA	from the Greek *topos* (place)

In nature, no organic substance is synthesized unless there is provision for its degradation; recycling is enforced.

BARRY COMMONER

ECOTOPIA

WESTON'S NEXT ASSIGNMENT: ECOTOPIA

The TIMES-POST is at last able to announce that William Weston, our top international affairs reporter, will spend six weeks in Ecotopia, beginning next week. This unprecedented journalistic development has been made possible through arrangements at the highest diplomatic level. It will mark the first officially arranged visit by an American to Ecotopia since the secession cut off normal travel and communications in 1980.

The TIMES-POST is sending Weston on this unique and difficult investigative assignment in the conviction that a candid, on-the-spot assessment of Ecotopia is essential as we enter the 21st century. Old antagonisms have too long deterred close examination of what has been happening in Ecotopia--a part of the world once near, dear and familiar to us, but closed off and increasingly mysterious during its two decades of independence.

The problem now is not so much to oppose Ecotopia as to understand it--which can only benefit the cause of international good relations. The TIMES-POST stands ready, as always, to serve that cause.

(May 3) Here we go again, dear diary. A fresh notebook with all those blank pages waiting to be filled. Good to be on the way at last. Alleghenies already receding behind us like pale green ripples on an algae-covered pond. Thinking back to the actual beginnings of this trip—almost a year ago? Those careful hints dropped at the White House like crumbs for the President's vacuum-cleaner mind to suck up. Until finally they coalesced into some kind of ball and came out as his own daring idea: okay, send some unofficial figure out there, purely informal—a reporter not too closely identified with the administration, who could nose around, blow up a few pretty trial balloons—can't hurt! A tingly moment when he finally broached it, after a big Brazil briefing session. That famous confidential smile! And then saying that he had a little adventure in mind, wanted to discuss it with me privately. . . .

Was his tentativeness only his habitual caution, or a signal that if anything went wrong the visit (and the visitor) were politically expendable?

Still, an important opening in our foreign policy—lots of weighty arguments for it. Breach that rent the nation in 1980 should be healed—so the continent can stand united against rising tide of starvation and revolution. Hawks who want to retake "lost lands of the west" by force seem to be growing stronger—need neutralizing. Ecotopian ideas are seeping over the border more dangerously—can't be ignored any longer, might be detoxified by exposure. Etc.

Maybe we can find a hearing for proposal to reopen diplomatic relations; perhaps trade proposals too. With reunification a gleam in the eye. Even just a publicizable chat with Vera Allwen could be useful—the President, with his customary flexibility, could use it to fend off both hawks and subversives. Besides, as I told Francine—who scoffed, naturally, even after three brandies—I want to see Ecotopia because it's there. Can things really be as weird there as they sound? I wonder.

Have been mulling over the no-nos. Must stay clear of the secession itself: too much bitterness could still be aroused. But fascinating stories there, probably—how the secessionists filched uranium fuel from power plants for the nuclear mines they claimed to have set in New York and Washington. How their political organization, led by those damned women, managed to paralyze and then supplant the regular political structure, and got control of the armories and the Guard. How they bluffed their way to a stand-off—helped, of course, by the severity of the national economic crisis that struck so conveniently for them. Lots of history there to be told someday—but now is not the time....

Getting harder to say goodbye to the kids when I take off on a long trip. Not that it's really such a big deal, since I sometimes miss a couple of weekends even when I'm around. But my being away so much seems to be beginning to bother them. Pat may be putting them up to it; I'll have to talk to her about that. Where else would Fay get the idea of asking to come along? Jesus—into darkest Ecotopia with typewriter and eight-year-old daughter....

No more Francine for six weeks. It's always refreshing to get away for a while, and she'll be there when I get back, all charged up by some adventure or other. Actually sort of exciting to think of being totally out of touch with her, with the editorial office, in fact with the whole country. No phone service, wire service indirect: uncanny isolation the Ecotopians have insisted on for 20 years! And in Peking, Bantustan, Brazil there always had to be an American interpreter, who couldn't help dangling ties from home. This time there'll be nobody to share little American reactions with.

And it is potentially rather dangerous. These Ecotopians are certainly hotheads, and I could easily get into serious trouble. Government's control over population seems to be primitive compared to ours. Americans are heartily hated. In a jam the Ecotopian police might be no help at all—in fact they apparently aren't even armed.

Well, ought to draft the first column. Mid-air perhaps not the worst place to begin.

WILLIAM WESTON ON HIS JOURNEY TO ECOTOPIA

On board TWA flight 38, New York to Reno, May 3. As I begin this assignment, my jet heads west to Reno—last American city before the forbidding Sierra Nevada mountains that guard the closed borders of Ecotopia.

The passage of time has softened the shock of Ecotopia's separation from the United States. And Ecotopia's example, it is now clear, was not as novel as it seemed at the time. Biafra had attempted secession from Nigeria in 1969. Bangladesh had successfully broken free of Pakistan in 1971. Ecotopia's secession in 1980 was followed by that of Quebec from Canada in 1983. Our intelligence reports tell of continual "minority" disturbances even in the Soviet Union. It is a worldwide tendency. The only important counter-development we can point to is the union of the Scandinavian countries in 1985—and even that is perhaps only an exception to prove the rule, since the Scandinavians were virtually one people culturally in any event.

Nonetheless, many Americans still remember the terrible shortages of fruit, lettuce, wine, cotton, paper, lumber, and other western products which followed the breakaway of what had been Washington, Oregon, and Northern California. These problems exacerbated the general U.S. economic depression of the period, speeded up our chronic inflation, and caused widespread dissatisfaction with government policies. Moreover, Ecotopia still poses a nagging challenge to the underlying national philosophy of America: ever-continuing progress, the fruits of industrialization for all, a rising Gross National Product.

During the past two decades, we as a people have mostly tried to ignore what has been happening in Ecotopia—in the hope it will prove to be mere foolishness and go away. It is clear by now, however, that Ecotopia is not going to collapse as many American analysts at first predicted. The time has come when we must get a clearer understanding of Ecotopia.

If its social experimentation turns out to be absurd and irresponsible, it will then no longer tempt impressionable young Americans. If its strange customs indeed prove as barbaric as rumors suggest, Ecotopia will have to pay the cost in outraged world opinion. If Ecotopian claims are false, American policy-makers can profit from knowledge of that fact. For instance, we need to assess the allegation that Ecotopia has no more deaths from air and chemical pollution. Our own death rate has declined from a peak of 75,000 annually to 30,000—still a tragic toll, but suggesting that measures of the severity adopted in Ecotopia are hardly necessary. In short, we should meet the Ecotopian challenge on the basis of sound knowledge rather than ignorance and third-hand reports.

My assignment during the next six weeks, therefore, is to explore Ecotopian life from top to bottom—to search out the realities behind the rumors, to describe in concrete detail how Ecotopian society actually operates, to document its problems and, where that is called for, to acknowledge its achievements. By direct knowledge of the situation in which our former fellow-citizens now find themselves, we may even begin to rebuild the ties that once bound them to the Union they so hastily rejected.

(May 3) Reno a sad shadow of its former goodtimes self. With the lucrative California gambling trade cut off by secession, the city quickly decayed. The fancy casino hotels are now mere flophouses—their owners long ago fled to Las Vegas. I walked the streets near the airline terminal, asking people what they thought of Ecotopia out here. Most replies noncommittal, though I thought I could sometimes detect a tinge of bitterness. "Live and let live," said one grizzled old man, "if you can call what they do over there living." A young man who claimed to be a cowboy smiled at my question. "Waaal," he said, "I know guys who say they've gone over there to get girls. It isn't really dangerous if you know the mountain passes. They're friendly all right, so long as you aren't up to anything. Know what, though? The girls all have guns! That's what they say. That could shake you up, couldn't it?"

Had a hard time finding a taxi driver willing to take me over the border. Finally persuaded one who looked as if he had just done 20 years in the pen. Had to promise not only double fare but 25 percent tip besides. For which I got a bonus of dirty looks and a string of reassuring remarks: "What ya wanta go in there for anyhow, ya some kind of a nut? Buncha goddamn cannibals in there! Ya'll never get out alive—I just hope I will."

CROSSING THE ECOTOPIAN BORDER

On board the Sierra Express, Tahoe-San Francisco, May 4. I have now entered Ecotopia—the first known American to visit the new country since its Independence, 19 years ago.

My jet landed at Reno. Though it is not widely known, the Ecotopian government prohibits even international flights from crossing its territory—on grounds of air and noise pollution. Flights between San Francisco and Asia, or over the pole to Europe, must not only use a remote airport 40 miles outside the city, but are forced to follow over-water routes; and American jets for Hawaii must fly via Los Angeles. Thus to reach San Francisco I was compelled to deplane at Reno, and take an expensive taxi ride to the train station at the north end of Lake Tahoe. From Tahoe there is frequent and fast service.

The actual frontier is marked by a picturesquely weathered wooden fence, with a large gate, obviously little used. When my taxi pulled up, there was nobody around. The driver had to get out, go over to a small stone guard-house, and get the Ecotopian military to interrupt their card game. They turned out to be two young men in rather unpressed uniforms. But they knew of my coming, they checked my papers with an air of informed authority, and they passed the taxi through the gate—though only after making a point of the fact that it had required a special dispensation to allow an internal combustion engine to pass their sacred portals. I replied that it only had to take me about 20 miles to the train station. "You're lucky the wind is from the west," one of them said. "If it happened to be from the east we might have had to hold you up for a while."

They checked my luggage with some curiosity, paying special attention to my sleeping pills. But I was allowed to keep everything except my trusty .45 and holster. This might be standard garb in New York, I was told, but no concealable weapons are permitted in Ecotopia. Perhaps noticing my slightly uneasy reaction, one of the guards remarked that Ecotopian streets are quite safe, by day or night. He then handed me a small booklet, *Ecotopia Explains.* This document was nicely printed but with rather quaint drawings. Evidently it had been prepared chiefly for tourists from Europe and Asia. "It might make things easier to get used to," said the other guard, in a soft, almost insinuatingly friendly tone that I now begin to recognize as a national trait. "Relax, it's a free country."

"My friend," I countered, "I've been in a hell of a lot stranger places than this country and I relax when I feel like it. If you're finished with my papers, I'll be on my way."

He snapped my passport shut, but held it in his hand. "Weston," he said, looking me in the eye, "You're a writer. We count on you to use words carefully while you're here. If you come back this way, maybe you'll be able to use that word 'friend' in good faith. We'd like that." He then smiled warmly and put out his hand. Rather to my surprise, I took it and found a smile on my own face as well.

We drove on, to the Tahoe station of the Ecotopian train system. It turned out to be a rustic affair, constructed of huge timbers. It might pass in America for a monstrous ski chalet. It even had fireplaces in the waiting rooms—of which there are several, one a kind of restaurant, one a large, deserted room with a bandstand where dances must be held, and one a small, quiet lounge with leather chairs and a supply of books. The trains, which usually have only two or three cars but run about every hour, come into the basement of the station, and in cold weather huge doors close behind them to keep out the snow and wind.

Special facilities for skiers were evident—storage racks and lockers—but by this time of year the snows have largely melted and there is little skiing. The electric minibuses that shuttle from the station to ski resorts and nearby towns are almost empty.

I went down to my train. It looked more like a wingless airplane than a train. At first I thought I had gotten into an unfinished car—there were no seats! The floor was covered with thick, spongy carpet, and divided into compartments by knee-high partitions; a few passengers were sprawled on large baglike leather cushions that lay scattered about. One elderly man had taken a blanket from a pile at one end of the car, and laid down for a nap. Some of the others, realizing from my confusion that I was a foreigner, showed me where to stow my bag and told me how to obtain refreshments from the steward in the next car. I sat down on one of the pillows, realizing that there would be a good view from the huge windows that came down to about six inches from the floor. My companions lit up some cigarettes, which I recognized as marijuana from the odor, and began to pass them around. As my first gesture of international good will, I took a few puffs myself, and soon we were all sociably chatting away.

Their sentimentality about nature has even led the Ecotopians to bring greenery into their trains, which are full of hanging ferns and small plants I could not identify. (My companions however reeled off their botanical names with assurance.) At the end of the car stood containers rather like trash bins, each with a large letter—M, G, and P. These, I was told, were "recycle bins." It may seem unlikely to Americans, but I observed that during our trip my fellow travelers did without exception dispose of all metal, glass, or paper and plastic refuse in the appropriate bin. That they did so without the embarrassment Americans would experience was my first introduction to the rigid practices of recycling and re-use upon which Ecotopians are said to pride themselves so fiercely.

By the time you notice you are underway in an Ecotopian train, you feel virtually no movement at all. Since it operates by magnetic suspension and propulsion, there is no rumble of wheels or whine or vibration. People talk, there is the clink of glasses and teacups, some passengers wave to friends on the platform. In a moment the train seems literally to be flying along the ground, though it is actually a few inches above a trough-shaped guideway.

My companions told me something about the background of these trains. Apparently the Boeing company in Seattle, at the time of Independence, was still staggering along after the mauling it took in the worldwide depression of the late seventies, not to mention cancellation of the lucrative but ecologically dangerous SST project in 1971. The Ecotopian government, though its long-range economic policies called for diversification and decentralization of production in each city and region, took temporary advantage of the Boeing facilities to help build the new national train system. While the Germans and Japanese had pioneered in magnetic-suspension trains with linear motors, Boeing began production on the system only a year after Independence. When I asked how the enormous expense of the system had been financed, my companions laughed. One of them remarked that the cost of the entire roadbed from San Francisco to Seattle was about that of ten SST's, and he argued that the total social cost per person per mile on their trains was less than that for air transport at any distance under a thousand miles.

I learned from my booklet that the trains normally travel about 360 kilometers per hour on the level. (Use of the metric system is universal in Ecotopia.) You get a fair view of the countryside at this speed, which translates as about 225 miles per hour. And we only attained that speed after about 20 minutes of crawling up and over the formidable eastern slope of the Sierra Nevadas, at what seemed less than 90 miles per hour. Donner Pass looked almost as bleak as it must have to the Donner pioneer party who perished there. We made a stop at Norden and picked up a few late-season skiers—a cheerful bunch, like our skiers, but dressed in raggedy attire, including some very secondhand-looking fur jackets. They carried home-made knapsacks and primitive skis—long, thin, with flimsy old-fashioned bindings. The train then swooped down the long canyons of the Sierra forests, occasionally flashing past a river with its water bubbling blue-black and icy between the rocks. In a few minutes we slid into Auburn. The time-table, which graphically lays out the routes and approximate schedules of a complex network of connecting trains and buses, showed three stops before San Francisco itself. I was glad to notice that we halted for less than 60 seconds, even though people sauntered on and off with typical Ecotopian looseness.

Once we reached the valley floor, I saw little of interest, but my companions still seemed fascinated. They pointed out changes in the fields and forests we passed; in a wooded stretch someone spotted a doe with two fawns, and later a jackrabbit caused great amusement. Soon we entered the hilly country around San Francisco Bay, and shot through a series of tunnels in the grass-covered, breast-shaped green hills. There were now more houses, though rather scattered—many of them seeming to be small farms. The orchards, fields and fences looked healthy and surprisingly well cared for, almost like those of western Europe. Yet how dingy and unprosperous the farm buildings looked, compared to the white-painted farms of Iowa or New England! The Ecotopians must be positively allergic to paint. They build with rock, adobe, weathered boards—apparently almost anything that comes to hand, and they lack the aesthetic sense that would lead them to give such materials a coat of concealing paint. They would apparently rather cover a house with vines or bushes than paint it.

The drabness of the countryside was increased by its evident isolation. The roads were narrow and winding, with trees dangerously close to the pavement. No traffic at all seemed to be moving on them. There wasn't a billboard in sight, and not a gas station or telephone booth. It would not be reassuring to be caught in such a region after dark.

An hour and a quarter after we left Tahoe, the train plunged into a tube near the Bay shore, and emerged a few minutes later in the San Francisco main station. In my next column I will describe my first impressions of the city by the Golden Gate—where so many earlier Americans debarked to seek their fortunes in the gold fields.

(May 4) General impression: a lot of Ecotopians look like oldtime westerners, Gold Rush characters come to life. God knows we have plenty of freaky-looking people in New York, but their freakishness is self-conscious, campy, theatrical—a way of showing off. The Ecotopians are almost Dickensian: often strange enough, but not crazy-looking or sordid, as the hippies of the sixties were. Fanciful hats and hair-dos, jackets, vests, leggings, tights; so help me, I think I even saw a codpiece—either that or the guy was supernaturally endowed. There's a lot of embroidery and decorations made of small shells or feathers, and patchwork—cloth must be terribly scarce they go to such lengths to re-use it.

And their manners are even more unsettling. On the streets there are electrical moments when women stare me directly in the eyes; so far I've looked away, but what would happen if I held contact? People seem to be very loose and playful with each other, as if they had endless time on their hands to explore whatever possibilities might come up. There's none of the implicit threat of open criminal violence that pervades our public places, but there's an awful lot of strong emotion, willfully expressed! The peace of the train ride was broken several times by shouted arguments or insults; people have an insolent kind of curiosity that often leads to tiffs. It's as if they have lost the sense of anonymity which enables us to live together in large numbers. You can't, therefore, approach an Ecotopian functionary as we do. The Ecotopian at the train ticket window simply wouldn't tolerate being spoken to in my usual way—he asked me what I thought he was, a ticket-dispensing machine? In fact, he won't give you the ticket unless you deal with him as a real person, and he insists on dealing with you—asking questions, making remarks to which he expects a sincere reaction, and shouting if he doesn't get it. But most of such sound and fury seems to signify nothing. There may be dangerous lunatics among the harmless ones, but I haven't seen any yet. Just hope I can preserve my own sanity.

THE STREETS OF ECOTOPIA'S CAPITAL

San Francisco, May 5. As I emerged from the train terminal into the streets, I had little idea what to expect from this city—which had once proudly boasted of rising from its own ashes after a terrible earthquake and fire. San Francisco was once known as "America's favorite city" and had an immense appeal to tourists. Its dramatic hills and bridges, its picturesque cable cars, and its sophisticated yet relaxed people had drawn visitors who returned again and again. Would I find that it still deserves its reputation as an elegant and civilized place?

I checked my bag and set out to explore a bit. The first shock hit me at the moment I stepped onto the street. There was a strange hush over everything. I expected to encounter something at least a little like the exciting bustle of our cities—cars honking, taxis swooping, clots of people pushing about in the hurry of urban life. What I found, when I had gotten over my surprise at the quiet, was that Market Street, once a mighty boulevard striking through the city down to the waterfront, has become a mall planted with thousands of trees. The "street" itself, on which electric taxis, minibuses, and delivery carts purr along, has shrunk to a two-lane affair. The remaining space, which is huge, is occupied by bicycle lanes, fountains, sculptures, kiosks, and absurd little gardens surrounded by benches. Over it all hangs the almost sinister quiet, punctuated by the whirr of bicycles and cries of children. There is even the occasional song of a bird, unbelievable as that may seem on a capital city's crowded main street.

Scattered here and there are large conical-roofed pavilions, with a kiosk in the center selling papers, comic books, magazines, fruit juices, and snacks. (Also cigarettes—the Ecotopians have *not* managed to stamp out smoking!) The pavilions turn out to be stops on the minibus system, and people wait there out of the rain. These buses are comical battery-driven contraptions, resembling the antique cable cars that San Franciscans were once so fond of. They are driverless, and are steered and stopped by an electronic gadget that follows wires buried in the street. (A safety bumper stops them in case someone fails to get out of the way.) To enable people to get on and off quickly, during the 15 seconds the bus stops, the floor is only a few inches above ground level; the wheels are at the extreme ends of the vehicle. Rows of seats face outward, so on a short trip you simply sit down momentarily, or stand and hang onto one of the hand grips. In bad weather fringed fabric roofs can be extended outward to provide more shelter.

These buses creep along at about ten miles an hour, but they come every five minutes or so. They charge *no* fare. When I took an experimental ride on one, I asked a fellow passenger about this, and he said the minibuses are paid for in the same way as streets—out of general tax funds. Smiling, he added that to have a driver on board to collect fares would cost more than the fares could produce. Like many Ecotopians, he tended to babble, and spelled out the entire economic rationale for the minibus system, almost as if he was trying to sell it to me. I thanked him, and after a few blocks jumped off.

The bucolic atmosphere of the new San Francisco can perhaps best be seen in the fact that, down Market Street and some other streets, creeks now run. These had earlier, at great expense, been put into huge culverts underground, as is usual in cities. The Ecotopians spent even more to bring them up to ground level again. So now on this major boulevard you may see a charming series of little falls, with water gurgling and splashing, and channels lined with rocks, trees, bamboos, ferns. There even seem to be minnows in the water—though how they are kept safe from marauding children and cats, I cannot guess.

Despite the quiet, the streets are full of people, though not in Manhattan densities. (Some foot traffic has been displaced to lacy bridges which connect one skyscraper to another, sometimes 15 or 20 stories up.) Since practically the whole street area is "sidewalk," nobody worries about obstructions—or about the potholes which, as they develop in the pavement, are planted with flowers. I came across a group of street musicians playing Bach, with a harpsichord and a half dozen other instruments. There are vendors of food pushing gaily colored carts that offer hot snacks, chestnuts, ice cream. Once I even saw a juggler and magician team, working a crowd of children—it reminded me of some medieval movie. And there are many strollers, gawkers, and loiterers—people without visible business who simply take the street for granted as an extension of their living rooms. Yet, despite so many unoccupied people, the Ecotopian streets seem ridiculously lacking in security gates, doormen, guards, or other precautions against crime. And no one seems to feel our need for automobiles to provide protection in moving from place to place.

I had noticed on the train that Ecotopian clothes tend to be very loose, with bright colors striving to make up for what is lacking in style and cut. This impression is confirmed now that I have observed thousands of San Franciscans. The typical Ecotopian man wears nondescript trousers (even denim is common—perhaps from nostalgia for American fashions of the pre-secession seventies?) topped with an often hideous shirt, sweater, poncho, or jacket. Despite the usually chilly weather, sandals are common among both sexes. The women often wear pants also, but loose-flowing gypsy-like skirts are more usual. A few people wear outlandish skin-tight garments which look like diving wet-suits, but are woven of some fabric unknown to me. They may be members of some special group, as their attire is so unusual. Leather and furs seem to be favorite materials—they are used for purses and pouches, pants and jackets. Children wear miniature versions of adult clothing; there seem to be no special outfits for them.

Ecotopians setting out to go more than a block or two usually pick up one of the white-painted Provo bicycles that lie about the streets by the hundreds and are available free to all. Dispersed by the movements of citizens during the day and evening, they are returned by night crews to the places where they will be needed the next day. When I remarked to a friendly pedestrian that this system must be a joy to thieves and vandals, he denied it heatedly. He then put a case, which may not be totally far-fetched, that it is cheaper to lose a few bicycles than to provide more taxis or minibuses.

Ecotopians, I am discovering, spout statistics on such questions with reckless abandon. They have a way of introducing "social costs" into their calculations which inevitably involves a certain amount of optimistic guesswork. It would be interesting to confront such informants with one of the hard-headed experts from our auto or highway industries—who would, of course, be horrified by the Ecotopians' abolition of cars.

As I walked about, I noticed that the downtown area was strangely overpopulated with children and their parents, besides people who apparently worked in the offices and shops. My questions to passersby (which were answered with surprising patience) revealed what is perhaps the most astonishing fact I have yet encountered in Ecotopia: the great downtown skyscrapers, once the headquarters of far-flung corporations, have been turned into apartments! Further inquiries will be needed to get a clear picture of this development, but the story I heard repeatedly on the streets today is that the former outlying residential areas have largely been abandoned. Many three-story buildings had in any case been heavily damaged by the earthquake of 1982. Thousands of cheaply built row houses in newer districts (scornfully labelled "ticky-tacky boxes" by my informants) have been sacked of their wiring, glass, and hardware, and bulldozed away. The residents now live downtown, in buildings that contain not only apartments but also nurseries, grocery stores, and restaurants, as well as the shops and offices on the ground floor.

Although the streets still have an American look, it is annoyingly difficult to identify things in Ecotopia. Only very small signs are permitted on the fronts of buildings; street signs are few and hard to spot, mainly attached to buildings on corners. Finally, however, I navigated my way back to the station, retrieved my suitcase, and located a nearby hotel which had been recommended as suitable for an American, but still likely to give me "some taste of how Ecotopians live." This worthy establishment lived up to its reputation by being almost impossible to find. But it is comfortable enough, and will serve as my survival base here.

Like everything in Ecotopia, my room is full of contradictions. It is comfortable, if a little old-fashioned by our standards. The bed is atrocious—it lacks springs, being just foam rubber over board—yet it is covered with a luxurious down comforter. There is a large work table equipped with a hotplate and teapot. Its surface is plain, unvarnished wood with many mysterious stains—but on it stands a small, sleek picturephone. (Despite their aversion to many modern devices, the Ecotopians have some that are even better than ours. Their picturephones, for instance, though they have to be connected to a television screen, are far easier to use than ours, and have much better picture quality.) My toilet has a tank high overhead, of a type that went out in the United States around 1945, operated by a pull chain with a quaint carved handle; the toilet paper must be some ecological abomination—it is coarse and plain. But the bathtub is unusually large and deep. Like the tubs still used in deluxe Japanese inns, it is made of slightly aromatic wood.

I used the picturephone to confirm advance arrangements for a visit tomorrow with the Minister of Food, with whom I shall begin to investigate the Ecotopian claims of "stable-state" ecological systems, about which so much controversy has raged.

(May 5) Maybe they have *gone back to the stone age. In the early evening I saw a group of hunters, carrying fancy bows and arrows, jump off a minibus, on*

which they had loaded a recently killed deer. Two of them hoisted it up, suspended on a long stick they carried on their shoulders, and began marching along the street. (A large hunting dog padded along with them—first pet I've seen in Ecotopia, where animals are evidently left as wild as possible, and people seem to feel no need of them as company.) A crowd gathered to watch them, little boys hung around excitedly. The hunters stopped near me for a rest—and also, I suspect, to allow people to admire their kill. One of them caught my eye and must have seen disgust in it. He rubbed his hand over the deer's wound, still damp with blood, then ran his finger across my cheek, as if to implicate me in the hunt. I jumped back, shocked, and the crowd laughed in what seemed an ugly way.

Later, talking with some of the people there, I learned the group had been hunting just outside town—where, apparently, deer are numerous. The hunters looked savage enough (long knives, beards, rough clothes) but they were evidently quite ordinary citizens off on a hunt. The deer would be butchered and the meat divided: game is said to be a source of considerable meat in the Ecotopian diet; it is prized for its "spiritual" qualities!

Whether such practices are forced upon them by scarcities, or are the result of some deliberate throwback policy, I don't yet know. But the scene, in the gathering dusk, was ghoulish enough. (Most Ecotopian streets are pitch dark at night—evidently their power policies have caused them to curtail night lighting almost entirely. Can't tell why this doesn't lead to the crime panic it would bring among us. Have asked people whether they feel safe at night, and they reply Yes without hesitation—claim they can see well enough, and turn the conversation onto something irrelevant: how bicycle lights look, bobbing through the night like fireflies, or how fine it is to be able to see the stars even in the city. Good thing they don't *have cars, or the accident rates would be spectacular.)*

A little trouble with the maid last night, when she thought I took liberties. We had had a conversation about my picking some flowers on the street and bringing them up to the room. Evidently Ecotopians don't pick flowers, preferring to enjoy them where they grow, and she rather playfully set me straight on this. Maybe she was just trying to be friendly, but seemed to be giving me the eye, yet wouldn't play. Well, sublimation makes the pen grow stronger? (No, it makes me wish I could import Francine for a day or two.)

I like dressing well, but my New York clothes were making me stick out here; so have picked up a new wardrobe. Dark-green serape with a hood, soft but so tightly woven I am told it will keep off the rain (and probably make me smell like a wet sheep). A couple of loose shirts in suitably gaudy colors, a vest, a floppy suede jacket, two pairs of denim pants. Also a pair of heavy shoes—my elegant Italian street shoes clearly won't go here! I look in the mirror and laugh—if I rang Francine's doorbell in this outfit she'd call the police. (One game we've never played is rape by Ecotopian agent who sneaks into N Y and seduces woman of prominent journalist to gain secret information.)

From what I could determine on my brief shopping spree, the clothes here do not include any nylon, orlon, dacron, or other synthetics. ("I need a couple of shirts, the drip-dry kind." Incredulous clerk: "You mean some kind of synthetic fiber shirt? We haven't sold them for 20 years." Followed by a lecture to the effect that too much electric power and water are required in the production of synthetics—and also they can't be recycled.) I noticed some garments with labels proudly declaring they were "re-used wool." Both fabrics and garments all domestic-made —and the prices seem sky-high.

Don't like the fetishistic avoidance of synthetics, but I had forgotten how nice a good cotton shirt feels to the skin. This quality is emphasized by the manufacturers—they make a point that the fabrics have been washed several times before being offered for sale. . .

FOOD, SEWAGE, AND "STABLE STATES"

San Francisco, May 6. When I arrived at the Ministry of Food for my interview with the Minister, I was unhappy to find that she was too busy to see me. I was introduced instead to an Assistant Minister, a man in his early thirties, who received me in a work overalls outfit. His office was also surprisingly unimpressive for a person of importance. It had no desk, no conference table, no soft chairs. Along one wall was a cluttered series of wooden filing cases, bookshelves, and tables covered with papers in utter disorder. Against another wall was a kind of laboratory set-up, with testing equipment of various kinds.

The Assistant Minister is, like many Ecotopians, unnervingly relaxed, with a deep, slow voice. He sprawled on woven cushions in a sunny corner of the floor, under a skylight with some kind of ivy hanging near it, and his lab assistant produced hot water for tea on a bunsen burner. I squatted awkwardly, and began by asking my carefully prepared questions about Ecotopian agricultural output. These were ignored. Instead the Assistant Minister insisted on giving me "a little background." He then began to discuss, not agriculture at all, but sewage. The first major project of his ministry after Independence, he said, had been to put the country's food cycle on a stable-state basis: all food wastes, sewage and garbage were to be turned into organic fertilizer and applied to the land, where it would again enter into the food production cycle. Every Ecotopian household, thus, is required to compulsively sort all its garbage into compostable and recyclable categories, at what must be an enormous expenditure of personal effort; and expanded fleets of garbage trucks are also needed.

The sewage system inherited from the past, according to the Assistant Minister, could only be called a "disposal" system. In it sewage and industrial wastes had not been productively recycled but merely dumped, in a more or less toxic condition, into rivers, bays and oceans. This, he maintained, was not only dangerous to the public health and the life of water creatures, but its very objective was wasteful and unnatural. With a smile, he added that some of the sewage practices of earlier days would even be considered criminal if carried out today.

"In my papers over there," he said, "you can find historical reports of great sums being spent on incinerators to burn up sewage sludge. Their designers boasted of relatively smog-free stacks. We were of course accused of 'sewer socialism,' like our Milwaukee predecessors. Nonetheless, we constructed a national system of sludge drying and natural fertilizer production. After seven years we were able to dispense with chemical fertilizers entirely. This was partly through sewage recycling, partly through garbage composting, partly through reliance on some novel nitrogen-fixing crops and crop rotation, and partly through methods of utilizing animal manure. You may have seen from the train that our farm animals are not kept in close confinement like yours. We like them to live in conditions approaching the natural. But not only for sentimental reasons. It also avoids the gigantic accumulation of manure which is such a problem in your feedlots and poultry factories."

Naturally, this smug account roused all my skepticism, and I questioned him about the economic drawbacks of such a system. My questions, however, met a flat denial. "On the contrary," he replied, "our system is considerably cheaper than yours, if we add in *all* the costs. Many of your costs are ignored, or passed on through subterfuge to posterity or the general public. We on the other hand must acknowledge all costs. Otherwise we could not hope to achieve the stable-state life systems which are our fundamental ecological and political goal. If, for instance, we had continued your practice of 'free' disposal of wastes in watercourses, sooner or later somebody else would have had to calculate (and bear) the costs of the resulting dead rivers and lakes. We prefer to do it ourselves. It is obviously not easy to quantify certain of these costs. But we have been able to approximate them in workable political terms—especially since our country is relatively sensible in scale."

I obtained the detailed analyses on which his assertions are based, and have studied them at leisure. Extensive objective research would be necessary to confirm or disprove them. They do appear to be surprisingly hard-nosed. Of course the Ecotopian situation has allowed their government to take actions that would be impossible under the checks and balances of our kind of democracy.

Next I asked the Assistant Minister about Ecotopian food production and processing. I knew he must be aware of the great achievements of our food industry in recent decades, not only in the introduction of synthetic meat and other protein foods, but also in pre-cooking and packaging generally. I was curious to see how he would justify the regressive practices that, according to many rumors, had returned Western agriculture to the dark ages, and cooks to their chopping blocks and hot stoves (microwave ovens being illegal in Ecotopia). Again I quote his reply at length. It is, I am discovering, characteristic of the way in which Ecotopians justify extremist policies.

"You must remember," he began, "that Ecotopia at the beginning was faced with a stupendous surplus of food production capacity. California alone had produced about a third of the food eaten in the United States. Oregon and Washington had enormous fruit and grain production. We could produce, therefore, something like five times the amount of food needed by our own population. With food export to the U.S. ended because of the political crisis, our problem was how to shrink our agricultural output drastically. At the same time we wanted to end extractive and polluting practices in farming. Luckily, the new employment policies, which reduced the normal work week to about 20 hours, helped a lot. Also we were able to absorb some surplus farm labor in construction work required by our recycling systems. Along with simplification in food processing, we also achieved many economies in food distribution. As your grocery executives know, a store handling a thousand items is far less difficult and expensive to operate than one handling five thousand or more, as yours do. But probably our greatest economies were obtained simply by stopping production of many processed and packaged foods. These had either been outlawed on health grounds or put on Bad Practice lists."

This sounded like a loophole that might house a large and rather totalitarian rat. "What are these lists and how are they enforced?" I asked.

"Actually, they aren't enforced at all. They're a mechanism of moral persuasion, you might say. But they're purely informal. They're issued by study groups from consumer co-ops. Usually, when a product goes onto such a list, demand for it drops sharply. The company making it then ordinarily has to stop production, or finds it possible to sell only in specialized stores."

"But surely these committees are not allowed to act simply on their own say-so, without scientific backing or government authorization?"

The Assistant Minister smiled rather wanly. "In Ecotopia," he said, "you will find many many things happening without government authorization. But the study committees do operate with scientific advice, of the most sophisticated and independent type imaginable. Scientists in Ecotopia are forbidden to accept payments or favors from either state or private enterprises for any consultation or advice they offer. They speak, therefore, on the same uncorrupted footing as any citizen. Thus we avoid the unfortunate situation where all your oil experts are in the pay of the oil companies, all the agricultural experts in the pay of agribusiness, and so on."

This was too much. "No doubt," I said, "it is scientists of this type who have frittered away the great industrial heritage you possessed at Independence, and wrecked your marvelous street and highway system, and dissolved your fine medical centers. What benefits of civilization are they prepared to undermine next?"

"I will not speak to any but food questions," he replied. "I can provide you with whatever evidence you require to prove that Ecotopians eat better food than any nation on earth, because we grow it to be nutritious and taste good, not look good or pack efficiently. Our food supplies are uncontaminated with herbicides and insecticides, because we use cultivation for weeds and biological controls for insects. Our food preparation practices are sound, avoiding the processing that destroys food values. Most important of all, our agriculture has reached an almost totally stable state, with more than 99% of our wastes being recycled. In short, we have achieved a food system that can endure indefinitely. That is, if the level of foreign poisons dumped on our lands by rain and wind doesn't rise above the present inexcusable figures."

The Assistant Minister scrambled to his feet, went to his shelves, and pulled down a half dozen pamphlets. "You will find some relevant information summarized here," he said. "Let me recommend that, after you have digested it, you follow Ecotopian ways in not wasting it."

This bad joke took me by surprise, but it did break the tension, and I laughed. He led me to the door. "You may phone if you develop further questions," he said gravely.

I returned to my hotel and read the pamphlets. One was a highly technical discussion of the relations between sewage sludge, mineral fertilizer requirements, groundwater levels and run-off, farm manure, and various disease organisms. Another, which struck me as particularly depressing because of its moralizing tone, surveyed food habits that had been common before Independence, analyzing the health hazards involved. Its humorless approach seemed to imply that soda drinks had been some kind of plot against mankind. Apparently, over a 30-year period, American soda manufacturers should have been held personally accountable for some 10 billion tooth cavities! This relentless tendency to fix responsibility on producers is, I begin to see, widespread in Ecotopian life—to the complete neglect of the responsibility, in this case, of the soda consumers.

My room boasts a trio of recycle chutes, and I have now, like a proper Ecotopian, carefully disposed of the pamphlets in the one marked P. It is a good thing Ecotopians do not have chewing gum—which chute would that belong in?

(May 7) The stable-state concept may seem innocuous enough, until you stop to grasp its implications for every aspect of life, from the most personal to the most general. Shoes cannot have composition soles because they will not decay. New types of glass and

pottery have had to be developed, which will decompose into sand when broken into small pieces. Aluminum and other nonferrous metals largely abandoned, except for a few applications where nothing else will serve—only iron, which rusts away in time, seems a "natural" metal to the Ecotopians. Belt buckles are made of bone or very hard woods. Cooking pots have no stick-free plastic lining, and are usually heavy iron. Almost nothing is painted, since paints must be based either on lead or rubber or on plastics, which do not decompose. And people seem to accumulate few goods like books; they read quite a bit compared to Americans, but they then pass the copies on to friends, or recycle them. Of course there are *aspects of life which have escaped the stable-state criterion: vehicles are rubber-tired, tooth fillings are made of silver, some structures are built of concrete, and so on. But it is still an amazing process, and people clearly take great delight in pushing it further and further.*

(I was wrong to think more garbage trucks needed: actually Ecotopians generate very little of what we would call garbage—material that simply has to be disposed of in a dump somewhere. But of course they do need more trucks to haul away material from the recycle bins.)

These people are horribly over-emotional. Last night after supper I was sitting in my hotel room writing when loud screams began in the corridor. A man and a woman, threatening each other with what sounded like murder. At first I thought I'd better keep out of it. They went off down the hall and I figured were probably going out or returning to their room. But they drifted back, yelling and screaming, until they were right outside my door. I finally stuck my head out, and found three or four other hotel guests standing around watching, placidly, and doing absolutely nothing to interfere. It seemed to be a matter of a passionate affair coming to a bitter ending. The woman, hair half-covering her teary but beautiful face, screamed at the man and kicked at him viciously—still no action from the onlookers, some of whom in fact actually smiled faintly. The man, his own face red with anger, took the woman by the shoulders as if he was about to bash her head against the wall—and at this, finally, two of the Ecotopians present stepped forward and put restraining hands on his shoulders. Instead of knocking her brains out, therefore, the man was reduced to spitting in her face—whereupon she unleashed a horrible stream of curses and insults, things more personally wounding than I have ever heard (much less said) in private, not to mention with a bunch of strangers looking on. But the man did not seem humiliated or surprised—and indeed gave back insults just as dreadful as he got. The scene had gone on for perhaps 15 minutes, with more spectators gathering. It was more theatrical than anything I've seen in Italy. Finally the man and woman evidently ran out of fury. They stood limply, looking at each other, and then fell into each other's arms, crying and nuzzling each other wetly, and staggered off down the corridor to their room. At this the spectators began exchanging lively observations, making the kind of appreciative and comparative remarks we make after a particularly vicious round in a boxing match. Nobody seemed to care what it had all been about, but they sure got a kick out of the expression of intense feeling! Evidently restraints on interpersonal behavior have been very much relaxed here, and extreme hostility can be accepted as normal behavior.

Maybe I'm not as good a traveler these days. Don't have much appetite for the sugarless Ecotopian food, despite their pride in their "natural" cuisine. Find myself worrying about what I'll do if I get sick or have an accident. The Ecotopians have probably turned medical science back fifty years. I have visions of being bled, *like in the middle ages.*

Even began thinking almost fondly, last night, of my years with Pat and the kids. Maybe I'm beginning to miss the comfort of just lying around at home. (Why should this particular jaunt make me so confused and tired? It's an exciting story, an unusual opportunity—all my colleagues envy me. I just can't quite seem to get my hands on it.) Kids used to come into bed with us Sunday mornings, and play Bear Comes Over the Mountain—giggly and floppy and lovable. Afterward when they'd gone out, Pat would infallibly ask when I was going away again. No man can live with reproaches before breakfast. But I loved her in my fashion.

The Ecotopian work schedule and the intermixture of work and play can make the simplest things practically impossible to accomplish here. Went to the wire office to file my story yesterday. It has to go via Seattle and Vancouver, since there have been no direct transcontinental connections since secession. Different clerk in the office, picked up the copy, started reading it, laughed, tried to argue with me about the way I quoted the food guy. "Look," I said, "I'm just doing my job—how about you just doing yours? Put it on the fucking wire!"

He looked at me with real hurt, as if I'd just told him his office smelled. "I didn't realize you were in such a hurry," he said. "We don't get American reporters in here every day, you know, and what you're writing is really interesting. I wasn't trying to be boorish."

You can't argue with these people. "Go ahead, read it," I said, figuring to shame him into quick action. But he gave me an appeased glance, said "Thanks," and settled down to read. I drummed on the counter with my fingers for a while, but Ecotopian leisure time had clearly set in. Finally he finished, went over to the machine, sat down, turned and said, "Well, it's okay for a beginning. I'll send it real fast for you." Then he zapped the thing out at about 80 words a minute! And came back to hand me the copy with a broad, pleased smile. "My name's Jerry, by the way. I went to school with George (the Assistant Minister) and you got him down very well." I suppose I believe him. Anyway, couldn't help smiling back. "Thanks, Jerry," I said. "See you tomorrow."

CAR-LESS LIVING IN ECOTOPIA'S NEW TOWNS

San Francisco, May 7. Under the new regime, the established cities of Ecotopia have to some extent been broken up into neighborhoods or communities, but they are still considered to be somewhat outside the ideal long-term line of development of Ecotopian living patterns. I have just had the opportunity to visit one of the strange new minicities that are arising to carry out the more extreme urban vision of this decentralized society. Once a sleepy village, it is called Alviso, and is located on the southern shores of San Francisco Bay. You get there on the interurban train, which drops you off in the basement of a large complex of buildings. The main structure, it turns out, is not the city hall or courthouse, but a factory. It produces the electric traction units—they hardly qualify as cars or trucks in our terms—that are used for transporting people and goods in Ecotopian cities and for general transportation in the countryside. (Individually owned vehicles were prohibited in "car-free" zones soon after Independence. These zones at first covered only downtown areas where pollution and congestion were most severe. As minibus service was extended, these zones expanded, and now cover all densely settled city areas.)

Around the factory, where we would have a huge parking lot, Alviso has a cluttered collection of buildings, with trees everywhere. There are restaurants, a library, bakeries, a "core store" selling groceries and clothes, small shops, even factories and workshops—all jumbled amid apartment buildings. These are generally of three or four stories, arranged around a central courtyard of the type that used to be common in Paris. They are built almost entirely of wood, which has become the predominant building material in Ecotopia, due to the reforestation program. Though these structures are old-fashioned looking, they have pleasant small balconies, roof gardens, and verandas—often covered with plants, or even small trees. The apartments themselves are very large by our standards—with 10 or 15 rooms, to accommodate their communal living groups.

Alviso streets are named, not numbered, and they are almost as narrow and winding as those of medieval cities—not easy for a stranger to get around in. They are hardly wide enough for two cars to pass; but then of course there *are* no cars, so that is no problem. Pedestrians and bicyclists meander along. Once in a while you see a delivery truck hauling a piece of furniture or some other large object, but the Ecotopians bring their groceries home in string bags or large bicycle baskets. Supplies for the shops, like most goods in Ecotopia, are moved in containers. These are much smaller than our cargo containers, and proportioned to fit into Ecotopian freight cars and onto their electric trucks. Farm produce, for instance, is loaded into such containers either at the farms or at the container terminal located on the edge of each minicity. From the terminal an underground conveyor belt system connects to all the shops and factories in the minicity, each of which has a kind of siding where the containers are shunted off. This idea was probably lifted from our automated warehouses, but turned backward. It seems to work very well, though there must be a terrible mess if there is some kind of jam-up underground.

My guides on this expedition were two young students who have just finished an apprenticeship year in the factory. They're full of informaton and observations. It seems that the entire population of Alviso, about 9,000 people, lives within a radius of a half mile from the transit station. But even this density allows for many small park-like places: sometimes merely widenings of the streets, sometimes planted gardens. Trees are everywhere—there are no large paved areas exposed to the sun. Around the edges of town are the schools and various recreation grounds. At the northeast corner of town you meet the marshes and sloughs and saltflats of the Bay. A harbor has been dredged for small craft; this opens onto the ship channel through which a freighter can move right up to the factory dock. My informants admitted rather uncomfortably that there is a modest export trade in electric vehicles—the Ecotopians allow themselves to import just enough metal to replace what is used in the exported electric motors and other metal parts.

Kids fish off the factory dock; the water is clear. Ecotopians love the water, and the boats in the harbor are a beautiful collection of both traditional and highly unorthodox designs. From this harbor, my enthusiastic guides tell me, they often sail up the Bay and into the Delta, and even out to sea through the Golden Gate, then down the coast to Monterey. Their boat is a lovely though heavy-looking craft, and they proudly offered to take me out on it if I have time.

We toured the factory, which is a confusing place. Like other Ecotopian workplaces, I am told, it is not organized on the assembly line principles generally thought essential to really efficient mass production.

Certain aspects are automated: the production of the electric motors, suspension frames, and other major elements. However, the assembly of these items is done by groups of workers who actually fasten the parts together one by one, taking them from supply bins kept full by the automated machines. The plant is quiet and pleasant compared to the crashing racket of a Detroit plant, and the workers do not seem to be under Detroit's high output pressures. Of course the extreme simplification of Ecotopian vehicles must make the manufacturing process much easier to plan and manage—indeed there seems little reason why it could not be automated entirely.

Also, I discovered, much of the factory's output does not consist of finished vehicles at all. Following the mania for "doing it yourself" which is such a basic part of Ecotopian life, this plant chiefly turns out "front ends," "rear ends," and battery units. Individuals and organizations then connect these to bodies of their own design. Many of them are weird enough to make San Francisco minibuses look quite ordinary. I have seen, for instance, a truck built of driftwood, almost every square foot of it decorated with abalone shells—it belonged to a fishery commune along the coast.

The "front end" consists of two wheels, each driven by an electric motor and supplied with a brake. A frame attaches them to a steering and suspension unit, together with a simple steering wheel, accelerator, brake, instrument panel, and a pair of headlights. The motor drives are capable of no more than 30 miles per hour (on the level!) so their engineering requirements must be modest—though my guides told me the suspension is innovative, using a clever hydraulic load-leveling device which in addition needs very little metal. The "rear end" is even simpler, since it doesn't have to steer. The battery units, which seem to be smaller and lighter than even our best Japanese imports, are designed for use in vehicles of various configurations. Each comes with a long reel-in extension cord to plug into recharging outlets.

The factory does produce several types of standard bodies, to which the propulsion units can be attached with only four bolts at each end. (They are always removed for repair.) The smallest and commonest body is a shrunken version of our pick-up truck. It has a tiny cab that seats only two people, and a low, square, open box in back. The rear of the cab can be swung upward to make a roof, and sometimes canvas sides are rigged to close in the box entirely.

A taxi-type body is still manufactured in small numbers. Many of these were used in the cities after Independence as a stop-gap measure while minibus and transit systems were developing. These bodies are molded from heavy plastic in one huge mold.

These primitive and underpowered vehicles obviously cannot satisfy the urge for speed and freedom which has been so well met by the American auto industry and our aggressive highway program. My guides and I got into a hot debate on this question, in which I must admit they proved uncomfortably knowledgeable about the conditions that sometimes prevail on our urban throughways—where movement at *any* speed can become impossible. When I asked, however, why Ecotopia did not build speedy cars for its thousands of miles of rural highways—which are now totally uncongested even if their rights of way have partly been taken over for trains—they were left speechless. I attempted to sow a few seeds of doubt in their minds: no one can be utterly insensitive to the pleasures of the open road, I told them, and I related how it feels to roll along in one of our powerful, comfortable cars, a girl's hair blowing in the wind. . . .

We had lunch in one of the restaurants near the factory, amid a cheery, noisy crowd of citizens and workers. I noticed that they drank a fair amount of the excellent local wine with their soups and sandwiches. Afterward we visited the town hall, a modest wood structure indistinguishable from the apartment buildings. There I was shown a map on which adjacent new towns are drawn, each centered on its own rapid-transit stop. It appears that a ring of such new towns is being built to surround the Bay, each one a self-contained community, but linked to its neighbors by train so that the entire necklace of towns will constitute one city. It is promised that you can, for instance, walk five minutes to your transit station, take a train within five minutes to a town ten stops away, and then walk another five minutes to your destination. My informants are convinced that this represents a halving of the time we would spend on a similar trip, not to mention problems of parking, traffic, and of course the pollution.

What will be the fate of the existing cities as these new minicities come into existence? They will gradually be razed, although a few districts will be preserved as living museum displays (of "our barbarian past," as the boys jokingly phrased it). The land will be returned to grassland, forests, orchards, or gardens—often, it appears, groups from the city own plots of land outside in the country, where they probably have a small shack and perhaps grow vegetables, or just go for a change of scene.

After leaving Alviso we took the train to Redwood City, where the reversion process can be seen in action. Three new towns have sprung up there along the Bay, separated by a half mile or so of open country, and two more are under construction as part of another string several miles back from the Bay, in the foothills. In between, part of the former suburban residential area has already been turned into alternating woods and grassland. The scene reminded me a little of my boyhood country summers in Pennsylvania. Wooded strips follow the winding lines of creeks. Hawks circle lazily. Boys out hunting with bows and arrows wave to the train as it zips by. The signs of a once busy civilization—streets, cars, service stations, supermarkets—have been entirely obliterated, as if they never existed. The scene was sobering, and made me wonder what a Carthaginian might have felt after ancient Carthage was destroyed and plowed under by the conquering Romans.

(May 8) Something peculiar *is going on in this place. Can't yet exactly locate the source of the feeling. It's like waking up after a dream and not being quite able to remember what it was about. The way people deal with each other—and with me—keeps reminding me of something—but I don't know what. Always takes me off guard, makes me feel I was confronted with some fine personal opportunity—a friendship, learning something's important, love—which by then has just passed. . . . And they often seem to be surprised, a little disappointed maybe—as if I was a child who was not proving a very fast learner. (But what am I supposed to be learning?)*

Then sometimes life here seems like a throwback to a past I might have known through old photographs. Or a skip ahead *in time: these people, who are so American despite their weird social practices, might be what we will become. (They miss no chance, of course, to tell me we should get on with it.) Also keep feeling I have gotten stuck on vacation in the country. Partly it's all the trees, and maybe the dark nights (which still make me feel a power blackout must have struck), and also it's hard to get used to the quiet. Must be doing something to my New York paranoia system, geared to respond to honking, screeching, buzzing, bangs, knocks, not to mention a shot or a scream now and then. You expect silence in the country. But here I am in a metropolitan area of several million, constantly surrounded by people—and the only really loud noises are human shouts or babies crying. There's no "New Man" bullshit in Ecotopia, but how do they stand the quiet?*

Or for that matter, how do they stand their isolation from us? Has bred a brash kind of self-sufficiency. They seem to be in surprisingly good touch with the rest of the world, but as far as we're concerned, they're strictly on their own—like adolescent children who have rejected their parents' ways. They'll probably get over it.

Ecotopians a little vague about time, I notice—few wear watches, and they pay more attention to things like sunrise and sunset or the tides than to actual hour time. They will *accede to the demands of industrial civilization to some extent, but grudgingly. "You'd never catch an Indian wearing a watch." Many Ecotopians sentimental about Indians, and there's some sense in which they envy the Indians their lost natural place in the American wilderness. Indeed this is probably a major Ecotopian myth; keep hearing references to what Indians would or wouldn't do in a given situation. Some Ecotopian articles—clothing and baskets and personal ornamentation—perhaps directly Indian in inspiration. But what matters most is the aspiration to live in balance with nature, "walk lightly on the land," treat the earth as a mother. No surprise that to such a morality most industrial processes, work schedules, and products are suspect! Who would use an earth-mover on his own mother?*

Hotel was okay for a while, but has gotten kind of boring. Have taken to spending a good bit of time a few blocks away, down near the waterfront, at "Franklin's Cove," a sort of press commune, where maybe 40 Ecotopian journalists and writers and TV people live. They've been extremely hospitable—really make me feel welcome. The place must have once been a warehouse, and is now broken up into rooms. They cook collectively, have work rooms (no electric typewriters, I notice, but lots of handy light video recorders), even a kind of gym. Beautiful wild garden in back where people spend a lot of time lying around on sunny days—part of it in crumbling ruins of one wing of the warehouse, which nobody has bothered to wreck and haul away. ("Time is taking its course, and we just let it," replied one of the residents when I asked why this unsightly condition was tolerated.) Center of things is a lounge-library filled with soft chairs and sofas. I've been there so much I even have a favorite chair.

Ecotopians, both male and female, have a secure sense of themselves as animals. At the Cove they lie about utterly relaxed, curled up on couches or floor, flopped down in sunny spots on little rugs or mats, almost like a bunch of cats. They stretch, rearrange themselves, do mysterious yoga-like exercises, and just seem to enjoy their bodies tremendously. Nor do they keep this to themselves, particularly—I've several times walked in on people making love, who didn't seem much embarrassed or annoyed—it was hardly different from walking in on somebody taking a bath. I find myself envying them this comfortableness in their biological beings. They seem to breathe better, move more loosely. I'm experimenting, trying to imitate them. . . .

Especially in the evenings, though of course they have a lot of free time during the day as well, people gather round and talk—the kind of leisurely talk I associate with college days. Jumps around from topic to topic, and people kid a lot, and cheer each other up when need be, but there's some thread to it usually. Last evening spent quite a while talking to an interesting guy I've met at the Cove—Bert Luckman (that seems to be his real *name). He was studying at Berkeley at the time of Independence—bright Jewish kid from New York. Had gone through Maoist phase, then got into secessionist movement. Politics and science writer (not an odd combination here) for the* S. F. Times. *Has written a book on cosmology, has a mystic streak, but still a reporter's reporter: tough, wry, well-organized writing. Is surprisingly skeptical about U.S. science, which he regards as bureaucratically constipated and wasteful. "You made the dreadful mistake," he said, "of turning your science establishment over to established scientists, who could be trusted. But it's mainly young and untrustworthy scientists who get important new ideas. —You still have a few things happening, but it's lost the momentum you need." (I wonder. Check when get back.)*

After some drinks the conversation got livelier and more personal. Thought I'd do some probing. "Doesn't this stable-state business get awfully static? I'd think it would drive you crazy after a certain point!"

Bert looked at me with amusement, and batted the ball back. "Well, don't forget that we *don't have to be stable. The system provides the stability, and we can be erratic within it. I mean we don't try to be perfect, we just try to be okay on the average—which means adding up a bunch of ups and downs." "But it means giving up any notions of progress. You just want to get to that stable point and stay there, like a lump."*

"It may sound that way, but in practice there's no stable point. We're always striving to approximate it, but we never get there. And you know how much we disagree on exactly what is to be done—we only agree on the root essentials, everything else is in dispute." I grinned. "I've noticed that—you're a quarrelsome lot!" "We can afford to be, because of that root agreement. Besides, that's half the fun of relating to each other—trying to work through different perspectives, seeing how other people feel about things."

"It's still flying in the face of reality, this striving for stability." Bert took this more seriously: "Is it? But we've actually achieved something like stability. Our

system meanders on its peaceful way, while yours has constant convulsions. I think of ours as like a meadow in the sun. There's a lot of change going on—plants growing, other plants dying, bacteria decomposing them, mice eating seeds, hawks eating mice, a tree or two beginning to grow up and shade the grasses. But the meadow sustains itself on a steady-state basis—unless men come along and mess it up."

"I begin to see what you mean. It may not look so static to the mouse."

After his student years Bert traveled a lot—in Canada, Latin America, Europe, Asia. Even thought of going to the U.S. sub rosa—but didn't do it (or says he didn't). Attached to a charming giddy woman named Clara, some years older and also a journalist—they have separate rooms at the Cove. Bert seems to be a wanderer—has also worked on papers in Seattle, Vancouver, and a little California coast resort town called Mendocino. We exchanged life histories, and he pumped me for inside intrigues on my travels, my relations with sources in our government, and so on. Caught me in a couple of prevarications, but seems to take their measure quickly and understand them. We went on talking in a frank and almost brotherly way, so I tried harder to be candid and scrupulous. Told him about Francine; he wanted to know precisely the nature of my relationship with her, and seemed surprised that it is so tentative, even though it's gone on for three years now. "It seems contradictory to me," he said. "You live in separate apartments, see each other a couple of times a week, spend weeks on end away from each other altogether. At the same time you don't have a group of people to live with, to support you emotionally, to keep your collective life going on actively and strongly while you're apart. I'd think that during one of these absences you'd have split up long ago—one of you would have taken up seriously with someone else, and then there'd be two other little separate worlds, instead of the two you have now. I'd find that very scary."

"It is *very scary," I said, "and once or twice we* have *gotten involved with someone else. But we have always come back to each other." "It still sounds frivolous to me," he said, frowning. "It gives too much power to loneliness. Here we try to arrange it so we are not lonely very often. That keeps us from making a lot of emotional mistakes. We don't think commitment is something you go off and do by yourselves, just two of you. It has to have a structure, social surroundings you can rely on. Human beings are tribal animals, you know. They need lots of contact."*

"You might be right," I said doubtfully. "I never thought of myself that way particularly. Though at one point I remember wondering if having lots and lots of children might not be a good thing." "Well, there are other kinds of families, you know," he said gently and with a slight smile. "I'll take you to visit some."

Have also had some good talks with Tom, a writer for a major magazine called Flow. *He's maybe 35 but has a face that already shows lines; also a temper, and he was swearing at somebody who had challenged his view of recent American strategy in Brazil. I kept quiet at first, but it happened I knew Tom was right: we* had *set up a system of electronically fenced enclaves in Sao Paulo as a means of controlling guerrilla movements, though it had been portrayed as an urban-redevelopment measure. "Look," said Tom finally, "we have a goddamn American reporter right here, why don't we ask him?" "All right," said the other guy to me, "do you know anything about it?"*

"Yeah," I said, "I do. Tom's got it straight. There are sensor fields all over Sao Paulo. Anything that moves, the army knows about." "How did you get your information? Are you sure?"

"Sure I'm sure. I heard the President give the or-

der—and I also heard him tell the press that he'd deny it if we reported it." Tom burst out laughing. He and his opponent didn't speak for several days after that, but Tom and I made up for it. Talked not only about Brazil—also about functions of journalists, and the changes in man-woman relationships that have occurred in Ecotopia. According to him, women in Ecotopia have totally escaped the dependent roles they still tend to play with us. Not that they domineer over men—but they exercise power in work and in relationships just as men do. Above all, they don't have to manipulate men: the Survivalist Party, and social developments generally, have arranged the society so that women's objective situation is equal *to men's. Thus people can be just people, without our symbolic loading on sex roles. (I notice, however, that Ecotopian women still seem to me feminine, with a relaxed air of their biological attractiveness, even fertility, though I don't see how they combine this with their heavy responsibilities and hard work. And men, though they express feelings more openly than American men—even feelings of weakness—still seem masculine.)*

Tom's bright, and cynical as any good newspaperman is, yet strangely optimistic about the future. Believes that the nature of political power is changing, that the technology and social structure can be put at the service of mankind, instead of the other way round. Skeptical but not, I notice, bitter. Must be comfortable to think like that.

Am missing Francine's reliably amiable "attentions." (Whenever I'm away I realize anew what a faithful playmate she is; despite our having deliberately resolved never to be faithful to each other.) Have the awful suspicion that every woman around me is secretly, constantly fucking and that I could have them if I only knew the password—but I don't. I must be missing something—can the women journalists at the Cove simply find me unattractive in some mysterious way? They are friendly enough, direct, open; they even touch me sometimes, which of course feels good and gives me a warm rush. But again, it's sisterly: if I touch them back, they seem to feel I'm making an improper advance, and back off. There must be some move, when a woman here comes close to you, that I don't know how to make? Yet I watch the Ecotopian men, and they don't seem to do anything, except maybe smile a little; and then things go on from there, or sometimes don't—it's all very casual and nobody seems to worry about it. Very confusing all around; makes me feel hung up on my own patterns. Many Ecotopian women are beautiful in a simple, unadorned way. They're not dependent for their attractiveness on cosmetics or dress—they give the impression of being strong, secure, pleasure-loving people, very honest and straightforward emotionally. They seem to like *me: in the Cove as on the streets they meet my eyes openly, are glad to talk, even quite personally. Yet I can't get past that stage to any real action. Have to think about that some more. Maybe I'll learn something.*

THE UNSPORTING LIFE OF ECOTOPIA

San Francisco, May 9. American sports fans would have a miserable time of it in Ecotopia. They would find no baseball and no football, no basketball, not even ice hockey. The newspapers have what they label "sports pages," but these are devoted to oddball individual sports. Skiing, especially cross-country style, gets big coverage. Hiking and camping, which are usually lumped with fishing and hunting, are treated as sports. Swimming, sailing, gymnastics, ping-pong, and tennis get a lot of attention. So does chess! There's no boxing or wrestling in Ecotopia, and no roller derby. In short, for the sports enthusiast Ecotopia is about as dull as you could imagine: the sports scene is set up purely for the benefit of the participants.

On the other hand, from a physical-fitness point of view ordinary Ecotopian citizens are remarkably healthy looking. An American like myself tends to feel a little flabby here. Ecotopians are used to walking everywhere, carrying heavy burdens like backpacks and groceries for long distances, and they have a generally higher level of physical activity than Americans. The women, especially, look marvelously healthy, even though they do not adhere to our standards of style. The fat and broken-down people we are accustomed to seeing on our city streets are absent here, and even oldsters seem surprisingly fit and hearty. To my questions about this, Ecotopians have replied "Well, nature has equipped us well, and we lead active physical lives," or some such phrases. It apparently does not occur to them that human beings in other countries are *not* in equally good shape.

But my inquiries, pursued further, have turned up an extensive network of unobtrusive physical activities which, in fact, seem almost Spartan in their intensity, and participation in some kind of minor sport is virtually universal among Ecotopians. Even volleyball, God help them, is a favorite pastime, and at noon or indeed other hours you can see teams cavorting in factory yards or on the streets. It doesn't look terribly competitive, but is obviously fun.

Ecotopians also love to dance, which is good exercise; and walking a lot, which is forced on them by the prohibition of cars, probably has the compensation of being good for the health. (Runners, whether for health or haste, are common sights here.) Ping-pong tables seem to be one of the commonest items of furniture, and I must confess that when I challenged an awkward-looking teen-ager to a friendly game, I got stomped!

Ecotopian schools, with their looser scheduling (and better climate) give children far more outdoor time than ours. So the youngsters have a high level of physical activity throughout their school years. School groups often go on expeditions: it's common to see six-year-olds, with heavy backpacks, trudging along with older kids on hikes which, I am told, may last four or five days, and in quite forbidding country. As they move on into higher levels of school (the term "grade" is not used in our sense) much of the children's time is allotted to training in fishing and hunting and survival skills, at the expense of basic educational skills. They are forced to learn not only the basic techniques but also how to improvise ecologically acceptable equipment in the wilds: hooks, snares, bows, arrows, and so on.

Some parents and other adults participate voluntarily in the children's field trips—for meat as well as sport, since wild game has returned to the reforested areas in great numbers. Thus mountain lions, wildcats, bears (including grizzlies), and wolves may now be hunted, along with deer, foxes, and rabbits. (Hunting is usually done with bows and arrows, not firearms, though most Ecotopian living units possess shotguns.) The experiences of the children are closely tied in with studies of plants, animals, and landscape. I have been impressed with the knowledge that even young children have of such matters—a six-year-old can tell you all about the "ecological niches" of the creatures and plants he encounters in his daily life. He will also know what roots and berries are edible, how to use soap plant, how to carve a pot holder from a branch.

A big sports role is played by Ecotopian rivers and lakes, which seem to be a magnetic attraction to young people even though the coastal waters are freezing cold. Shortly after Independence, an expropriation law made all waterfront properties into "water parks." Beautiful exclusive estates were seized and turned into fishing communes, schools, hospitals, oceanographic and limnological institutes, museums of natural history. Public boating, fishing and swimming were permitted in lakes that had formerly been enclosed in fenced, guarded private developments. The new government even went so far as to dynamite some of the dams which had been built on the rivers—on the dubious grounds that they prevented "white-water" recreational boating or interfered with the salmon runs—which have been reestablished with great effort and enjoy much public support.

A curious physical fitness aspect of Ecotopian life is that in school the classes in carpentry and other tool work (which are taken by most students, girls as well as boys) carry out construction projects that often involve the handling of timbers, masonry and other heavy materials.

But the strangest thing about Ecotopian sports for an American is to understand how Ecotopians get along without the thrills, drama and suspense provided by our pennant seasons, the pageants of our bowl games, or the opportunity for boys to identify with star players. Apparently, the excitement we focus on our major sports has been entirely diverted in Ecotopia to what they call "the war games." These are never described in the sports pages, however, nor indeed anywhere else in print. People have been evasive when I have asked about these "games," but rumors that have reached us outside Ecotopia suggest that rather bestial practices are involved. From conversations I have overheard, especially among young men, it is clear that Ecotopians are intensely concerned with these bloody rituals—in which it appears that hundreds of Ecotopian youths perish every year. Soon I hope to make an eye-witness report on one of these controversial spectacles.

(May 10) No progress in my efforts to set up an appointment with President Allwen. Her assistant friendly enough, however. Says it will happen in due course, but why don't I look around the country some more first, "so you have something to talk about." Asked me pointedly to make sure they get early copies of all my dispatches. Are they waiting to see what I write before they decide whether to give me my precious appointment?

Saw Allwen on a TV event—dedication of a solar-energy plant. Altogether unlike our ribbon-cutting ceremonies. Here the people who do the ceremony are the people who did the work. Cameramen wander around among everybody; it's all quite helter-skelter, there seem to be no passive bystanders, everybody is talking to everybody else. The camera has been with various groups for a while, one of them including this rather plain but strong unidentified woman who's chatting and laughing with them. They're showing her some papers, she's joking with them. After a while it turns out she is Vera. But nobody calls on her for a speech. She turns to a woman nearby and says, "Why don't you tell everybody how this all got started?"

Seriously but with absolutely no pompousness, the woman describes the background of the plant—why it was needed here, how the people involved in the communities it would serve decided what kind of plant it should be, how some novel scientific developments got worked up. Then she turned to other people, and they talked about the actual construction —funny stories, mainly, not at all our kind of solemn, contribution-to-the-ages sort of stuff. Certain aspects of the installation are evidently far from perfect—at least in some eyes—and the criticisms weren't kept under cover in the slightest. When this got a little heavy, Allwen re-entered the conversation. But she didn't play the stern arbiter or mother role, she talked about some other case where something had gone wrong, and told a political anecdote about how the people had finally gotten together and more or less fixed it up. The mood lightened, mutual confidence returned.

And then, when everybody seemed to have said what they wanted to say, the group just sort of amorphously decided it was time to turn on the switch. Amid jokes that maybe it wouldn't work after all, a child was brought forth to actually push the switch. It worked. Lightbulbs lighted; people cheered and hugged each other; and then, as champagne was brought out, the camera crews put down their equipment and picked up glasses, and we saw no more.

I've also been using spare time watching some of Allwen's collected speeches on my videodisc player. (Bought a full set to take back with me.) Clearly a remarkable woman: a powerful personality with a gift for folksy yet highly political speaking. There is a lot of warmth, yet a certain menace too: you wouldn't want to be her enemy. Maybe the old Queen Elizabeth was like that? At the same time Allwen never seems to rely on the us-against-them gambit. The underlying point is always some kind of unity; there's a family feeling even when she's chastising someone. I doubt if anyone, whatever their politics, could be entirely in her bad graces! She has a way of seeming to take the viewer into her confidence, so that you share the logic and conviction of her argument. It would be hard to feel she was selling *you something, the way too many of our television speeches do. Instead she seems to be giving—clarity, strength, wisdom. Maybe as much a religious leader as a politician? Head of the state ecological church, chief priestess? Doesn't look it, God knows! But anyway a force to be reckoned with.*

ECOTOPIAN TELEVISION AND ITS WARES

San Francisco, May 10. Ecotopians claim to have sifted through modern technology and rejected huge tracts of it, because of its ecological harmfulness. However, despite this general technological austerity, they employ video devices even more extensively than we do. Feeling that they should transport their bodies only when it's a pleasure, they seldom travel "on business" in our manner. Instead, they tend to transact business by using their picturephones. These employ the same cables that provide television connections; the whole county, except for a few isolated rural spots, is wired with cable. (There is no microwave broadcasting.) Video sets are everywhere, but strangely enough I have seldom seen people sitting before them blotted out in the American manner. Whether this is because of some mysterious national trait, or because of the programming being markedly different, or both, I cannot yet tell. But Ecotopians seem to use TV, rather than letting it use them.

Some channels are apparently literal parts of the government structure—something like a council chamber with a PA system would be. People watch these when the doings of local governments or the national legislature are being transmitted. (Virtually no government proceedings are closed to press and public anyway.) Viewers not only watch—they expect to participate. They phone in with questions and comments, sometimes for the officials present, sometimes for the TV staffs. Thus TV doesn't only provide news—much of the time it *is* the news. The routine governmental fare includes debates that involve public figures, or aspirants to public office; many court proceedings and executive meetings; and meetings of the legislatures and especially of their committees. Running comment is interspersed from a variety of sources, ranging from the narrators to vehemently partisan analysts. There is no rule of objectivity, as with our newscasters; Ecotopians in general scorn the idea as a "bourgeois fetish," and profess to believe that truth is best served by giving some label indicating your general position, and then letting fly.

Other channels present films and various entertainment programs, but the commercials are awkwardly bunched entirely *between* shows, rather than scattered throughout. Not only does this destroy the rhythm we're used to on TV—commercials giving us timely respites from the drama—but it increases the tendency for the commercials to fight each other. And this is bad enough anyway, because they are limited to mere announcements, without impersonated housewives or other consumers, and virtually without adjectives. (Some prohibition must exist for all the media, since ads in magazines and newspapers are similarly bland.) It's hard to get excited about a product's specifications-list, but Ecotopian viewers do manage to watch them. Sometimes, I suspect, they watch merely in hopes of a counter-ad to follow—an announcement of a competing product, in which the announcer sneeringly compares the two.

Also, the commercials may seem watchable because they are islands of sanity in the welter of viewpoints, personnel, and visual image quality that make up "normal" Ecotopian TV fare. Some channels even change managements entirely—at noon, or 6 P.M., a channel that has been programming political events or news will suddenly switch over to household advice, loud rock music, or weird surrealistic films bringing your worst nightmares to garish life. (Ecotopians don't seem to believe overmuch in color tuning. The station engineers sometimes joke around and transmit signals in which people deliberately come out green or fuchsia, with orange skies.) Then again you may come upon a super-serious program imported from Canada or England. And there are a few people who tune in American satellite signals and watch our re-runs, or laugh it up at our commercials. But this seems to be an acquired, minority taste—and it also requires an expensive special adapter to pick up the signals directly.

Television, incidentally, may be an important reason for Ecotopians' odd attitudes toward material goods. Of course many consumer items are considered ecologically offensive and are simply not available, so nobody has them: thus electric can openers, hair curlers, frying pans, and carving knives are unknown. And to curb industrial proliferation the variety which is so delightful in our department stores is much restricted here. Many basic necessities are utterly standardized. Bath towels, for instance, can be bought in only one color, white—people have to dye their own in attractive patterns (using gentle natural hues from plant and mineral sources, I am told). Ecotopians generally seem to travel light, with few possessions, though each household, naturally, has a full component of necessary utensils. As far as personal goods are concerned Ecotopians possess or at least care about mainly things like knives and other tools, clothing, brushes, musical instruments, which they are concerned to have of the highest possible quality. These are handmade and prized by their owners as works of art—which I must admit they sometimes are.

Objects that *are* available in stores seem rather old-fashioned. I have seen few Ecotopian-made appliances that would not look pretty primitive on American TV. One excuse I've heard is that they are designed for easy repair by users. At any rate they lack the streamlining we're used to—parts stick out at odd angles, bolts and other fasteners are plainly visible, and sometimes parts are even made of wood.

I have, however, observed that Ecotopians do repair their own things. In fact there are no repair shops on the streets. A curious corollary is that guarantees don't seem to exist at all. People take it for granted that manufactured items will be sturdy, durable, and self-fixable—which of course means they are also relatively unsophisticated compared to ours. This state of affairs has not been achieved easily: I have heard many funny stories about ridiculous designs produced in the early days, lawsuits against their manufacturers, and other tribulations. One law now in effect requires that pilot models of new devices must be given to a public panel of ten ordinary people ("consumers" is not a term used in polite conversation here). Only if they all find they can fix likely breakdowns with ordinary tools is manufacture permitted.

An exception of sorts is made for video and other electronic items. These are required to be built of standard modularized parts and shops must stock component modules as well as test equipment, so users can isolate and replace defective components. And of course much electronic gear is now so small that it must simply be recycled if it stops working. The Ecotopians, indeed, have produced some remarkably miniaturized electronic devices, such as stereo sets no larger than a plate, ingeniously responsive controls for solar heat systems and industrial processes, and short-range radiotelephones built into a tiny earphone. These evidently satisfy a national urge for compactness, lightness, and low power requirements.

(May 11) This morning got my first look at that curious Ecotopian practice known as cooperative criticism. Had stopped in at one of their little open-front cafes where you can get an overwhelmingly hearty breakfast. Family-style tables, but it was still early, and conversation desultory. A man near me who had ordered scrambled eggs broke the quiet after the waiter brought his plate.

"Look at those eggs!" he demanded—not of the waiter, as we might do, but of the cafe at large. He held them up for all to see. "They're totally dried out!" At this point, I expected the waiter to try to soothe the customer and offer him a new plate of eggs. Instead, both customer and waiter headed for the kitchen area, which was off to the side of the room but separated only by a counter. (Ecotopians take pleasure is being able to inspect ingredients and see their food being cooked. Their kitchens are always open to view, and they watch the cooks rather as we watch a pizza-thrower.) "Who cooked these eggs?" the customer asked. One of the cooks, a woman, put aside a pot and walked over to look.

"I did. What's wrong with them?" The man repeated his complaint, the woman took a fork, sampled the eggs. "You must have left them lie on the plate," she said. "The plate's got cold too." Several hands reached out to touch the plate, and sub-arguments broke out about that, the consensus being that the plate was still pretty warm, and the woman must indeed have overcooked the eggs. "Why weren't you watching them?" the customer asked. "Because I have two stoves and about 14 orders going!" retorted the woman.

At this, some happy customers chimed in, saying that Ruth was a phenomenally careful cook and had done their *eggs to perfection. So then the problem of Ruth's workload was examined by all present, loudly. (Meanwhile, new customers were drifting in and all were joining into the discussion, and every breakfast in the place was getting stone-cold; nobody cared.) Somebody asked Ruth why she didn't yell for help when she got behind, and she blushed and said, with a resentful glance at her fellow cooks, that it was* her *job and she could do it. One of the other customers, who seemed to know Ruth, said he knew she wouldn't ask for help from the other cooks, who were also busy, but what would be wrong with admitting that occasionally the load got extra heavy, and accepting help when it's offered?*

Here many customers chimed in, telling her they'd be glad to step into the kitchen and pitch in for a few minutes. At this, Ruth began to weep, whether from shame or relief. A couple of customers came into the kitchen, hugged her, lent a hand; she probably dropped salty tears into the next couple of orders, but everybody else went back to their tables, seeming very satisfied with the whole episode, and the complainer ate his new eggs with gusto, after thanking Ruth loudly and elaborately when she personally brought them out to him—with many smiles all around them.

Little emotional dramas like this seem to be common in Ecotopian life. There's something embarrassing and low-class about them, but they're delightful in a way, and both participants and observers seem to be energized by them.

Usually on my trips I feel pretty frustrated sexually after a couple of days and try to get taken care of, somehow or other. Am still totally puzzled why these independent Ectopian women don't react to my signals. It certainly isn't because they are out of touch with their own sexuality! Was kidding around with one I picked up on the street. "Look," she said after a bit, "if you just want to fuck why don't you say so?" and marched off in disgust. That got to me, somehow. Realized I don't just *want to fuck, as I usually think when I'm away. I really want to figure out what goes on between men and women out here, and try getting with it: they obviously deal with each other in ways I don't know about. I feel envious and left out, but also challenged and curious. Sometimes my confusion settles into a feeling of readiness, patience, calmness: as if I must soon run into somebody who will make it all clear. But it doesn't make it any easier that Ecotopians are very noisy at their love-making. Groans and gasps and shudders and moans percolate through my hotel walls, even though they aren't particularly thin. Evidently they don't have any inhibitions about others hearing what's going on.*

THE ECOTOPIAN ECONOMY: FRUIT OF CRISIS

San Francisco, May 12. It is widely believed among Americans that the Ecotopians have become a shiftless and lazy people. This was the natural conclusion drawn after Independence, when the Ecotopians adopted a 20-hour work week. Yet even so no one in America, I think, has yet fully grasped the immense break this represented with our way of life—and even now it is astonishing that the Ecotopian legislature, in the first flush of power, was able to carry through such a revolutionary measure.

What was at stake, informed Ecotopians insist, was nothing less than the revision of the Protestant work ethic upon which America has been built. The consequences were plainly severe. In economic terms, Ecotopia was forced to isolate its economy from the competition of harder-working peoples. Serious dislocations plagued their industries for years. There was a drop in Gross National Product by more than a third. But the profoundest implications of the decreased work week were philosophical and ecological: mankind, the Ecotopians assumed, was not meant for production, as the 19th and early 20th centuries had believed. Instead, humans were meant to take their modest place in a seamless, stable-state web of living organisms, disturbing that web as little as possible. This would mean sacrifice of present consumption, but it would ensure future survival—which became an almost religious objective, perhaps akin to earlier doctrines of "salvation." People were to be happy not to the extent they dominated their fellow creatures on the earth, but to the extent they lived in balance with them.

This philosophical change may have seemed innocent on the surface. Its grave implications were soon spelled out, however. Ecotopian economists, who included some of the most highly regarded in the American nation, were well aware that the standard of living could only be sustained and increased by relentless pressure on work hours and worker productivity. Workers might call this "speed-up," yet without a slow but steady rise in labor output, capital could not be attracted or even held; financial collapse would quickly ensue.

The deadly novelty introduced into this accepted train of thought by a few Ecotopian militants was to spread the point of view that economic disaster was not identical with survival disaster for persons—and that, in particular, a financial panic could be turned to advantage if the new nation could be organized to devote its real resources of energy, knowledge, skills, and materials to the basic necessities of survival. If that were done, even a catastrophic decline in the GNP (which was, in their opinion, largely composed of wasteful activity anyway) might prove politically useful.

In short, financial chaos was to be not endured but deliberately engineered. With the ensuing flight of capital, most factories, farms and other productive facilities would fall into Ecotopian hands like ripe plums.

And in reality it took only a few crucial measures to set this dismal series of events in motion: the nationalization of agriculture; the announcement of an impending moratorium on oil-industry activities; the forced consolidation of the basic retail network constituted by Sears, Penneys, Safeway, and a few other chains; and the passage of stringent conservation laws that threatened the profits of the lumber interests.

These moves, of course, set off an enormous clamor in Washington. Lobbyists for the various interests affected tried to commit the federal government to intervene militarily. This was, however, several months after Independence. The Ecotopians had established and intensively trained a nationwide militia, and airlifted arms for it from France and Czechoslovakia. It was also believed that at the time of secession they had mined major Eastern cities with atomic weapons, which they had constructed in secret or seized from weapons research laboratories. Washington, therefore, although it initiated a ferocious campaign of economic and political pressure against the Ecotopians, and mined their harbors, finally decided against an invasion.

This news set in motion a wave of closures and forced sales of businesses—reminiscent, I was told, of what happened to the Japanese-Americans who were interned in World War II. Members of distinguished old San Francisco families were forced to bargain on most unfavorable terms with representatives of the new regime. Properties going back to Spanish land-grant claims were hastily disposed of. Huge corporations, used to dictating policy in city halls and statehouses, found themselves begging for compensation and squirming to explain that their properties were actually worth far more than their declared tax value.

Tens of thousands of employees were put out of work as a consequence, and the new government made two responses to this. One was to absorb the unemployed in construction of the train network and of the sewage and other recycling facilities necessary to establish stable-state life systems. Some were also put to work dismantling allegedly hazardous or unpleasant relics of the old order, like gas-stations. The other move was to adopt 20 hours as the basic work week—which, in effect, doubled the number of jobs but virtually halved individual income. (There were, for several years, rigid price controls on all basic foods and other absolute necessities.)

Naturally, the transition period that ensued was hectic—though many people also remember it as exciting. It is alleged by many who lived through those times that no one suffered seriously from lack of food, shelter, clothing, or medical treatment—though some discomfort was widespread, and there were gross dislocations in the automobile and related industries, in the schools, and in some other social functions. Certainly many citizens were deprived of hard-earned comforts they had been used to: their cars, their prepared and luxury foods, their habitual new clothes and appliances, their many efficient service industries. These disruptions were especially severe on middle-aged people—though one now elderly man told me that he had been a boy in Warsaw during World War II, had lived on rats and moldy potatoes, and found the Ecotopian experience relatively painless. To the young, the disruptions seem to have had a kind of wartime excitement—and indeed sacrifices may have been made more palatable by the fear of attack from the United States. It is said by some, however, that the orientation of the new government toward basic biological survival was a unifying and reassuring force. Panic food hoarding, it is said, was rare. (The generosity with food which is such a feature of Ecotopian life today may have arisen at that time.)

Of course the region that comprises Ecotopia had natural advantages that made the transition easier. Its states had more doctors per capita, a higher educational level, a higher percentage of skilled workers, a greater number of engineers and other technicians, than most other parts of the Union. Its major cities, except for Seattle, were broadly based manufacturing and trade complexes that produced virtually all the necessities of life. Its universities were excellent, and its resources for scientific research included a number of the topnotch facilities in the United States. Its temperate climate encouraged an outdoor style of life, and made fuel shortages caused by ecological policies an annoyance rather than the matter of life or death they would have been in the severe eastern winters. The people were unusually well versed in nature and conservation lore, and experienced in camping and survival skills.

We cannot, however, ignore the political context in which the transition took place. As Ecotopian militants see the situation, by 1980 there had been almost a quarter century of military action in Indochina. American involvement in Southeast Asia was in its fifteenth year. Cease-fires had come and gone. Evading Congressional fiscal controls, the U.S. administration had continued with attempts to find a "final solution" to Asian uprisings. The burden of military outlays to support an enormous arms establishment caused economic disruption even after the citizenry lost the power to control them. The persistent inflation and recession of the seventies had caused widespread misery and undermined Americans' confidence in economic progress; wildcat strikes and seizures of plants by workers had required the almost constant mobilization of the National Guard. After the abortive antipollution efforts of the early seventies, the toll of death and destruction had resumed its climb. Energy crises had bred economic disruption and price gouging. And chronic Washington scandals had greatly reduced faith in central government.

"All this," one Ecotopian told me, "convinced us that if we wished to survive we had to take matters into our own hands." I pointed out that this had always been the claim of conspiratorial revolutionaries, who presume to act in the name of the majority, but take care not to allow the majority to have any real power. "Well," he replied, "things were clearly not getting any better—so people really were ready for change. They were literally sick of bad air, chemicalized foods, lunatic advertising. They turned to politics because it was finally the only route to self-preservation."

"So," I replied, "in order to follow an extremist ecological program, millions of people were willing to jeopardize their whole welfare, economic and social?"

"Their welfare wasn't doing so well, at that point," he said. "Something had to be done. And nobody else was doing it. Also"—he shrugged, and grinned—"we were very lucky." This gallows humor, which reminds me of the Israelis or Viennese, is common in Ecotopia. Perhaps it helps explain how the whole thing happened.

(May 13) Mysteriously, the Ecotopians do not feel "separate" from their technology. They evidently feel a little as the Indians must have felt: that the horse and the teepee and the bow and arrow all sprang, like the human being, from the womb of nature, organically. Of course the Ecotopians work on natural materials far more extensively and complexly than the Indians worked stone into arrowpoint, or hide into teepee. But they treat materials in the same spirit of respect, comradeship. The other day I stopped to watch some carpenters working on a building. They marked and sawed the wood lovingly (using their own muscle power, not our saws). Their nail patterns, I noticed, were beautifully placed, and their rhythm of hammering seemed patient, almost placid. When they raised wood pieces into place, they held them carefully, fitted them (they make many joints by notching as well as nailing). They seemed almost to

be collaborating with the wood, rather than forcing it into the shape of a building. . . .

Got a strange call on the hotel phone last night, from a gruff-sounding man who asked if he and a couple of friends could see me. He had his phone picture switched off to start, but after I said I'd be glad to talk to him, he turned it on. We met at a coffeehouse he suggested, which turned out to have the atmosphere of a men's club: dark wood panelling, newspapers on racks along the wall, beer, good coffee, pastries. They started out by saying how pleased they were to hear of my visit, and that they hoped relations between the two countries would now begin to improve.

This was news: no Ecotopians I've met so far have seemed to give much of a damn about relations with the U.S. one way or the other. I began to study my companions more closely. They were evidently businessmen of some kind—there is a way in which business people tend to assume proprietorship which seemed familiar. I began to see who they probably were: the Opposition!

The gruff one introduced us all. Then, rather gingerly, they began to explain their position: that, while many of the ecological reforms of the new government were of course necessary and desirable, others stifled their spirit of enterprise. "The economy, as you have seen by now, has been going downhill steadily. It's terrible, what we have lost. Worse, we are on a collision course with the U.S."

"How is that?" I asked.

"Let's face it. We are a small nation on the periphery of a very large one. Persisting in this ecological craziness will sooner or later lead to an armed conflict, and we will be wiped out. We know what you did to Vietnam, what you're doing now in Brazil. Our atomic mines might turn out to be a bluff. Then it could happen here too."

"So what can you do?"

"We could take a softer line—make a few compromises. We're excited by your coming because it could lead to resumption of normal relations between the two countries. From that, we could see the exchange of pilot plants, to show what happens when you let the managers manage—and gradually a growth of economic interdependence. In time, we could get our economy going again on modern lines."

"Isn't the Progressive Party working in that direction?"

There was a pause. "Yes, but they only put up a token struggle. They pay lip service to the idea of change, but when it comes to real changes, they drag their feet. They're really almost as bad as the Survivalists. We've just about given up on them."

"So what are you going to do?"

They shifted uneasily. "We have great hopes from your visit, first of all. We urge you to speak for the idea of normalization of relations, here and when you get back to Washington. We hope that will get things moving. But we also want you to know that we are prepared to fight for our ideas."

I looked at them, startled. "Fight?"

They looked back, very solemnly, and then must have decided to take their big chance. "We have been led to believe that the U.S. government supports clandestine groups in countries with governments thought to be unfriendly. The time is coming when normal means of political action may no longer serve. Ecotopia has to be made to realize that it must change course. We are ready for anything. But we need help."

"You aren't afraid of being taken simply for American agents?"

"It's a chance we'll have to take. We would of course ask for materials that can't be traced to U.S. sources." It was my turn to pause. "You mean you are asking for explosives, guns?" They looked at me a

little disappointed. "Of course. We will then be in a position to dramatize that the present course has unacceptable costs. There is only one way to do that."

"Well," I said, "you must realize I am a journalist, not a C.I.A. agent!" They smiled politely but skeptically. "However, I suppose I could pass on what you have told me to people who might be interested. How much popular support can you demonstrate for your proposed actions?"

"You know how people are—they go along with what's popular at the time, even when it's against their own best interests. But dramatic action will generate immense enthusiasm."

I looked them over. They are not a terribly convincing lot of prospective terrorists—but then probably that's the way most any *terrorists look. A couple of them are over 50, people who in the U.S. would be members of Rotary or country club—normal, productive citizens—but here find themselves misfits. A couple are young, hot-eyed, resentful, dangerous. —How they got that way, I have no idea, but they would probably be against the regime whatever it was or did. So far, I see no signs they would have any substantial social backing. All the same, I made notes of how they can be found. Coming out of the coffeeshop, we could have been businessmen who had just worked out a division of the territory. . . .*

(May 15) Marissa Brightcloud. A self-adopted Indian-inspired name—many Ecotopians use them. Met me at train yesterday, to bring me to the forest camp, where I am to observe lumbering and forestry practices for a few days. Assumed at first she must be some kind of PR or government person. Later learned she is one of seven members of elected committee that runs camp and tens of thousands of acres of forest. Strong, warmly physical woman—slender but with solid hips; dark curly hair, large intense eyes: I'd guess at an Italian family background. It was still

damp morning—she wore a rough knitted sweater, denim pants, some kind of hiking or work shoes. Only decoration a light silk scarf at her neck—flowery, subtle pattern.

She had arranged bicycles for us. Panic: I haven't been on a bike in years! Wobbly at first. She watched me get onto it again with calm amusement, then we headed out through the station town and into the woods. She said little, but watched me curiously. Once we stopped on a hill, at a good view over a tract of forest. She gestured, then put a hand on my arm, as if awaiting my reaction. Nice forest, but all I could think of to say was, "Beautiful view." She looked at me a trifle impatiently, as if wondering what kind of person I could be, anyway.

"This forest is my home," she said quietly. "I feel best when I'm among trees. Open country always seems alien to me. Our chimp ancestors had the right idea. Among trees you're safe, you can be free." This with a mysterious smile.

I could think of no reply. She pedaled off. Seemed faster—or was I just getting tired? Had a little trouble keeping up, thought I concealed it. Finally we reached the camp.

It's a group of ramshackle buildings in a grove of very large trees. Old and unpainted, but with a certain sturdy grace, like old summer camps; arranged erratically around large central mess-hall meeting-room building. Off at one side a barn filled with machinery; beyond that an open nursery area of many acres, with thousands of tiny trees sprouting. The whole place foresty-smelling, as of needles slowly decomposing into a springy layer of humus underfoot. Light filtering down through the great trees—strange, soft atmosphere—made me feel a little odd, like a dark church.

As we arrived, several dozen people poured out of the buildings to greet us. A visitor is an event for them, evidently. Marissa stood rather protectively be-

side me as they came up and surrounded us. Barrage of questions—what I've seen so far, where I live in the U.S., what I want to see here, what is my favorite tree (all I could think of was "Christmas tree"—botany was not a good subject for me—but it got appreciative laughs). Wisecracks about how I don't look like much of a lumberjack. Suddenly realized that about half the group are women. Assumed at the time they must deal chiefly with the nursery and the planting of young trees; later learned they also cut trees, operate tractors, and drive big diesels.

"Before we show him our work, our guest must have his bath," Marissa declared with a smile. Led me away for the ceremonial bath with which Ecotopians greet people who come to stay with them—even if, like me, they've only been an hour on the way. More talkative now. She has lived in this camp for several years, but has an occasional month in the city—part vacation and part a change-of-pace assignment, evidently. Obviously very hard-working person. At the same time lively and female, rather mischievous about the members of the camp crew who are city people doing their "forest service." Before people can buy a large quantity of lumber (for instance to build a house) they are obliged to put in a period of some months of labor in a forest camp—planting trees, caring for the forest lands, and supposedly setting in motion the new growth that will one day replace the wood they are buying. (Poetic but foolish notion—though it may make people have a better attitude toward lumber resources.)

She wanted to know whether I had a family, who made up my household (seemed surprised that I didn't even live with wife and children, much less grandparents, cousins, friends, colleagues, but in my own place, 30 miles away, all by myself, though I spend a good deal of time with another woman). Asked what my pleasures were—a question I found hard to answer frankly, but I tried, and her curiosity made it seem easier. "First a sense of power—of reaching out to people, to masses of them and to key people who can act—through my work. Then feelings of craftsmanship in my writing, of intelligence, of knowing I have the background and the originality to grasp strange events and put them into perspective. And love of luxury, or at least fine things: eating in the best restaurants, wearing the best clothes, being seen with the best people." Marissa interrupted teasingly, "Is your woman friend one of the best people?"

"Well, in a way. Or rather, the best people like her a great deal, even though she is not really one of them."

The bath house is a couple of hundred yards off in the woods. By the time we got there the conversation had taken an oddly personal turn. "You haven't mentioned pleasures between yourself and other people, men or women. Don't you have friends, don't you like to love people?" "Well, of course!" I replied, feeling taken off guard. She opened the door to the bath house, and led me into the dark interior, holding my hand. Turned on the bath water tap, threw some more wood on the heating fire, gave me a warm, wry smile, came nearer, put a hand on my shoulder. "Do you want to make love with me?"

I have *been feeling frustrated the last few days, but her assertiveness unnerved me a moment. She's not at all submissive or attentive. She just wanted to get close to me, to play, and to make love. I figured this will happen after the bath, but found myself pushed down onto the wood floor of the bath house. Jesus, I said to myself, this woman is stronger than I am!*

But I mustered my forces, rolled her over. We were both instantly very excited. She giggled at the rapid fumbling we did with our clothes. We got enough of them off to manage—she looking at me intensely now, no more smiles. Her legs are muscular; as I went into her she wrapped them tightly around me. It was hard and brief and sweaty; her sexual odors are powerful. I lost consciousness of the hard floor beneath, and of the hot water steadily running into the huge round tub. Afterward she laughed and disengaged herself. "That was nice," she said; "I guessed you wouldn't mind some contact, when I met you at the train." She looked at me curiously. "Did you think of making a move when I stopped to show you the forest? I know a nice spot there, and I thought—"

"I guess I still felt like too much of a guest to focus on anything like that."

"Well, I thought of it. I liked you, you're a serious person, even if you're not a great bicycler! You just seemed so—distraught or something. Anyway, we don't make that much of a distinction about guests. You're expected to join into everything. We'll have you at work tomorrow. Now I'll show you how we wash."

We scrubbed each other with an odd-shaped sponge, using a dishpan to scoop water from the tub. (There seems to be no shower.) Then we climbed in to soak, Marissa smiling contentedly. Seemed to me a ravishing presence in a way I have never before encountered. Not exactly beautiful, at least by my usual standards. But sometimes, when she looks at me, my hair stands up as if I'm confronting a creature who's wild and incomprehensible, animal and human at once. Eyes dark brown, hard to fathom. She was a little rough as we splashed around in the water—bit me, jumped away. Finally realized she wanted me to stop being gentle with her. Kept relapsing into a kind of silly tenderness. She'd bring me out of it with a push or a bite.

This got very exciting. Eyes shining, she leapt out of tub and ran out the door, dripping. I looked after her, surprised. She jumped back in door, did a comic but enticing little dance, out the door, laughing, in again, and never saying a word. I sprang out and after her, down a forest path. She's damn fast, and also good at dodging around trees. We got into deeper forest. Suddenly, ducking around a particularly huge redwood tree, she disappeared into a hollow at its base. Springing in after her, I found myself in some kind of shrine. She was lying there on a bed of needles, taking deep, gasping breaths. Dimly visible, suspended on the charred inside of the tree, were charms and pendants made of bone and teeth and feathers, gleaming polishing stones. It was as if I was being sucked into the tree, into some powerful spirit, and I fell on her as if I were falling freely through the soft air from a great height, through darkness, my reportorial self floating away.

We must have made love for hours. Cannot describe. Will *not.*

Finally we got up and returned to bath house, Marissa pausing as we left the tree, mumbling something I couldn't catch. Dawned on me that it was a prayer of some kind, and that this incredible woman is a goddamn druid or something—a tree-worshipper!

My feet hardly touched the ground as we went back to camp. When we got there everyone was in mess hall having lunch. Noisy, cheerful scene, big long tables. People smiled at us, made room. (Couple of women didn't smile—but looked me over appraisingly, or so it seemed. Are they all like Marissa, I wonder?)

Later in day, talking with one of the men, learned that Marissa has a reputation for being one of the most responsible and hard-working people on the executive committee. Difficult for me to focus on that side of her personality, even though I saw her operating in that role later in the afternoon. It turns out she has a regular lover in the camp. But has somehow arranged it so she can be with me during my stay. Lover is blond, shy, blushes a lot about other things but doesn't seem at all jealous about his woman having made love with me. Evidently there are other women he can console himself with! Wasn't sure till nightfall who would sleep with whom. But she came to the little cabin I'm assigned to, quite unanxious about the whole situation.

What we do sexually is different from anything that has ever happened to me. Now that the beginning is over, we are utterly relaxed. We hug, we wrestle, we lie absolutely quietly looking at each other, we touch each other with feathery touches that are sometimes erotic and sometimes not. There seems to be no agenda: I feel no compulsion to fuck her, though she is enormously desirable to me. She never says in words whether anything pleases her or not. It's as if the whole recent American sexual "revolution," with its demands and counterdemands and its training and its working at sex like a problem to be solved, has dropped out of my head. Everything comes from our feelings. Sometimes there is excitement in a mere look. Sometimes we get to almost terrifying orgiastic climaxes. But one doesn't really seem more important than the other. In any case, what happens between us is so extraordinary that I find myself utterly unconcerned with her regular lover, or what she might do with him.

Only one thing I don't like: she won't let me use my mouth on her breasts. "You're not a baby," she said, and pushed me away, moving my hand onto one of them instead: they are firm, fit my hand perfectly, very sensitive to arousal. "Have you had any children?" I asked. "Not yet," she said, "but I will soon." "With Everett?" "Oh, no! We're just good friends—fucking partners, not mates." "How will you find your mate?" She shrugged: "What a question! Don't you know?"

I thought about Pat. "I believed I knew, once, but we turned out to be just—well, living partners. We had two children, but then we broke up." "That must be terribly hard for the children, in your country? It's bad enough here, where children have many others besides their parents to love them." "Yes, it is:

If I was doing it again I wouldn't leave." She looked at me—I thought approvingly—in the dim light that filtered through the forest canopy and into the cabin. Then she gave me a hug, and turned over to go to sleep.

IN ECOTOPIA'S BIG WOODS

Healdsburg, May 17. Wood is a major factor in the topsy-turvy Ecotopian economy, as the source not only of lumber and paper but also of some of the remarkable plastics that Ecotopian scientists have developed. Ecotopians in the city and country alike take a deep and lasting interest in wood. They love to smell it, feel it, carve it, polish it. Inquiries about why they persist in using such an outdated material (which of course has been entirely obsoleted by aluminum and plastics in the United States) receive heated replies. To ensure a stable long-term supply of wood, the Ecotopians early reforested enormous areas that had been cut over by logging companies before Independence. They also planted trees on many hundreds of thousands of acres that had once been cleared for orchards or fields, but had gone wild or lay unused because of the exodus of people from the country into the cities.

I have now been able to visit one of the forest camps that carry out lumbering and tree-planting, and have observed how far the Ecotopians carry their love of trees. They do no clear-cutting at all, and their forests contain not only mixed ages but also mixed species of trees. They argue that the costs of mature-tree cutting are actually less per board foot than clear-cutting—but that even if they weren't, it would still be desirable because of less insect damage, less erosion, and more rapid growth of timber. But such arguments are probably only a sophisticated rationale for attitudes that can almost be called tree worship—and I would not be surprised, as I probe further into Ecotopian life, to discover practices that would strengthen this hypothesis. (I have seen fierce-looking totem poles outside dwellings, for instance.)

Certainly the Ecotopian lumber industry has one practice that must seem barbarian to its customers: the unlucky person or group wishing to build a timber structure must first arrange to go out to a forest camp and do "forest service"—a period of labor during which, according to the theory, they are supposed to contribute enough to the growth of new trees to replace the wood they are about to consume. This system must be enormously wasteful in terms of economic inefficiency and disruption, but that seems to disturb the Ecotopians—at least those who live in and run the lumber camps—not a bit.

The actual harvesting of timber is conducted with surprising efficiency, considering the general laxness of Ecotopian work habits. There is much goofing off in the forest camps, but when a crew is at work they work faster and more cooperatively than any workmen I have ever seen. They cut trees and trim them with a strange, almost religious respect: showing the emotional intensity and care we might use in preparing a ballet.

I was told that in rougher country ox-teams and even horses are used in lumbering, just as they were in Gold Rush times. And in many areas a tethered balloon and cables hoist the cut trees and carry them to nearby logging roads. But in the camp I visited (which may be a showplace) the basic machine is a large electric tractor with four huge rubber tires. These are said to tear up the forest floor even less than oxen, which have to drag timber out on some kind of sled. Though heavy, these tractors are surprisingly maneuverable since both front and rear wheels steer. They have a protected operator's cabin amidship; on one end there is a prehensile extension bearing a chain saw large enough to cut through all but the hugest trees, and mounted so it can cut them off only a few inches above ground level. (This is of course pleasant aesthetically, but it is also claimed that it saves some millions of board feet of lumber each year, and helps in management of the forest floor.) This saw can also cut trees into loadable lengths.

On the other end of the tractor is a huge claw device that can pick up a log, twirl it around lengthwise over the tractor, and carry it to the logging road where big diesel trucks wait to be loaded.

Ecotopian foresters claim that this machinery enables them to log safely even in dry weather, since there are no exhausts likely to set fire to undergrowth. It does seem to be true that their methods disturb the forest very little—it continues to look natural and attractive. Several types of trees usually grow in stands together, which is supposed to encourage wildlife and cut the chances of disastrous insect and fungi invasions. Curiously, a few dead trees are left standing—as homes for insect-gobbling woodpeckers! —and there are occasional forest meadows to provide habitats for deer and other animals. The older trees seed young ones naturally, so the foresters generally now only do artificial planting in areas they are trying to reforest. The dense forest canopy keeps the forest floor cool and moist, and pleasant to walk in. Although it rained for a few hours during my stay, I noticed that the stream passing near the camp did not become muddy—evidently it is true, as they claim, that Ecotopian lumbering leaves the topsoil intact, cuts down erosion, and preserves fish. (I didn't actually see any fish—but then I am the kind of person who seldom sees fish anywhere.)

The lumber camps themselves do not have sawmills, though they possess portable devices with which they can saw rough boards in small quantities for their own needs. The main squaring and sawing of timber, and the production of slabs for pulp, takes place at mills located in more open country, which buy logs from the forest camps. The resulting boards are then sold, almost entirely in the county-sized area just around the mill. Lumber sales are solely domestic; Ecotopia ceased lumber export immediately after Independence. It is claimed that, since the U.S. formerly exported half as much lumber as was used in housing, much of it from the West, some surplus actually existed from the beginning of the new nation. Ecotopian foresters argue that their policies have, since then, more than doubled their per capita resources of timber. There are, however, no present plans for a resumption of export.

Interestingly enough, the Ecotopians themselves have a debate in progress about the huge diesel trucks they use to haul logs. Several forest workers apologized to me that they are still dependent on these noisy, smelly, hulking diesels. Yet there are people all over them at the end of the work day, shining them up—one of the few outlets still allowed in this carless society for man's love of powerful machinery. One truck I saw has lost its bumper, and the replacement is a large, sturdy piece of wood. As they wear out, the trucks will be eliminated in favor of electric vehicles. Meanwhile, people argue hotly over the bumpers—extremist ideologues saying that the bumpers (which are actually stainless steel, not chrome plate) should all be replaced with wood, and the traditionalists maintaining that the trucks should be treated as museum relics and kept in original condition. The factions seem about equally matched, which means that the traditionalists have won so far—since a change on such a "drastic" matter is only carried out if there is a virtual consensus.

Our economists would surely find the Ecotopian lumber industry a labyrinth of contradictions. An observer like myself can come only to general conclusions. Certainly Ecotopians regard trees as being alive in almost a human sense—once I saw a quite ordinary-looking young man, not visibly drugged, lean against a large oak and mutter "Brother Tree!" And equally certainly, lumber in Ecotopia is cheap and plentiful, whatever the unorthodox means used to produce it. Wood therefore takes the place that aluminum, bituminous facings, and many other modern materials occupy with us.

An important by-product of the Ecotopian forestry policies is that extensive areas, too steep or rugged to be lumbered without causing erosion, have been assigned wilderness status. There, all logging and fire roads have been eradicated. Such areas are now used only for camping and as wildlife preserves, and a higher risk of forest fire is apparently accepted. It is interesting, by the way, that such Ecotopian forests are uncannily quiet compared to ours, since they have no trail-bikes, all-terrain vehicles, airplanes overhead, nor snowmobiles in the winter. Nor can you get around in them rapidly, since foot trails are the only way to get anywhere.

Has Ecotopian livestock or agricultural production suffered because of the conversion of so much land to forest? Apparently not; vegetables, grains and meat are reasonably cheap, and beef cattle are common features of the landscape, though they are never concentrated in forced-feeding fattening lots. Thus an almost dead occupation, that of cowboy, has come back. And cattle ranches in the Sierra foothills have reverted to the old summer practice of driving their stock up to the high valleys where they pasture on wet mountain meadow grass. Grasslands research is said to be leading to the sowing of more native strains, which are better adapted to the climate and resist the incursion of thistles. Pasture irrigation is practiced only in a few areas, and only for milking herds.

But the true love of the Ecotopians is their forests, which they tend with so much care and manage in the prescribed stable-state manner. There they can claim much success in their campaign to return nature to a natural condition.

(May 18) Marissa says I am squeamish about violence. Makes fun of American war technology, claims we had to develop it because we can no longer bear just to bayonet a man—have to spend $50,000 to avoid guilt, by zapping him from the stratosphere. This because last night I expressed dismay at the ritual war games. "Listen, you'll love *it," she said gaily, "you're just ripe for it!" With this, a flash of teeth: she can still scare me a little, sometimes is very aware of her strength—plain animal strength. And then great peals of laughter. Phoned to arrange to take me to a war games session not far north of here, which some friends of hers will be participating in. Her eyes shone with mischief as she set it all up. Before she even hung up the picturephone we were all over each other again. Giggling uncontrollably.*

She finds my dubious confrontations with Ecotopian manners and morals endearingly comic. I am childishly wasteful in her eyes. This morning I had written a few sentences on a page, got disgusted, and tossed it away. She picked it up, frowned. "You've only used a little part of this one." "Well, it didn't go right, so I wanted a fresh start." "Why can't you make your fresh start further down? It's you that's making the start, not the poor paper! Think of the tree it came from." I tore the sheet up and threw it at her. . . . On the other hand, if I lapse into inattention or mere American businesslikeness, she gets furious and accuses me of being detached and inhuman. But sometimes, if I am just lying quietly or thinking or writing, she looks at me as if I am not ludicrously un-Ecotopian but merely a fellow human being. It is at such times, I notice, that we have had our tenderest love-making.

I got up early next morning, to take train back to city and work on my next story. We bicycled together to the station. When the train warning bell rang I felt surprisingly bereft and blurted out, "Marissa, come with me." She hugged me hard and said, "I want to, but I can't. I'll come tomorrow though. About sundown." The train swept in, its air blast pushing us back. I got in and we stared at each other through the big windows until the train pulled away. Her grave, intense expression is still in my mind as I sit trying to finish my report on Ecotopian population policy. Tomorrow night she'll be here, in my room. . . .

It feels good to be back at the Cove. I'm beginning to know the people here, and feel accepted as a colleague and a person, despite being an American. Bert is formidably generous, like most Ecotopians, really brotherly—but without the competitiveness that can be mixed with. Spends much time cluing me in on things here, introduces me to key people, lends me shirts, gave me a pen that I admired. Maybe it is their economy of biological abundance that gives them this generosity?

He has been reading my dispatches, jokes about putting an expose in the Times *titled "Weston's Progress," but thinks I am trying seriously to overcome my "prejudices." He finds the lumber story the best yet, says teasingly that Marissa must have inspired me a little. (I have told him about our encounter, though not in any detail.) Also likes the story on Alviso. "But the sports story was terrible. You'd better keep away from that kind of thing. —Are you really going to try to handle the ritual war games?" I told him that Marissa had already arranged for me to see one, in a couple of days. He looked at me uncertainly. "I hope it goes all right," he said. "It's about the trickiest story you'll face here, I imagine.*

I might be able to help a little on it, if you want. I'd be glad to look over the draft, give you a little background maybe."

"Sure you can see it," I replied, "but I'll write it the way I write it."

We shook hands on that, Ecotopian fashion.

(Later) Unpleasant night visit from the Ecotopian counter-intelligence, who have somehow heard about my encounter with the underground. (Or have I been tailed?) "Of course," they said, "you are perfectly free to talk with anyone at all while you are in Ecotopia. But you shouldn't think we are naive about your government's clandestine operations. It would be wise of you to forget to deliver that message in Washington."

"And if I don't forget?" "It will just make more trouble for your friends here." "They're not my friends." "Then why transmit their message?" "I don't like being intimidated."

They smiled. "A little country like ours 'intimidating' a big one like yours? Don't be absurd." There was a pause. I wondered how much they knew of what I had said. "Weston, you are not a fool. We also know you are not a spy. But would you expect somebody who acts like a spy to be received in the President's office?"

"Okay," I replied. "You've made your point. No message."

A sweaty experience—I'll have to watch my step. These Ecotopians are not so easy-going as they look. And to tell the truth it relieves my mind—didn't much like those people. I've burned the list of names and contact points.

DECLINE WITHOUT FALL? THE ECOTOPIAN POPULATION CHALLENGE

San Francisco, May 20. Ecotopia's population is slowly declining, and has done so for almost 15 years. This startling fact—which by itself would set Ecotopia apart from the U.S. and all other nations except Japan—has led to speculation that rampant abortion and even perhaps infanticide may be practiced here. However, I have now investigated sufficiently to report that Ecotopia's decline in population has been achieved through humane measures.

We tend to forget that even before Independence the rate of population growth in the area that became Ecotopia had slowed, as it had in most of the rest of the U.S. This was due, according to American demographers, partly to the persistent inflation-recession, partly to the relaxation of abortion laws, and perhaps most of all to increased recognition that additional children, in a highly advanced industrial society, could be more of a burden than an advantage to a family—the reverse of the situation in agricultural or less advanced societies. In addition, the horrible "Green Revolution" famines, in which tens of millions perished in Pakistan, India, Bangladesh, and Egypt, had provided new and grim lessons in the dangers of overpopulation.

After secession, the Ecotopians adopted a formal national goal of a declining population—though only after long and bitter debate. It was widely agreed that *some* decline was needed, to lessen pressure on resources and other species and to improve the comfort and amenity of life. But opinions differed widely on exactly how a decline could be achieved, and how far it shuld go. Deep fears of national extinction gave heavy ammunition against advocates of population decline, and economists warned of fiscal dislocations.

Finally a three-stage program was adopted. The first stage, to last through 1982, was a massive educational and medical campaign aimed at providing absolutely all women with knowledge of the various birth-control devices. Abortion upon demand was legalized; its cost soon became very low, and it was practiced in local clinics as well as hospitals. As far as statistics could reveal in such a short period, this program reduced the number of births to a few tenths of a percent below the number of deaths—almost enough to counterbalance the still growing longevity. (Ironically, an unusual number of pregnancies were initiated during the exciting months when Independence was achieved!)

The second stage, 1983 through 1984, was linked to the radical decentralization of the country's economic life, and was thus more political in nature. During this period the Ecotopians largely dismantled their national tax and spending system, and local communities regained control over all basic life systems. This enabled people to deliberately think about how they now wished to arrange their collective lives, and what this meant for population levels and distribution. With better conditions in the countryside, the great concentrations of people in San Francisco, Oakland, Portland, Seattle, and even the smaller metropolitan areas began to disperse somewhat. New minicities grew up in favorable locations, with their own linkage necklaces of transit lines: Napa, on its winding, Seine-like river, at last pollution-free; Carquinez-Martinez, stretching out along rolling hills dropping down to the Strait; and others throughout the country. Some old city residential areas were abandoned and razed, and the land turned into parks or reforested. Some rural towns, like Placerville, which had been in the 10–20,000 people range, gained satellite minicities that would in a decade bring them to a total of 40-50,000—which was felt to be about ideal for an urban constellation.

Decentralization affected every aspect of life. Medical services were dispersed; the claim is that instead of massive hospitals in the city centers, beseiged by huge lines of waiting patients, there were small hospitals and clinics everywhere, and a neighborhood-oriented system of medical aides. Schools were broken up and organized on a novel teacher-controlled basis. Agricultural, fishery, and forestry enterprises were also reorganized and decentralized. Large factory-farms were broken up through a strict enforcement of irrigation acreage regulations which had been ignored before Independence, and commune and extended-family farms were encouraged.

All these changes, according to my informants, meant notable readjustments in problems of crowding, and the predictions of some anti-decline arguments were indeed borne out: there didn't seem to be as many too many people as before!

Thus, the pressures for further population control measures waned during 1984. When final statistics were in, however, the population had indeed taken its first actual drop—by about 17,000 people for Ecotopia as a whole. This fact was not greeted by the hysteria that had been widely predicted, and people probably took grim satisfaction from the news that American society, with its widely publicized overpopulation, had grown by another three million during the same period.

The third stage, if we can call it that, was one of watchful waiting, which has continued to the present. Abortion costs have fallen further, and the number per year has stabilized. The use of contraceptive devices now seems universal. (They are all, incidentally, female-controlled; there is no "male pill" here.) Population has tended to drop gently at a rate of around

65,000 per year, so that the original Ecotopian population of some 15 million has now declined to about 14 million. It is argued by some extremists that the declining population provides a substantial annual surplus per capita and helps account for the vitality of Ecotopian economic life. Though the decline undoubtedly influences the confident political and economic atmosphere, I remain skeptical of direct effects—the decline, after all, is only .3% per year.

What will happen to Ecotopian population levels in the future? Most people here foresee a continued slow decline. They consider that a more rapid drop might endanger the nation, making it more vulnerable to attack by the United States—which is still widely feared to be desirous of recapturing its "lost territories." On the other hand, some people hope that American population will itself soon begin to decline—and if that happens, many Ecotopians are prepared to accept an indefinite drop in their own numbers. In fact, some radical Survivalist Party thinkers believe that a proper population size would be the number of Indians who inhabited the territory before the Spaniards and Americans came—something less than a million for the whole country, living entirely in thinly scattered bands! Most Ecotopians, however, contend that the problem is no longer numbers as such. They place their faith for improvement of living conditions in the further reorganization of their cities into constellations of minicities, and in a continued dispersion into the countryside. In connection with this, the radicals are currently mounting a campaign to make train travel entirely free: this, they argue, could make country living more agreeable to people who find city pleasures and facilities important, since they could then visit the cities virtually whenever they wished.

Americans are, of course, accustomed to believe that only economic and population growth can lead to improvement in life. The Ecotopian experiments, whatever their apparent achievements, have a long way to go in order to change this basic conviction. Ecotopian circumstances have been, after all, unusually favorable compared to those in the rest of the U.S.; the Ecotopians' special advantages in fertile agricultural land, a backlog of buildings suitable for housing, and a more self-reliant Western tradition, have all led them to a focus on surpluses, not shortages —which they have encountered (or perhaps brought about) only in energy and metals.

Americans would find Ecotopian population policies alarming in that, along with Ecotopia's decline in population, the nuclear family as we know it is rapidly disappearing. Ecotopians still speak of "families," but they mean by that term a group of between five and 20 people, some of them actually related and some not, who live together. In many such families not only eating and household duties are shared, but also the raising of children—in which men and women seem to participate equally as far as time spent is concerned, but within a strange power context. Ecotopian life is strikingly equalitarian in general—women hold responsible jobs, receive equal pay, and of course they also control the Survivalist Party. The fact that they also exercise absolute control over their own bodies means that they openly exert a power which in other societies is covert or nonexistent: the right to select the fathers of their children. "No Ecotopian woman ever bears a child by a man she has not freely chosen," I was told sternly. And in the nurturing of children while they are under two, women continue this dominance; men participate extensively in the care and upbringing of the very young, but in cases of conflict the mothers have the final say, and mince no words about it. The fathers, odd though it appears to me, acquiesce in this situation as if it was perfectly natural; they evidently feel that their time of greater influence on the young will come later, and that that is the way it should be.

It's difficult for an outsider to determine the bonds that hold the communal groups together, but children may be a key factor, though economic necessity clearly plays an important part also. In one such family I visited, I was reminded of the earlier American practice of having godparents—related or unrelated persons who assume a certain responsibility for children, take a special interest in them, and help to enrich their lives—or give them a refuge from their parents! Ecotopian children normally live surrounded by informal "godparents," and a cheerier bunch of kids I have never seen. A willingness to help nurture children may well be the crucial qualification for membership in one of these "families." But there are also "families" with no children at all. These have an entirely different atmosphere, tend to be larger, and are evidently more transient. Some are professionally oriented—journalist groups, musicians, scientists, craftspeople, or people concerned with an enterprise like a school or factory. Their members are mostly younger, whereas the families with children have members who span a wide range of ages. (It is rare for Ecotopian old people to live alone, as so many of ours do; they mostly live in the families, where they play an important role in child care and early education.)

Americans are familiar with rumors of sexual depravity in Ecotopia, but I must report that the sexual practices of these families seem about as stable as ours. Generally there are more or less permanent heterosexual couples involved—though both male and female homosexual couples also exist, and I gather that same-sex relationships pose less of a problem psychologically than they do with us. Monogamy is not an officially proclaimed value, but the couples are generally monogamous (except for four holidays each year, at the solstices and equinoxes, when sexual promiscuity is widespread). Single members of the families often take up with lovers from outside, and sometimes this results in the addition or subtraction of a family member. There seems to be a continual slow shifting of membership, probably something like what must have happened with our "extended families" a few generations back.

I have made extensive inquiries about Ecotopian attitudes on the kind of eugenic population planning which has been discussed so passionately in the U.S.—either the aiding of natural selection by deliberate breeding, or farther-out possibilities such as cloning, whereby actual genetic duplicates of superior individuals might be produced, or even modification of gene structures to produce a race of supermen. However, no Ecotopian scientist or citizen has been willing to discuss such matters, which they view with great distaste. Nor, when I have ventured the hypothesis that man may be only a "missing link" between the apes and a later, superior humanity, have I obtained any response except condescending incredulity. Their reluctance to enter into such speculations may show the extent to which Ecotopians have blinded themselves to the exciting possibilities offered by modern scientific advances. But it also shows that they are more willing than we to live with the biological constitutions we now possess.

(May 21) Everybody suddenly glued to TV sets. Ecotopian monitor systems, which seem to be extremely sophisticated for both nuclear and general pollution, have detected a sudden increase in the radiation level of air blowing in from the Pacific. Cause still unknown. Much speculation on the streets and in media: Chinese nuclear blast gone out of control? Accident in a Japanese fission plant? Conflict on the Chinese-Russian border? Nuclear submarine accident offshore? People anxious, depressed, angry. They turn in a crisis to the TV, which they

watch in tense groups, but not in the passive, dependent fashion of Americans—they actually shout at it, and the switchboards are flooded with picturephone callers. Vera Allwen and her foreign minister were obliged to appear within an hour and on the defensive, answering angry citizens who put pointed, difficult questions about why their government can't do anything. (Also hotheads who think commando teams should be sent to disable plants in Japan, China, Siberia which emit wastes into air or sea!) Allwen says she is preparing a stiff protest to whoever turns out to be responsible. Meanwhile Ecotopian ships and agents are on a crash program to locate the pollution source. So far dead silence from the U.S. wire services, which are received in Vancouver and relayed here, though our satellite reconnaissance must have spotted what happened.

There is a widespread tendency to blame technological disasters on Americans, so I haven't been made to feel terribly welcome in the last few hours. Groups I have been with, watching Allwen and other national politicos, seem to think the Ecotopian government is too tolerant of pollution coming in from outside. Talk about "reparations" on TV—apparently some international pollution-fine system is really being proposed. The Japanese will love that.

Have been watching all this mostly from Franklin's Cove, where I moved today, at their invitation (and urged by Marissa, who doesn't like hotels at all). "You're a journalist, aren't you?" they said; "Well then, you ought to live with us!" A welcome thought, and I guess I can find the time for their cooking and cleaning work crews. My little room's on the top floor; dormer window looks out toward Alcatraz—a green hump looming out of the Bay, with its cheerful orange lighthouse tower. Hard to believe such a peaceful grassy island once housed our worst desperadoes, and was covered with concrete and steel.

(Later) Have found the work crew experience a little unnerving. First time I joined one it was for after-dinner clean-up. I pitched in, American-style, scurrying around carrying dishes to the sink area. After a few moments I realized people had stopped their general chatter and were staring at me. "My God, Will," said Lorna, "whatever are you doing, running a race?" Everybody else laughed.

I blushed, or felt like it. "What do you mean?" "Well, you're hauling dishes like you were being paid by the dish. Very un-Ecotopian!" I looked around, suddenly conscious that everyone else had been working very leisurely by comparison: Lorna and Brit had developed a sort of game in which they took turns washing and giving each other little back rubs. Bert was meanwhile telling about a funny encounter he had had that day with a reader who threatened to beat him up. And Red was drinking beer and not doing much of anything; occasionally, when his attention fell on a dirty pot or something, he would bring it over to the sink.

"Don't you want to get it done with?" I replied defensively. "When I have a job to do I like to get it over with. What's wrong with a little efficiency?" "A little goes a long way, Will," Lorna said. "Our point of view is that if something's worth doing, it ought to be done in a way that's enjoyable—otherwise it can't really *be worth doing."*

"Then how does anything get done?" I asked, exasperatedly. "You don't mean to tell me washing dishes is exactly fun?" "It is the way we do it," said Bert. "Almost anything can be, if you keep your eye on the process and not on the goal."

"Okay," I said. "I'll try it." So I goofed off in the Ecotopian manner—drank a little beer, tossed some knives and forks into the sink, told a joke I'd heard that day, then wiped a few tables. But it was hard to keep my pace down, and harder still to keep in good touch with the other people—I'd focus on the

task, and blot them out. But they noticed this, and invented a game around it. "Hey Will!" they'd yell, "We're here!" And somebody would tickle me, or give me a pat. They'll retrain me yet.

(May 23) Marissa's got positively hypnotic powers: when she's here I lose track of time, obligations, my American preconceptions. She exists in a contagious state of immediate consciousness. Somewhere far back in her head must be the forest camp, her responsibilities there, her plans to return tomorrow. But she seems to be able to turn them absolutely off and just be. *She seems capable of anything—she's the freest and least anxious person I've ever known. To the extent I can get in on this, I begin to feel high and a little strange, as if I was on some kind of drug. I keep thinking she is like a wild animal: of course she responds to the influences and constraints of the other animals around (me included) but these are not inside her head, somehow. She's highly unpredictable, moody, changeable, yet wherever she is, she's always right* there, *with me or whoever it is. (I don't know how to deal with the jealousy I feel when she turns her attention, like a beautiful searchlight beam, on somebody else. But I bear it.)*

Not that we lie around in bed all the time—have actually been fairly busy, wandering around to visit people she knows, taking expeditions so she can show me her favorite San Francisco places, eating at peculiar little restaurants, laughing, sometimes just sitting and watching people or birds or even trees. She has special trees all over the place, and they're really important to her. (Thinks I should write a column on the trees of Ecotopia!) She studies their characters, revisits them to see how they've grown and changed, likes to climb in some of them (she's agile and surefooted), is immensely happy if they're thriving and cast down if they're not. Even talks to them—or rather mutters, since she knows I think it's kind of crazy.

I realize I am growing terribly attached to her. What seemed at the beginning like a lark, the usual brief liaison of a travelling man, has quickly gotten terribly serious. Marissa is clearly a powerful and remarkable person: sees through my bullshit, but sees something valuable under it. By comparison I look back at Pat as almost an artificial person, vapid and rigid and horribly, horribly controlled. Even Francine, my beloved nutty Francine, with whom I've had such giggles and pleasures, begins to seem lightweight. With Marissa I get into feelings I never knew were there: a deep, overwhelming, scary sharing of our whole beings, as well as our bodies. There's no denying it—we're beginning to love each other. And despite her free ways, and her still living with Everett at the camp, she has some fierce possessive streak for me—gets angry whenever my return comes up.

Went sailing on the Bay yesterday, with a couple of people from the Cove. Marissa invited her brother Ben. Older brother; turns out to be surly and viciously anti-American. As soon as we had pushed off he came right at me with arguments and charges. I tried to parry politely but it didn't help. It's early in the season and the wind doesn't come up strongly yet, so we veered around trying to set the sails for a while. Then everybody lay down on the foredeck, getting some sun and watching the water go by. I went aft to sit with Ben, and offered to take the tiller. He scowled and said abruptly, in a low voice, "What the hell are you messing around with my sister for? Goddamn Americans can't keep their hands off anything!" I answered mildly, "We like each other—what's wrong with that?" "You know what's wrong with it, you stupid bastard—you're really getting to her, and then you're going to take off." "I've never concealed my intentions from anybody, Ben." He looked at me. "I ought to just push you overboard, and not turn back!" He made a sudden movement with his hands. I grabbed the rail, thinking he might really try something. He grinned wickedly. "You creep!" I said. "What do you mean, trying to run your sister's life? Making threats? Think you're the Mafia or something?" At this the others, hearing us, sat up and came back aft. Ben and I exchanged mean looks. "We were just having a little argument," he said. I got up and sat beside Marissa on the other side of the cockpit. She looked at me, then at Ben. "I'll tell you about it later," I said. "So will I," Ben shot back.

We sailed on, over to an abandoned whaling station on the east side of the Bay, and put in there for a while. It's a museum now, with chilling exhibits about whaling and the extinction of mammals generally. Ben lost no chance to point out how Americans and their technology had been in the forefront of this tragic and irreversible process. And indeed I hadn't realized how far it has gone: it is a horrible story. Our role in it was heavy, and thousands of marvelous creatures that once inhabited this earth have now vanished from the universe forever. We have gobbled them up in our relentless increase. There are now 40 times more weight of humans on the earth than of all the wild mammals together!

Marissa mostly stared at the displays of whale life (Ecotopians have incredible wildlife photographers—they must literally live with the species they are filming—though as far as I can tell Ecotopians don't take ordinary snapshots of our quick-freeze-the-moment type.) It turns out she has swum with dolphins, but won't say much about the experience except that it was enormously exciting and quite scary.

On the way back we passed shrimp boats and other small fishing craft—apparently the Bay, once an open cess-pool, has again become the fertile habitat which estuaries naturally are (thus my ardent informant). Was proudly told how many metric tons of tiny, succulent Bay shrimp are consumed and shipped out daily; even clams, whose shells the local

Indians once piled into huge refuse mounds, have returned to the mudflats.

Windblown, a little sunstruck, a little drunk, we returned at dusk to the Cove and to bed. "Ben is really a good brother to have, but I've never been able to get him to know where to stop," Marissa said apologetically. (I had noticed her lecturing him on the dock as we were stowing the boat's gear away.) "He cares about me a lot, even if I've never gotten him to understand me. He never likes to see me taking risks. It's a relic of the family past, I guess—when women supposedly had no independence at all. But without taking risks, I wouldn't feel I was alive." She smiled at me, with a sweet but inscrutable companionableness, and laid down in my arms.

What can I possibly mean to this incredible woman? She evades my questions about what she thinks of me. When she is back at the lumber camp, she evidently sleeps and lives with Everett as before; yet little by little, she spends more of her free time with me. Yet she makes goodhumored fun of me, correcting my ecological mistakes (like wasting wash water or electricity) as if she was the highly advanced person and I a kind of bumpkin, not yet fully acclimated to civilized life.

Sometimes, when I say something about how Ecotopians, or she herself, appear to me, she becomes very quiet and attentive. The other night I mentioned their way of holding eye contact for what seems to me excessively long times, and how this stirred up feelings it is hard for me to handle. "What feelings?" she asked. "Nervousness, a desire for relief, to look away for a while." "And if you withstand the nervousness and go on looking?" (All this, of course, with her great dark eyes intent upon mine.) "Then I guess tenderness, and a desire to touch. —It makes me afraid I'll cry." "You strange person—of course you can cry!" She gave me a long, strong hug.

I had to explain. "Not in our country! Maybe here you can teach me, though. I don't have to be so guarded here, with you." "All right," she said, a faint puzzlement in her eyes. Can I be, for her, some kind of Mysterious Stranger—exotic in spite of myself?

SAVAGERY RESTORED: ECOTOPIA'S DARK SIDE

Marshall-by-the-Bay, May 24. After much negotiation, I have now been permitted to observe that monstrous custom which has inspired so much horror toward Ecotopia among civilized nations: the Ritual War Games. Yesterday I became, so far as I know, the first American ever to witness this chilling spectacle. My companions and I rose before dawn and took a train north from San Francisco to the town of Marshall. Then a walk of 20 minutes (passing two of the small, home-made shrines that dot the Ecotopian landscape) brought us to a hill overlooking a rolling, open piece of country with a creek flowing through it down to the marshy edge of the water.

When we got there, preparations for the ritual were well under way. Two bands of young men had gathered, one on each side of the creek. Perhaps 25 were on each side. Each group had built a fire, and prepared some kind of drink in a large cauldron—apparently a stimulant to anesthetize themselves against the terrors to come. Each man (they ranged from about 16 to 30) had a large, dangerous spear, with a point of sharpened black stone. And each man was painting himself with colors, in primitive, fierce designs.

After a time, when several hundred spectators had gathered, a signal was given on a large gong. At this, the spectators became tense and silent. The "warriors" deployed along both banks of the creek, taking up positions about a spear-length apart. One group, seeming more aggressive, began a war chant that sounded quite blood-thirsty, though also perhaps a bit reminiscent of our athletic cheers. When the other side seemed to hesitate and back off from the creek, the aggressive group crossed it, brandishing their spears, and began a series of rushes up the other side.

The defenders, however, could not be panicked. Whenever a number of attackers pressed hard against one of their men, his neighbors gathered to his defense, shouting and bringing their spears to bear; and this flexible, fluid, shifting pattern of offense and defense seemed to prevail all along the line. Occasionally a group would gather and rush at the opponents' line. But this rush would soon be countered, though often at the cost of very close calls with the sharp obsidian blades.

This went on, with much shouting and the crowd growing increasingly excited, for perhaps half an hour—the warriors returning occasionally to their cauldrons for refreshment. Then suddenly a scream went up from one end of the line. My attention had been elsewhere, so I did not actually see the fatal blow, but others later told me a warrior had slipped on the grass during one of the rushes, and an opponent had seized the chance and managed to run a spear entirely through his shoulder.

At this, all hostilities miraculously ceased. The two tribes retreated to their original positions. Partisans of the "winning" side appeared joyful, almost ecstatic, slapping and hugging each other; the losers' partisans were downcast. Doctors appeared from among the onlookers, and began attending to the wounded man. There was a lot of blood on the grass, but from comments around me I gathered that the victim was not in grave medical danger despite his nasty wound.

The victors now began a dance of celebration. Their partisans came down the hill to join them. Musicians struck up, and dancing began. The warriors shared their cauldron with all, in an atmosphere of excited jubilation. Some of the leading warriors on the winning side went off with women into the bushes. On the losing side there appeared to be a good deal of lamentation, crying, and writhing around. After a time the fires were stoked up again, food was brought out, and a feast began to take shape. This was held at the camp of the winners; they magnanimously offered to feed the defeated side—who accepted deferentially.

I learned that an ambulance which had been standing by would shortly carry away the wounded man (now neatly bandaged up) so I went over to speak to him. They had laid him out on a kind of stretcher made of red cloth with a white cross on it. His body was arranged in a startlingly crucifix-like way, with straps on wrists and ankles. Several women leaned over the stretcher, moaning and from time to time wiping his forehead with a damp rag.

"Oh, how you have suffered!" cried one. "I have done a man's thing," he replied, in a rather rote tone. "Your poor body has been hurt, you might have died!" the women said. "Do not think of me, think of our family: I bear wounds for them." "We all suffer!"

At this, the young man looked at them in an almost pitying way. "It is finished," he said quietly, and closed his eyes. From the way he spoke, I thought for a moment that the doctors had been mistaken, and he was dying. But apparently it was just a signal for the women to leave him—for after they did, he opened his eyes again and looked around in perfectly cheery spirits.

I seized the opportunity and went up to him. "How do you feel?"

"I feel like a man," he said, relapsing into his former rote manner. "Once more I have survived." "Can you tell me what the fighting was about?" "It was us against them, of course, to see who would win." "No other reason?"

He gave me a curious look. "It also is to test ourselves—don't you understand how good it feels to be frightened, and come through?" "Would you do it all over again?" "Sure. We *will* do it again, probably on the second full moon from now. —Are you some kind of stranger here?"

"I'm an American newspaper reporter," I said, "writing articles for my paper. Can I take your picture?" I pulled out my camera, expecting no objection, but the young man replied "NO! Absolutely not! Have you no decency?" At this a group of men nearby turned toward us in a menacing way.

"Excuse me," I said, realizing I had made a serious blunder. I put the camera away quickly. (Later I learned that Ecotopians think photography has a dark-magic side, as a way of trying to freeze time—to cheat biology and defy change and death, so it would be especially out of place at such a time.) The Ecotopians, however, did not leave it at that. One of the older men asked me to come and sit beside him. He offered me a meat-stuffed pastry, and proceeded to lecture me on the meaning of the war games I had been witnessing.

Ecotopians, he began, had always regarded anthropology as a field with great practical importance. After Independence they had begun to experiment in adapting anthropological hypotheses to real life. It was only over a great deal of resistance that a radical idea such as ritual warfare had become legally practicable, even with the ingenuity of the best lawyers. But its advocates had persisted, convinced as they were that it was essential to develop some kind of open civic expression for the physical competitiveness that seemed to be inherent in man's biological programming—and otherwise came out in perverse forms, like war.

They hoped that Ecotopians would not be forced to fight any actual wars, since they knew the utter destruction that would result. On the other hand, it seemed indisputable that man was not a creature built for a totally and routinely peaceful life. Young men, especially, needed a chance to combat "the others," to charge and flee, to test their comradeship, to put their beautiful resources of speed and strength to use, to let their adrenalin flow, to be brave and to be fearful. "In America," my companion pointed out with a smug grin, "you accomplish some of the same objectives with your wars and your automobiles. They let you be competitive and aggressive and you are allowed to risk smashing each other. Of course, you also have professional football. But it is only a spectator sport—and besides, the players do not possess lethal weapons. Though I admit we took some ideas from it."

Ecotopian experimentation with ritual warfare was planned to last about a single generation (some 25 or 30 years), after which its effects would be evaluated and a social decision made as to whether it was desirable to continue it or not. If the evaluation was negative, my informant assured me, they would move on to new experiments.

He went on to argue that Ecotopian ritual war games actually result in very few fatalities—something like 50 young men die in the games each year, a figure he insisted on comparing with our highway toll of about 75,000 a year and our war dead, which tend to average out to around 5,000 a year. It appears, by the way, that women never participate in the war games; but before our feminist militants leap on this point, they should know that the games were established as part of the Survivalist Party's generally cooperation-oriented program, and that Ecotopians prefer to focus women's competitiveness in other ways: through contests for political leadership, through organizing work—at which women are believed to excel—and through rivalry over men to father their children.

It is thus chiefly young men who participate in the games, and the meets are set up largely between neighboring groups, something like our highschool athletic contests but on an even smaller scale. The game today, for instance, was between two communes that occupy neighboring territories. One group raises sheep for wool and cows for milk; the other "farms" oysters in an estuary of the bay. Apparently in the cities competition is usually between neighborhoods or work groups—factory against factory, store against store, as happens in our industrial bowling leagues. However, there are no leagues, pennants, and so forth. Each ritual session is a self-contained event, an end in itself.

"What about the cross?" I asked.

"Well, Ecotopia came into existence with a Judeo-Christian heritage," was the reply. "We make the best of it. You will find many expressions of it in our culture still. In this case, obviously the young man *is* indeed suffering for his family or 'tribe.' We have a lot of poetry and music that focuses precisely on this suffering, as well as on courage and bravery. There's also a little ceremony for when a wounded man comes back from hospital. You might guess what it's called: the raising. He stands up and walks."

It is clear, thus, that the abhorrent spectacle of fine young men deliberately trying to kill each other is a semi-religious rite and a practice not lightly instituted, no matter what we Americans may think of it. It may indeed have antecedents in the institution of bullfighting, in football, in the Mass, or in the ritual wars of savage tribes. But its senseless violence, the letting of blood without a justifying cause, must surely remain a blot on Ecotopia's name among civilized nations.

(May 25) Goddamn woman is impossible! Got really turned on at the war games—stayed beside me during the fighting, explaining it to me in low, excited voice. Then afterward rushed away to the cauldron, drank an enormous cupful, looked around in an inviting fashion, and made no resistance when one of the winning warriors came up, propositioned her, and literally carried her away. (She weighs about 130, as I happen to know, but this didn't faze him.) Not a glance in my direction.

Later, when rest of us were eating, she sauntered back, flushed and sweaty. Ignored my obvious ill humor. Later, when we went back to the Marshall hotel, she was relaxed and floppy, and I tossed her around on the bed a little roughly, wouldn't let her up, more or less raped her. She seemed almost to have expected this. I felt odd when it began, confused between hatred and desire, but then they merged in a kind of hard, tightly holding embrace—a welcoming back on her part, and a deep acceptance of her on mine. I love her freeness, even when it hurts.

Just before waking up and writing the war-games story, had awful dream about it. Myself all painted up, ready for battle. Body greased and shining and beautiful—feel very alive, very strong. Women smile from the sidelines, I want to make love to all of them. Then there's a terrible gong sound—reverberates in my head, and panic strikes. Grab my spear and rush off with the other men. But when we get to the fighting line and begin to feint and jab, suddenly they turn and look at me with amazement, realizing I am not one of them. Then utter despair seizes me, for I know this means they will not fight for me: I am not one of their Tribe, and I am out there alone, ex-

posed to the sharp spears of the enemy, and my time has come....

Woke up sweating, hands clutched tight on dream spear. Wished I was home safe in New York.

Savages!

THEIR PLASTICS AND OURS

San Francisco, May 25. One surprising similarity between Ecotopia and contemporary America is that they both use huge amounts of plastics. At first I took this as a sign that our ways of life have not diverged so drastically after all. However, closer investigation has revealed that, despite surface resemblances, the two countries use plastics in totally different ways.

Ecotopian plastics are entirely derived from living biological sources (plants) rather than from fossilized ones (petroleum and coal) as most of ours are. Intense research effort went into this area directly after Independence, and it continues. According to my informants, there were two major objectives. One was to produce the plastics, at low cost and in a wide range of types: light, heavy, rigid, flexible, clear, opaque, and so on—and to produce them with a technology that was not itself a pollutant. The other objective was to make them all *biodegradable*, that is, susceptible to decay. This meant that they could be returned to the fields as fertilizer, which would nourish new crops, which in turn could be made into new plastics—and so on indefinitely, in what the Ecotopians call, with almost religious fervor, a "stable-state system."

One interesting strategy for biodegradability involved producing plastics which had a short planned lifetime and would automatically self-destruct after a certain period or under certain conditions. (With typical biology-centered thinking, Ecotopians refer to such plastics as "dying" when they begin to decompose.) Plastics of this type are used to make containers for beer, food of many types, to produce packaging materials that resemble cellophane, and so on. These materials "die" after a month or so, especially when exposed to sunlight's ultraviolet rays. I have noticed that the usually tidy Ecotopians have no hesitation about dropping (and stamping on) an empty beer container; it turns out they know that in a few weeks its remnants will have crumbled and decayed into the soil. Similarly, Ecotopian householders toss wrapping materials onto their compost heaps, knowing they will join in the general decay into rich garden fertilizer.

Another line of plastics development led to a variety of durable materials, which were increasingly needed in place of metals. Metals became deliberately scarce in early Ecotopia, when the little mining and smelting that had taken place were replaced by an entirely scrap-based metals industry. An amusing aspect of this scarcity was the nationwide campaign to recycle junked cars, which had littered the Ecotopian landscape just as they do ours. These formerly worthless heaps of junk skyrocketed in value, and were hauled up from creekbeds, pulled out of vacant lots, unearthed in abandoned barns, and of course salvaged from scrap yards. In a parallel campaign, several billion beer and soda cans were collected and recycled.

Ecotopian durable plastics, which are used for minibus bodies, "extruded houses," coins, bottles, and mechanical objects of many kinds, have molecular structures similar to those of our plastics, and are virtually decay-proof under ordinary circumstances —in particular, so long as they are not in contact with the soil. However, by chemical advances that have so far remained secret, Ecotopian scientists have built into these molecules "keyholes," which can be opened only by soil micro-organisms! Once they are unlocked, the whole structure decomposes rapidly.

This weird but ingenious system means that even a large plastic object will, if left in contact with damp earth over a long period of time, eventually decay. Usually, however, when plastic objects are to be recycled they are broken up into easily handled pieces and thrown into "biovats," huge tubs of a special earthen mush that soil micro-organisms find a good habitat. In time the results of this process are dried into sludge and recycled onto the land. (It is in such vats that the contents of the recycle bins marked P are dumped.)

Whatever their advantages these plastics do not impress all Ecotopians, especially those who are fond of wood. It is recognized, of course, that since plastics can be molded they are capable of taking shapes that wood is not; and that they can be stronger, more flexible, and often more durable. Extremists, however, still take exception to *any* use of plastics, believing they are unnatural materials that have no place in an ecologically ideal world. These purists will live only in wood houses, and use only containers such as wooden chests, string bags, woven baskets, and clay pots. The defenders of plastics, on their side, have many effective economic arguments, and they have also produced plastics that have a less "plasticky" feel and look—with some success, it seems to me.

Nonetheless, I have the impression that despite the undeniable Ecotopian scientific achievements in plastics, the future may well belong to the purists. For in this as in many areas of life, there is still a strong trend in Ecotopia to abandon the fruits of all modern technology, however innocuously they may be made, in favor of a poetic but costly return to what the extremists see as "nature."

(May 26) Got into big fight with Bert about the ritual war games story—not the story itself, but that I hadn't gone over it with him as I had said. "Do you always go off and do things purely on your own?" he said crossly. "Don't you think you might be missing something? Don't you know what you might get out of collective work?" "Well," I said defensively, "I was in a big hurry and you weren't around, and—" "Fuck your excuses," he said bluntly. "I offered to work with you as a brother. That was important. Do you have any idea how competitive and detached you seem to us?" He was furious, and I had the uncomfortable feeling he was right—I had missed an important opportunity. We talked for a while and I told him how I felt about it, but it will take some doing to get back onto a decent basis together. Which saddens me more than I would have expected; we have become friends.

Beginning to miss the kids a lot more than usual on this trip, and don't know why. God knows I neglect them when I'm home—pass up my weekends with them whenever something unusual is afoot, then try to make up for it with presents. (Haven't bought them anything in Ecotopia, though—nothing here worth carrying home. Or rather, there are many worthwhile things here, but none can be bought or carried away.) Have a feeling I'd like them to be here with me, see what I am seeing, meet the people I know. What would they think of Marissa? She would take their measure exactly, even their spoiledness (which wouldn't get anywhere with her!) and they'd respect and like her. Fay once said, when she was about six, that she didn't trust Francine. Marissa is easy to trust. But she never pretends there is no risk in it. . . .

Spoke earlier today with Kenny, a kid living at the Cove. His mother is away for a week, and I asked him if he was lonely with her gone. "Why should I be lonely? Everybody else is here." Suddenly tearful to think of my children so far away, without me, living what is after all a dangerous life and getting worse. It's not just the crime and the crazed people everywhere, but the expectation that our children's children will go on being poisoned by smog and chemicals. (Or will New York and Tokyo produce a race of mutants who can breathe carbon monoxide?)

What would their lives be like if they had been born Ecotopian kids? No ballet classes, stationwagons, shopping expeditions to department stores. They'd do actual hard adult work in gardens and shops and schools. They'd live in a welter of a dozen or more people, exposed to a lot of sexual vibrations and happenings that would make them grow up faster —and I guess stronger, though it scares me. (I want them protected—) But it would be a realer world than New York, I have to admit. In better touch with basic natural processes and the nitty gritty with fellow humans. It would be an incredible switch in their lives. But how do I know they might not thrive on it?

Some random notes that don't seem to fit in plans for columns:

Have discovered what those wet-suit-like garments are. People call them "bird-suits," and often embroider birds on them; also "unitards." Not uniforms after all, but a new type of garment. Many Ecotopians dislike them, in spite of their technical advantages. ("Bird-suits" because they are said to be almost as good a body covering as a bird's feathers!) Woven of some new combination of fibers—story confused, some say from keratin, which would mean bones, hooves, hair—some think from wood fibers. At any rate the inner layer is woven, thick, spongy, (quarter of an inch thick). Alleged properties quite magical: when it rains, surface layer cotton fibers swell and lie so tightly together that rain runs off; when it is hot, the inner layer fibers unkink, trap less air, thus allow faster escape of body heat, whereas when it is cold they curl up, trap more air, thus keep body heat in! (This is why suits must be skin-tight, evidently.) Then there is another smooth inner layer, to feel good on the skin. I have tried them on, and in fact bought two to take home—even if I wouldn't want to be seen on a New York street in them! Will be interesting to try in our zero temperatures—but I'll take an overcoat along.

"Preventive transportation." That's how Doctor Jake, Marissa's cousin, sardonic of mind but optimist, describes bicycles. Claims that every heart attack costs the medical system, the patient's living group, the patient's work group, etc. something between a year and two years' salary. Saving one heart attack can thus pay for something like 500 free Provo bikes. Besides, he claims that the bicycle is aesthetically beautiful because it is the most efficient means, in calories of energy per person per mile, ever devised for moving bodies—even jumbo jets eat up more energy, he says. (Looked me over as a physical specimen, said I was not in too bad shape for an American. "You'll probably feel livelier after a few more weeks here. The food, the air, getting in better touch with yourself." "What do you mean?" "Knowing yourself as an animal creature on the earth, as we do. It can feel more comfortable than your kind of life." "Well, I'll let you know," I said.)

Foreign trade note: Natural rubber comes in from Vietnam and Indonesia. Plastics and plastics-manufacturing machinery seem to be major export. Some Japanese electronics imported. Books, records, video-discs, musicians, performers from all over the world —except the U.S! How do they do it?

Good one the other night: Bert got to ridiculing the old Dupont slogan, Better Things for Better Liv-

ing Through Chemistry. "All that meant," he proclaimed, "was nylon, orlon, and the total prostitution of the state of Delaware. We want better living through biology. We don't think in terms of 'things,' there's no such thing as a thing—there are only systems." For the first time, this didn't sound like gibberish to me. It would apply to myself too: I am part of systems; no one, not even myself, can separate me off as an individual thing. (This realization came with a sort of sinking feeling that was not unpleasant. Hmmm?)

An intolerably smug people: Young clod about 20 telling me "automobiles are such a 19th-century contraption—why are you still so hung up on them?" Still, Ecotopians really very American in some ways. With a curious French influence—things like train schedules and price lists have a severe systematization. Perhaps this intellectual rigor necessary as counterbalance to the frivolity and looseness of personal life?

Money: Ecotopian bills seemed comic when I first saw them. Yet three weeks later I find them more attractive than the greenbacks left in my wallet. Very romantic in style: lush, Rousseau-like scenes, almost tropical, with strange beasts and wondrous plants. No images of famous Ecotopian leaders—when asked why not, people just laugh. Maybe it's a consequence of their informal, utilitarian attitude toward money—they bundle it up into rolls and toss it to each other in an offhand manner I've only observed among gamblers.

Habitations: You seldom see any store-bought furniture in Ecotopian houses. They have mattress beds on bare floor, enormous barbaric beds built of heavy timbers as if for ancient Vikings; there are houses with no beds at all, only bedrolls brought out at night, Japanese style. But never a proper, ordinary bed, with frame, slats, springs, and an innerspring mattress!

Have now visited several Ecotopian family groups, and am still amazed at their quietness. After Independence, I am told, great efforts were made to noise-proof things, and a lot of work was put into developing virtually soundless versions of many machines and appliances. Thus refrigerators, which among us produce a daily quota of shimmies, jiggles, grunts and rumbles, are silent models, which run on household septic-tank methane. (Very simple design, so not frost-free, but uses far less energy, I am told.) That other great source of urban noise, cars, have of course been eliminated. Clothes washers and dryers, which can't be made silent, are usually kept outside in separate huts. Dishwashers, perhaps our most annoying appliance, are not manufactured at all.

If I can get over minding the quiet, it may be nice to be subjected only to natural noises—the wind, music from other houses, footsteps, a baby crying. . . .

Could I get any writing done out at the forest camp? When I'm there Marissa's friends tease me because I don't join in on all their work. And she herself, though she sees my position, thinks I should participate more. I was shocked to learn that she had told pretty much everybody in her "family" many details about our relationship. "Don't you have any sense of privacy?" I blurted out. She got furious at me for this. "What are you talking about? These people live with me and love me. Naturally they want to know what is happening with me! So I tell them. They give me reactions, advice, they look at me, I see myself through them as well as through myself." "I still don't like it. You could at least have told me you were going to talk about it." More fury: "Listen, are you ashamed *of this relationship? What is so terrible about telling people about it?"*

We worked it out finally. I began to feel I do have an exaggerated need to keep romantic involvements to myself, and I think I got her to see how strange their practices are to me. She is always assuming I can just fit in perfectly. This galls—though it also feels good whenever I do manage to fit in, by working on some job I get praised for, or really being perceptive about some interpersonal development.

Want badly to spend more time with Marissa, but most of my sources are here in the city. It's painful to talk to her on the picturephone and not be able to touch. But she won't come in again right away. Maybe I'll go out tonight, at least for one night.

Have realized that it is a little scary to be in close touch with the land, as the Ecotopians are. Not sure how I would handle that. Their little shrines are not merely pious nature-appreciation, I have discovered. There is even one commemorating a famous murder —not too far, I suppose, from the mythic way we think about Tombstone, Arizona—though most are devoted to spirits who presumably presided over especially good times (and sometimes bad times, like the death of children). Some are little more than poems, scratched on scraps of wood that will soon decay—but that is evidently part of the tradition. "They're like dried cornstalks," one young girl told me, "they stand there for a while so you can see that something grew there, but another season always follows." My favorite so far is an ornate, subtly elegant maze laid out in shiny oyster shells on a hill overlooking the sea. In the center a piece of driftwood reads:

> *Sun, here we watched you go down*
> *As if it was the last time.*
> *Thank you for the morning.*

WOMEN IN POWER: POLITICIANS, SEX AND LAW IN ECOTOPIA

San Francisco, May 27. The fact that Ecotopia's chief of state Vera Allwen is a woman is, of course, common knowledge. But most Americans are unaware that the Survivalist Party she heads is a woman-dominated organization—and that it played a key role in the struggle for Independence.

While a majority of Survivalist Party members are women, many men are members also, and some indeed hold high party positions. The basic cooperation- and biology-oriented policies of the party, however, are usually considered to be derived mainly from female attitudes and interests; the chief opposition party, the Progressive Party, continues to express what are alleged by Survivalists to be outdated and destructive male attitudes toward individualism, productivity, and related issues.

Women are, as in the U.S., a substantial majority of the population in Ecotopia. The initial growth and success of the Survivalists, I have been told by some long-term members, came from a frank and vitalizing recognition of this fact, together with its corollary: that women have distinct interests and needs which have been, despite some advances, unmet during the 200 years of American rule. "We had had two centuries of it, and it wasn't good enough," one influential Survivalist woman told me.

Although dissatisfaction with life under Washington control was especially deep in the Western states by the time of the abortive bicentennial celebrations of 1976, it was apparently only the Survivalists who forcefully argued that secession offered the sole hope of stable, long-range decent survival. But the acceptance of this perilous political alternative by citizens of the area that became Ecotopia was, or at least so I am now told, accomplished only by drastic tactics. By 1978 almost a third of the state legislators, and a good many national representatives, were women. In their caucuses they had worked out in preliminary form many of the measures that in 1980 became the basis of Ecotopian government. The debates over how to put these into practice, and especially whether secession was necessary in order to do so, were long and emotionally arduous.

While the women were thus engaged, the male politicians were not idle. A crisis ensued when it was revealed that certain important male leaders had been devising a sort of sexual gerrymandering plan that would have reduced female representation almost by half. This proposal shocked the populace into fierce polarization. When Washington attempted to interfere on behalf of the gerrymanderers, widespread defiance of federal regulations began to take place—on every issue from taxes to pollution. A few months of such chaos led to the armed confrontations and growth of new locally controlled organs of state—workers' councils and citizens' councils—which carried out what we must now, with the Ecotopians, refer to as their Independence.

When conditions had stabilized, the Survivalists swept the constitutional convention elections of late 1980. They then reorganized the governmental structures of the states and counties, which they considered outmoded because unrelated to the organic structures of production and consumption, and also inherently inadaptable for dealing with regional ecological systems. They divided the country into five metropolitan and four rural regions. Within these they also greatly extended many powers of governments of the local communities.

They also began a second phase of national debate: whether "Ecology in One Country" is possible, or whether Ecotopia's own survival hinges on the exporting of survivalist doctrines to the rest of the world. The radicals who take the second position have been in the minority so far, but as ecocatastrophes overtake other countries with increasing frequency their strength keeps rising.

Since Americans may be skeptical of how a woman-dominated political system actually operates, I have attended several meetings of Survivalist Party groups. Judging by these, the Party is unlike any other I have ever observed. A meeting has no formal agenda; instead, it opens with a voicing of "concerns" by many participants. As these are discussed (often amid friendly laughter, as well as a few angry outbursts) general issues begin to take shape. But there are no Robert's Rules of Order, no motions, no votes—instead, a gradual ventilation of feelings, some personal antagonisms worked through, and a gradual consensual focusing on what needs to be done. Once this consensus is achieved, people take pains to assuage the feelings of those members who have had to give ground in order to achieve the consensus. Only after this healing process takes place is there formal ratification of the decisions taken—the only action during three hours or so that has the feeling of ordinary political business as we know it. And yet I must admit that, in those three hours, a great deal gets done: a political problem is indeed faced, defined, and a decision made about it, though only along with a great amount of attention to things that would be considered, among us, as more in the realm of social life than politics. On the other hand, it must also be admitted that people *enjoy* such meetings, and we might conceivably learn some lessons from them.

Although some Americans may expect Ecotopian law to be only a cover for government tyranny, closer acquaintance reveals that it operates on much the same principles as ours. Our Bill of Rights was incorporated into the Ecotopian constitution, though in its original form which would seem dangerously sweeping and unqualified to most Americans today. Ecotopians, like Americans, maintain an enormous army of lawyers and tend to work out many kinds of disputes in the courts.

The content of the law, of course, has changed somewhat. Ecotopians treat as severe breaches of the peace many actions we consider white-collar crimes seldom deserving of police or court action. Deliberate pollution of water or air is punished by severe jail sentences. "Victimless" crimes such as prostitution, gambling, and drug use are no longer on the books, but embezzlement, fraud, collusion, and similar "gentleman's crimes" are dealt with just as severely as crimes like assault and robbery—which are, by the way, rare in Ecotopia, perhaps because of the personal nature of their neighborhoods and the virtual impossibility of anonymity in them. (Strangers get a lot of attention in Ecotopia, but the motives for this may not be entirely friendliness.) Ecotopian courts mete out fines very seldom, it appears, preferring to rely on imprisonment, which is felt to affect convicted persons more equally. I hope to visit an Ecotopian prison soon; I am told that all prisons require the inmates to work, and rumors have circulated that some verge on slave-labor camps.

American policy flirted briefly, in the seventies, with attempts to control pollution. But Ecotopian economic law has proliferated wildly in the obsessive attempt to shape all agricultural and industrial enterprise into stable-state, recycling forms. It was first hoped that industries could be persuaded by public pressure to reduce their ecological damage. Educational campaigns pointed out that synthetic fiber production used far more electricity and water, and produced far more noxious by-products than natural fiber production; that high-compression engines required more steel, electricity, and high-priced fuel; that aluminum production required enormous electrical supplies; that synthetic chemicals tended to damage both man and environment, often in totally unexpected ways.

A few improvements were secured in the heady months following Independence. However, even the enterprises that sprang up after the flight of capital were reluctant to go further on pollution measures than their competitors. Moreover, attempts to use fines and special taxes also failed, because polluting firms could always pass costs along to their customers —who thus complained they not only had to suffer from the pollution the factories emitted, but had to pay higher costs for the products too.

In 1981, therefore, the Survivalist Party introduced a package of laws that flatly prohibited many types of highly polluting manufacturing and processing operations. Firms affected were to be bought off or helped through the transition to non-harmful operations by a system of financial risk-spreading. Even so, a number of firms went out of business rather than attempt such drastic changes.

Despite such momentous events, it appears that early Ecotopian policy involved much utilization rather than abolishment of existing governmental machinery. For example, after Independence the staffs of the huge state highway-building departments were not disbanded, but rather were set to work, along with their old construction-company allies, to restore the dismally polluted waterfronts, lake shores, and riverbanks. In Ecotopia at that time, as in the United States now, such areas were mainly devoted to factories, warehouses, sewage plants, railroad yards, dumps, and other unsavory uses. Armed with the condemnation powers that had earlier been used, as one Ecotopian told me, "to make the world safe for autos and impossible for people," the highway departments soon cleared the banks of all major and many minor waterways, and created Seine-like embankments, strip parks, piers for small craft, grassy and sandy beaches, and other improvements. Where highways had encroached on waterways, the pavement was used in part as foundations for pavilions, restaurants, dance halls, and other amusement facilities, while the remaining concrete was broken up and used in building the embankments. Bicycle paths, minibus lines, and transit stops were laid out so as to provide easy access to the water for all citizens.

Thus, in areas such as Puget Sound, the Columbia and Williamette rivers near Portland, and San Francisco Bay and Delta, waterways became useful for transportation—small water-taxis abound, and ferries cover longer distances. Ecotopians are almost as devoted to water as they are to trees, and rowing or sailing about in boats are favorite pastimes. There is hardly an Ecotopian who doesn't spend some of his time fishing, sailing, rowing, swimming, wading, or just looking at water. The national bird, I am told, is the egret—who spends his days knee-deep in marshes.

While the policies of the Survivalists and the Ecotopian government may seem extreme or foolish to us, they have not been carried out in a ruthless manner, as many suspect. For instance, while the national train system was under construction, existing freeways were used as highspeed bus routes. Articulated trailer-buses running at 100 miles per hour were given exclusive right to the lefthand lanes. Experience gained with this intermediate system was reportedly useful in the management of the train system when it was completed. The Ecotopians thus seem adept at using moderate and gradual changeovers to reach extreme goals. We may disagree with those goals, but I believe we must respect their manner of achieving them.

(May 28) Letter from Francine yesterday morning—smuggled through our prearranged emergency drop in Canada. Was somehow a shock to get it—hadn't

really expected to hear from her unless something went terribly wrong. Same madness in her life as usual: new schemes to astound the art world, a great sexual coup at a consular cocktail party—her first full-rank ambassador! Maybe she misses me—that would be a switch. But she would never admit it on paper, if at all. Maximum latitude: the rules of the game. . . .

Went over to an Ecotopian fair afterward. These are held monthly in many cities and towns. This one surprisingly large and well organized. Lasts three days, in the City Hall plaza, which is partly paved but tree-shaded with a number of fountains and a creek; it also has the steps of the grand old City Hall—which serve as bandstand, stage for performing actors, pantomimists, even jugglers. Plaza was covered with booths and stands of all kinds: craftsmen, farmers with produce to sell, food and drink vendors, fortune-tellers, portrait-sketchers, musicians. Takes on the appearance of a village: the booth people set up tents just behind their wares, in which they live for a couple of days.

How many of the thousands strolling about are potential customers, and how many just friends and families and children of the sellers, I couldn't tell. In any case the economic functions didn't seem overwhelmingly pressing. Mainly an enormous party, at which some selling, bartering, and trading went on. Gives people a chance to see friends from other areas (many of the merchants come from groups that live out in the country, but attend fairs regularly to sell their wares). Around the fringes there are musical groups performing, and there's dancing in the evenings, when most of the people seem to get together.

This is not one of the four weekends of the year when sexual license is said to prevail (the winter equinox was two months ago) but things certainly looser than usual. Maybe reacting to Francine's nutty letter, I got drunk and reckless, and followed two flirtatious young women into a tent. Nice sometimes to blot out thoughts of Serious Relating, and they were willing to play the game of anonymity. I guess it's a result of my puritan heritage that I've never been with two women at once (though I have often wished I had the nerve to try it). These girls were absolutely cool and matter of fact about it, which made it easier. Sometimes they would both concentrate on me, sometimes I would share one with the other. They seemed to regard sex the same way we'd regard eating, or maybe walking—a pleasant biological function, but without any heavy emotional expectations. Very relaxing. . . .

Curious note of natural delicacy: they never excluded me from any of the possible permutations and combinations, or ever expected me to be a mere voyeur. And nothing I did, even though a total stranger from another country, seemed to take them aback: they're maybe 22 or so, but they don't seem surprisable by anything men do.

It was an exhausting night; left me feeling lightheaded. Toward dawn I got dressed and walked all the way across the city to the Cove, listening to the fog horns and thinking about Marissa. Though I have twinges of jealousy about her, her behavior after the war games and mine this evening seem parallel and equal in some odd way. I don't feel guilty, anyway

Once home, I scribbled a note to Francine, offering her diplomatic immunity and telling her about my *escapade, and fell asleep. In the morning I tore up the note, and got back to work.*

WORKERS' CONTROL, TAXES, AND JOBS IN ECOTOPIA

San Francisco, May 28. Is the Ecotopian economy socialist? I asked a high government spokesman this question. I told him that it is widely considered to be so, by Americans, but that obviously the information gap of recent decades made a clear understanding difficult. This gentleman gave me a polite lecture, making it clear that he was speaking to what he considered the major American confusions.

The Ecotopian economy, he began, must be considered a mixed one, like that of the United States; but some elements of the mix are novel, and because of ecological and political considerations the balance of the mix is quite different. Not long after Independence, he reminded me, there was a massive flight of capital, similar to what happened after the Cuban revolution. Most families of great wealth fled, going either to Los Angeles, to the East, or in some cases to their Swiss or French estates. This undoubtedly damaged the managerial capabilities of Ecotopian enterprises, he admitted, though the total number of such refugees was only a few thousands, including women and children.

The Ecotopian government, faced with the necessity of feeding, housing, and clothing its population, at first teetered between a cautious attempt to carry on enterprises on the old lines, and breaking through into new and uncharted methods.

But as it happened, my informant argued, in a few months it became clear they had no real choice; for the people, seeing the former owners depart, realized that a new era was indeed upon them and began spontaneously taking over farms, factories, and stores. This process was chaotic, but it was not anarchic; it was controlled by the local governments and local courts. The assumption was usually made that those who had been working in the organization "owned" it; and since they had no other means of support, their immediate problem after Independence was to go on running it pretty much as it had been run. There were, he pointed out, some examples to go on, of enterprises taken over by employees in France in the late sixties, and of course a number of U.S. corporations had become employee-owned by purely legal and gradual means.

Such take-overs set the tone for the ongoing tasks of production and distribution of essentials; and they worked. But more massive and deliberate economic changes soon took place, above all in the diversion of money and manpower toward the construction of stable-state systems in agricultural and sewage practices, and in the scientific and technical deployment of a new plastics industry based upon natural-source, biodegradable plastics. (The transportation system, which remains an infringement on the stable-state principle, also consumed many resources in that period.)

I inquired about the sources of government revenue for such large-scale projects. The tax system of former years, it seems, was entirely abandoned at the time of Independence. Laws formalizing the forfeiture of property by owners, plus confiscatory inheritance taxes, were legislated. (Aside from personal articles, no Ecotopian can now inherit any property at all!)

Ecotopian revolutionaries took the position, which still appears to prevail, that a little-recognized yet fundamental defect of capitalism is that you cannot tax its owners justly—for wealth under capitalist governments always manages to provide sufficient tax loopholes for itself. The new tax system, upon which Ecotopian government now depends, relies entirely on what we would call a corporation tax—that is, a tax upon production enterprises (including individual craftsmen, incidentally). It is based partly upon net income, but also partly upon "turnover," or gross income. Like most functions of governing, tax-levying is carried out by the communities (mainly cities), which delegate very limited powers to the regional or national levels.

The reasoning behind this system, according to my

informant, is complex, but it turns upon the view that all taxes are fundamentally a means of the government seizing a share of economic output and putting it to publicly determined purposes—and that this seizure should therefore be at the immediate source, simple, understandable, just, and open to public view. (Ecotopian tax returns are not confidential, as with us.)

In recent years, this tax policy has been complemented by laws that have redefined the position of the employee—very drastically from an American viewpoint. The workers in an Ecotopian enterprise must now all be "partners"; a man cannot just set up a business, offer wages to employees, fire them when he no longer needs them, and pocket whatever profits he can make. Grotesque as it may seem, all Ecotopians who join an enterprise now do so on the same sort of basis as our high executives. Just as these gentlemen inquire about profit-sharing, stock options, tax shelters, retirement plans, and so on, so do ordinary Ecotopians inquire about the partnership terms in an enterprise they are considering joining!

There are no personal income, sales, or property taxes in Ecotopia, though there is a land tax that encourages concentration and probably accounts for the remarkable compactness of Ecotopian cities. There is a widespread aversion to other types of tax on the grounds that they are either regressive or promote divisiveness among people—whereas the enterprise tax, bearing as it does on collective groups, is thought to promote solidarity. (A paradoxical notion, perhaps, since these groups compete with each other strenuously enough.)

It is alleged, though of course this would be extremely difficult to prove, that there is no super-rich class in Ecotopia. It is admitted that certain occupational groups, such as artists and scientists and some doctors, have slightly higher incomes, though national training policies deliberately seek to keep such differentials moderate. But there are now said to be no individuals in Ecotopia who grow personally rich because they control means of production and hire other men's labor power. Occasionally, however, strange anomalies occur—when an enterprise comes up with some remarkable product or service for which there is an immediate and strong demand. The inventors and fabricators of the "bird-suits," for instance, are a small research collective, originally about 30 people. Because of the appeal of their ingeniously insulating garments, they are said to have made a great deal of money recently, even though they have now chosen to take in some new members and to work even less than the usual 20 hours per week.

Don't such successful groups use their profits to control other enterprises, or become absentee owners, and thus end up as capitalists just like ours? The answer on this point was complex, but seems to boil down to the fact that direct absentee investment by one enterprise or person in another enterprise is not permitted. Surpluses can thus only be "invested" by lending them to the national banking system, which in turn lends funds to enterprises. This arrangement, which resembles the one pioneered by the Yugoslavs in the seventies, obviously gives the bank an immense leverage on the economy, and makes possible the sometimes surprisingly large public investments that have characterized Ecotopian development. (The most it allows lucky producers, like the bird-suit people, is the chance to retire and live off the interest their profits can earn from the bank.) This process clearly needs close study by our economists; it appears to contradict many Ecotopian protestations of decentralization, even if the national bank does maintain regional branches which are said to have great autonomy.

Ecotopian enterprises generally behave much like capitalist enterprises: they compete with each other, and seek to increase sales and maximize profits, although they are hampered by a variety of ecological regulations. I suspect they are not immune to a certain amount of chicanery and false claims about their products.

However, the fact that the members of an enterprise actually own it jointly (each with one vote) puts certain inherent limits on what these enterprises do. For instance, they do not tend to expand endlessly: since the practical maximum size of a joint-ownership firm seems to be less than 300 people—beyond that they tend to break down into bureaucratic, inflexible forms and lose both their profitability and their members, who seek more congenial environments. "Small is beautiful," I was reminded. Also, the enterprises tend to be just as concerned with conditions of work as they are with profits, and in many instances members seem willing to accept lower profit and wage levels in exchange for a comfortable pace of work or a way of organizing work which offers better relations among the people doing it.

Competitive threats from other enterprises keep such laxity within bounds, but even so some Ecotopian products are utterly noncompetitive with the products of more efficient industries abroad. The prices of clothes and shoes outside the core stores, for example, are sky-high and draconian tariffs are used to keep out the sweat-shop products from Asia—the consequence being that many Ecotopians wear homemade garments, which has by now become considered a virtue.

It is impossible to assess the relative tax burden of Ecotopia, since taxes fall only upon enterprises. However, since the Ecotopian arms establishment is small (about the size of Canada's) and many functions of government which for us are very costly (such as education) are organized, strangely enough, on free-market principles, it seems certain that the relative total tax burden is much lower than ours. This may of course help to explain why the drop in Gross

National Product after Independence did not agitate the population more.

The tax revenues are used by the community governments to support their recycling services, housing, power, water, telephone, medical services, police, courts, and so on. A pro rata share of tax funds goes to the regional and national governments, to support operation of larger-scale systems such as the trains, defense, telecommunications, and most of the research establishment.

Curiously, despite the importance Ecotopians attach to agriculture and other rural affairs, the Ecotopian constitution is city-based where ours, inherited from an agricultural era, is rural-based. With us, the states have broad powers over cities (including the right to give them legal existence and set their boundaries). The Ecotopian main cities, however, dominate their regions through a strict application of one-person-one-vote principles. Furthermore, the county level of government is omitted entirely.

This curious system evidently leads to continual conflict and jealousy over the disposition of tax revenues. Instead of relying on a powerful central tax-collection agency that can attach incomes directly, the central government must continually placate and cajole the local governments to ensure a continued flow of funds. Thus the Ecotopian federal structure, which superficially resembles the small government bodies found under primitive capitalism, makes most of its outlays on uncontroversial activities that benefit all citizens absolutely equally. There is a surprisingly small national welfare system, considering that Ecotopians enjoy a lifetime "guarantee" of minimal levels of food, housing, and medical care. While some citizens, especially those working on untried developments in the arts, utilize this guarantee to exist without jobs (sometimes for years—the envy of our young artists!) most people either feel the guarantee level is too abject to exist on, or find it's desirable to work in order to provide themselves with a lively social life. The old and disabled, of course, must survive by taking advantage of the guarantee; and by my observation the living standard involved, while low, is perhaps slightly better than that of our Social Security recipients.

Despite the severe criticisms made of the Ecotopian economic and tax system by our experts, direct observation can thus only support the claims of Ecotopian spokesmen, however unwelcome these may be: the system is now a proved and integral part of Ecotopian life, and it is not going to go away.

(May 29) Just reread last couple of columns. Realize that my attitudes toward the place have changed a lot in three weeks. (And it doesn't seem to be just Marissa!) Am I getting soft in my writing? Maybe I didn't know what were the really penetrating questions to be asked on that economics stuff. Or maybe I'm even getting some kind of over-all snow job. The whole Ecotopian experiment seemed to me at first a silly provincial attempt to construct a decent society when every place else was going down the drain. From what I had seen of the rest of the world, I knew it couldn't work, it must be some kind of fraud! I hadn't believed the rumors about forced labor and stone-age degeneracy and all that crap, but I guess I really did expect to find there was something terribly wrong with it, some obvious horrible flaw which meant that we didn't after all really have to pay any serious attention to it; and my reports would end up documenting that, would make it all go away....

But it's not going away. In fact the more closely I look at the fabric of Ecotopian life, the more I am forced to admit its strength and its beauty. But that just leaves me at a total loss. I don't seem to have an attitude to write from any more; all I can do is call the individual separate shots as I see them. Is that losing my objectivity? Will Max start cutting my copy? Maybe I don't really understand anything anymore, or at least not in the way I used to think I did?

Have come out to visit Marissa at the forest camp. Found her deep in the woods, selecting trees for cutting. She let me come along if I wouldn't talk. She walks slowly through the trees, looking at them all very carefully. Then she'll sit or stand for a while, meditatively. In time she will walk to this tree and that, attach to each a red ribbon marking its doom, and murmur a phrase I couldn't catch. Her expression at these moments is sorrowful yet determined. Then she relaxes and we walk on to another tract of forest. This is a major part of her work—but it might as well be a ritual of some kind; there is a holiness to it.

Difficulties have at last begun to arise between her and Everett—he still doesn't seem to feel triumphed over, as I would in his place, but there has been dark talk about one of them having to leave. (I wish he would—I now find myself terribly jealous of her having anything to do with him.) At supper an argument came up over whether it would be a good idea to re-establish relations with Washington. Rather to my surprise, Marissa strongly in favor, with some ingenious arguments. I got many dirty looks, even though I didn't say much. Everett is, after all, a member of the family, and I am an interloper.

Was invited along on a provision trip to the nearby town. Four of us, bumping along in a little electric truck. Went to one of the core stores. Apparently the goods in them are produced by automated factories to government specifications. Standardized, very plain though often attractive, and incredibly, astoundingly cheap. Thus socks about a quarter of our prices, but only in black or white; standard plain pants, shirts, underwear similarly priced. I happen to need a new T-shirt, and got two, considering the bargain (saffron color!). Food sections of core stores offer a modest coverage of dried, frozen, preserved items. You could, if you wished, subsist on these for a tiny sum—and I have met a few artists and other oddball types who claim they do, being unwilling to spend their time earning the income needed for better fare. Many Ecotopians however seem to buy only bread, beans, rice, fruit and similar staples from these stores, relying on small independent shops for meat, produce, etc.—or shipments from fellow communes. (Lumber camp gets its meat, milk and vegetables from a farm commune 15 miles away.)

Standardization is carried amazingly far in the core stores. Preserved foods come in only three sizes of containers (all biodegradable, naturally)—one about the size of a small pickled-herring jar, one like a large jam jar, and one huge, the kind our restaurants get fruits in. These go by metric contents, not our "giant," "jumbo," etc. or our intricate can numbers. The labels, however, very lovely in design. And some of the goods have style, like the shoes.

Had lost my hairbrush somehow, and the core stores carry only natural-bristle types. When I said that I wanted a proper plastic-bristle one, my companions looked at me a bit strangely, took me to an "antiquarium." Turned out to be a special store where you can buy items no longer available in ordinary stores—including, it turns out, many items we sell in drugstores.

(Ecotopian "pharmacies," as they are called, are cramped little places that sell almost nothing but prescription drugs. The Ecotopian medical profession went through the pharmacopeia after Independence and ruthlessly eliminated many tranquillizers, energizers, sleep-inducers, and other drugs such as cold remedies. In fact they now license no *behavior-control drugs at all. Which may have been a contributing factor in reorganizing their schools: unable to make difficult children adapt to the schools, they had to adapt the schools to the children! I asked one doctor*

what happens with insomnia. "Well, usually this indicates a social problem, not a medical one," he said. "So we try to help the person change his life rather than his body chemistry, which is probably working fine. Besides, in Ecotopia it can be fun to stay up all night, you know. The 20-hour week has loosened things up a lot.")

Anyway, the antiquarium was patronized mainly by elderly women and a few rather decadent-looking young people, who laughed a lot and seemed to be looking for campy artifacts. With my plastic brush I got a lecture about it being impossible to recycle because it's the old type of plastic. "Damn thing will last for hundreds of years," said the clerk with distaste. Well, I'll remove it from his precious country when I leave. . . .

Marissa and friends telling me about origins of policy that all buildings must be of renewable and biodegradable materials. There was a time after Independence when only wood structures were permitted—the guiding genius of the period being one Archibald Fir, an architect. He wrote a remarkable influential study of earlier wood building, and helped lay down the specifications that plastics had to meet to be allowable as building materials. I asked why he took the name Fir, and not perhaps Redwood? Marissa: "Well, he was a modest man really, you see, and a realist." (He was also, it turns out, author of a magnificently biting attack on megastructures.)

Must go back to the city tonight. Trying to get Marissa to come too. But I am getting to be more part of life at the camp. Today before supper we were all sitting around playing (there's really no other word for it). "Well, Will," somebody says, "what can you do to entertain us?" I went hopelessly blank. People had been singing; I can't sing. There had been jokes; I've never been able to remember jokes. People had laughed and teased each other, in a kind of vaudeville routine way; I've never been able to do that hostile-friendly act. The fantasy flashed through my mind, "I could tell you the story of my life," but I realized I couldn't do that either—it would be too boring, it has no climax. Knowing Marissa was ashamed for me, I blurted out lamely, "Well, I don't know—I'm afraid I'm just not very entertaining. Nobody ever taught me how to entertain people—we relied on television, I guess." They absolutely wouldn't accept this; they thought I wanted to be coaxed. When it got through that I meant it, people were sad and embarrassed for me. "Listen," said one of the men, "we won't let you get away with that. You can't deny you know how to sing 'Row, Row, Row Your Boat,' okay? All right, start us on a round with that." So I took a deep breath, happened to come out more or less on key, and after a minute it went marvelously, everybody doing funny harmonies and fooling with the rhythm, and laughing at me. I shall have to extend my repertoire....

RACE IN ECOTOPIA: APARTHEID OR EQUALITY?

San Francisco, May 29. There are surprisingly few dark-skinned faces on San Francisco streets, and I have now learned why. After Independence, the principle of secession became a lively factor in Ecotopian political life. Thomas Jefferson and other early American patriots were quoted in its defense. The black population, whose economic deprivation under white control had made it increasingly nationalist and separatist even before Independence, apparently joined in the general exultation when the great break with Washington came. But in the months following, black separatist parties grew up to dominate the ghettoes of Oakland and San Francisco—having been strangled by the white suburbs earlier, the black population now wanted to control their own territory. After a long and bitter political struggle, the black areas (and also Chinatown in San Francisco) were officially designated as city-states within Ecotopia. They had their own city governments, levied the usual taxes, had their own police and courts, their own industries, and owned farms in the nearby countryside. In fact they possessed all the attributes of tiny independent countries—even including the issuance of postage stamps and currency—except for the carrying on of foreign relations.

This situation, though it satisfies many blacks, seems to others inherently unstable, and they argue for full independence as the only long-range solution. One scheme, which is currently being debated, would relocate the entire black population in a new territory including Monterey Bay and the Salinas Valley, which would provide abundant agricultural resources and direct access to the Pacific sea lanes. The political and economic problems posed are monstrous, of course, but such things were carried out in Eastern Europe after World War II.

A few black people have preferred to continue living or working outside the black areas (which are often referred to as Soul City). They seem to be fully integrated into white society, with intermarriage frequent. Life within the black territories, judging by my limited observations, has more hold-overs from pre-Independence days than Ecotopia as a whole. In fact a few private cars are still mysteriously tolerated, and people cling to certain symbols of the old ways: there is a brisk trade in high-quality Scotch whisky and other imported luxury goods which are hard to find in Ecotopia elsewhere. The per capita income is said to be about 10 per cent higher than in the white areas, largely because of longer working hours—probably a consequence of the lag in black consumption before Independence. "We're still making up for lost time," one stylish black man put it to me.

The culture of Soul City is of course different from that of Ecotopia generally. It is a heavy exporter of music and musicians, novels and movies and poetry, both to the rest of Ecotopia and to Europe and Asia. Black architects, bred in the ghettoes, have been leading proponents of rebuilding Ecotopian cities on people-centered rather than car-centered principles. Black enterprises, it is sometimes said, seem to be more naturally collectivist than those in white areas.

Since a high proportion of convicted criminals in early Ecotopia, as in the U.S., tended to be black, Soul City faced a major problem in this field. After Independence, with the legalization of marijuana and some other drugs, amnesties were declared for prisoners whose acts would no longer constitute crimes. A few guilty of "sex crimes" and crimes like loitering, drunkenness, and vagrancy were also freed. While the curbing of heroin traffic by taking it over as a government monopoly reduced the crime rate of Soul City as of other areas, a substantial black inmate population remained, and black penologists were forced to take the lead in prison reform.

What is most surprising to an American observer is the severity of current sentences for violent crime. An ordinary street mugging, of the type which in New York may bring a one-to-five-year sentence, and a time served of perhaps 18 months, here may bring a flat five-year sentence with no possibility of parole.

However, the serving of such sentences is quite different from its equivalent in our prisons. No large prisons of our type are maintained, either in Soul City or elsewhere in Ecotopia. Prisoners are dispersed in many small institutions housing only a few dozen inmates each. During the day inmates participate (under light guard and sometimes none at all) in the general life of society—holding jobs with ordinary job rights and pay. However, they (together with their wives, husbands, or lovers if they so desire) are confined at other times. This curious policy is justified by arguing that people guilty of violent crimes generally commit another one when freed, and thus end up in prison again; indeed traditional prison life increases their tendency to commit violence. (Except for murderers, perhaps, who usually kill spouses or acquaintances, and seldom repeat.) In the American system, the argument goes, prisons were only training schools for the inmates' next crimes. Soul City penologists, on the other hand, believe their relatively humane policies actually give inmates the time and opportunity to develop non-criminal modes of life in realistic life circumstances. They present impressive figures on the relative re-imprisonment rates for their inmates and ours, but naturally I have no way of verifying their accuracy.

Interestingly enough, ritual war games are practiced among the Soul City population also, but spears are considered too savage a weapon. Long, heavy sticks, rather like the quarterstaffs of Robin Hood's men, are used instead, and the participants wear crash helmets. Thus the games are usually ended not by a messy wound, but by one of the participants suffering broken ribs or limbs, or being knocked out.

Although virtually all inhabitants of Ecotopia still regard English as their native language, the establishment of Soul City brought a considerable emphasis on Swahili in the schools, and many adults now speak it. Other blacks, however, regard this an an artificial and useless step; they point out that black youngsters are already in effect bilingual since they master both standard English and the street dialect—which is, however, steadily becoming more widely acceptable in business and professional dealings in Soul City. Swahili may be useful in growing trade with African states. Awareness of Africa is acute among Ecotopian blacks, and I gather that Ecotopia is the source of considerable financial and munitions aid to revolutionaries in South Africa.

This, like other aspects of the Ecotopian race situation, is an uncomfortable irony for Americans. We look with horror on the apartheid society of South Africa, where the dominant white minority has enforced rigid segregation in every aspect of life. In Ecotopia, the black minority has itself enforced a similar segregation—though of course it makes some difference that this was voluntary whereas that of the Africans was forced upon them by the whites. But this admission that the races cannot live in harmony is surely one of the most disheartening developments in all of Ecotopia, and it clouds the future of our nation as well. Its example bodes ill for our own great metropolitan areas, whose black center cities are themselves already rife with talk of secession.

(May 30) At first Marissa refused to come to city with me, almost as a matter of principle. "It's the weekend," I said, "surely you can get away for two days!" "Why should I be the one who has to get away? Why don't you get away? Why should I have to come to you? I live here—you're just visiting at the Cove!" Our arguments become surprisingly bitter, punctuated by shoves, curses, growls, venomous looks: there is much at stake. I tried to patch things up and get a little warm feeling going with a hug; she slapped at me, took her sleeping bag and went out into the forest somewhere to sleep. I lay down, glumly, and got to sleep very late. Sometime near dawn I felt her slide into bed beside me. She laid a cool hand on my shoulder. "We must learn to take turns," she said. We circled arms around each other, and fell asleep.

But nothing is resolved, of course. Her sense of self-determination is unshakable. Later in the day she said she still didn't want to go into the city with me now, even if it was her turn. I had invited her to come along tomorrow to Punta Gorda where they're going to show me a thermal sea-power set-up. This is a welcome development—seems to show a certain warming up in my official reception, and makes it more likely I'll get to see Vera Allwen soon.

But the whole idea displeased Marissa: she came out with a crack about "foreign dignitaries." The train ride north is supposed to be inordinately beautiful—through lush farmland, mountain passes, orchard country, but none of that appealed to her. She said, though, she'd like to come to the Cove when I'm back from the trip. This dispelled my glumness a little. But it is hard to take her insistence on coming and going only as she pleases. Which is strange, because that is after all how Francine operates: is it maybe that I have never wanted anything more from her? Can't imagine what it would be like to live with someone like Marissa: the notion is exhilarating but scary, like an earthquake. (Felt my first one the other day, and broke out in a sweat though it just jiggled the room a little.)

ENERGY FROM SUN AND SEA

Punta Gorda, May 31. One of the least known and yet staggering achievements of Ecotopian science and technology is the massive thermal-gradient power plant at Punta Gorda, which I have just been allowed to visit. (Similar but smaller plants also exist near Monterey and at other points along the coast.) This is perhaps the most impressive of the means by which the Ecotopians have pursued their ideal of pollution-free sources of energy.

Like the rest of the world, Ecotopia is watching closely the ever more promising attempts to harness atomic fusion energy for practical purposes. The prospect does not entirely overjoy the Ecotopians, however, for they have a sentimental dislike of stringing power lines over their landscape and believe there is something unnatural in processes that concentrate gigantic quantities of energy at any one point; they are more interested in the technologies of generating energy near where it is needed.

Nonetheless, in this as in other matters, they are not exactly the senseless romantics some Americans think. When I visited the Ministry of Energy I discovered that officials there are well aware of the historical tendency for energy-rich cultures to conquer or dominate energy-poor ones. The Ecotopians are *not*, contrary to popular belief, headed back toward a Stone Age life. They use far more power than would be expected from travelling across their countryside—but both its sources and its uses tend to be diffused, concealed, and novel.

The Ecotopians inherited a system of oil- and gas-fired power plants (which they closed within a few years) and a number of atomic-fission plants. They believe that ultimately fission cannot be tolerated because of radioactive byproducts and heat pollution, but they have been willing to live temporarily with the fission plants located in remote and little-inhabited areas—though they have redoubled engineering precautions against nuclear explosions and extended hot-water discharge pipes more than a mile to sea. (With what I am beginning to realize is typical Ecotopian ingenuity, the seacoast plant discharges are carried in huge pipes made of rigid plastic which is extruded with air bubbles in it so that it is slightly buoyant. Thus it tends to float, and is anchored in place just below keel depth by cables to the ocean floor.)

Also inherited from pre-Independence days is an unconventional, and ecologically respectable, source of geothermal power. In the hot-springs region north of San Francisco, turbines are spun by steam coming up from the bowels of the earth. It is a hellish scene—billows of steam issue from pipes and wells, with loud hissing noises; the earth seems ready to explode. Despite the contrast with our quietly humming powerhouses, this geothermal system has advantages: cost is low, it adds virtually no pollutants to the atmosphere, and only a small amount of warm water to the run-off in nearby streams—one of which has become the site of swimming resorts that are open even in winter.

Ecotopia also took over numerous hydroelectric installations at dams in its great mountain ranges. However, these are regarded as temporary expedients too, since they tend to silt up after a few generations, and have unfortunate effects on salmon and other wildlife. Ecotopian thinking has moved uniformly toward power sources which, like solar energy, earth heat, tides, and wind, can be tapped indefinitely without affecting even the local biosphere. (Ecotopians thus take a childish delight in the windmills and rooftop wind-driven generators that are common in both cities and remote areas.)

The major thrust of Ecotopian energy research and development has involved two main sources. One is the energy of direct solar radiation, and several systems now exist for capturing it. Some require large installations and some small, but most are impressive in size. One type is a silvered parabolic mirror about 30 feet across that focusses the sunlight. Since the sun moves during the day, the receptor at the rays' focus must move too—so this odd-shaped device sits like a spider on a web of thin cables on which it pulls itself about, seeking maximum warmth, and sending steam through a flexible pipe to drive a generator on the side. Much of the southern part of Ecotopia is virtually desert, but these installations have reportedly proved effective in more northerly areas as well.

Another type is a bank of massive photo-cells, similar to those used on satellites but enormous in size.

I have visited one cell-bank south of Livermore, which uses a secret type of receptor material. The softly rolling grassy hills are faced on their south sides with literally city blocks on end of a glassy substance, in squares about two meters on a side. Narrow aisles run along the hillside, evidently mostly for the convenience of cleaning crews, whom I saw one evening wetting and wiping down the plates.

During the day the heat and glare are intense, but the setting is silent, placid and peaceful. Grass continues to grow in the aisles and under the plates, which are mounted a few feet off the ground. I heard a meadowlark, and noticed the tracks of field mice underfoot. This cell bank must cover an area several miles on each side, perhaps 20 or 30 square miles in all: it's the size of a major airport. It generates enough power for a chain of minicities, and Ecotopian planners believe that in cloudier climates too such installations are becoming economically feasible.

Even this huge set-up, however, is hardly remarkable beside the Punta Gorda thermal sea-power station, which might be taken for a reconstruction of some mad duke's medieval fortress. It squats on the shoreline at a point where deep and very cold water lies only a few miles offshore, and sucks up seawater through a monstrous pipe. Smaller pipes run this way and that, connected to generators and pumps. Engineers explained to me that the system is something like a giant refrigerator running in reverse. Since water can store enormous quantities of heat energy, even a relatively small temperature differential can be made to yield large amounts of power if suitably ingenious heat exchangers are employed—but great quantities of water must be pumped up to take advantage of this principle. The sheer architectural mass of the plant is overwhelming; it seems almost an extension of the tides themselves. (The deep cold water is very nutrient-rich. Some of it is therefore pumped into nearby ponds to warm up before being injected into the system along with already warm surface water—but while in the ponds it feeds fish and shellfish, which are an important byproduct of the plant.)

Going from the sublime massiveness of this great project, which must win the admiration of anyone who sees it, to the ridiculous, I must describe a peculiarly Ecotopian power-generating device, which in its way also helps to explain what a fanciful people we are dealing with. Recently I visited an Ecotopian "family" in their country house. (Many Ecotopian living groups either have some kind of shack in the woods or are associate members of a country commune, where they spend some of their time.) This delightful retreat was located in an utter mountain wilderness, many miles from the nearest power line; but when I got there I found a radio was pounding out music. This radio, it turned out, was powered by a *waterwheel!* Some clever inventor has built a small wheel which floats in midstream suspended from cables, thus avoiding costly and ecologically damaging embutments. It generates 24-volt power which, stored in a couple of batteries, is plenty to run the radio, a pump, and the few electric lights needed in a country place where people go to bed early. My hosts expressed great glee when I admired this incredible contraption. In fact they tried to give it to me to take home, but since it weighs about 30 pounds, this is fortunately out of the question.

This house, like many city dwellings, is heated by the system now widespread in Ecotopia—using solar radiation stored in a large water-tank underground, from which heated water can be pumped through radiators in the living areas. Much of the south walls and roofs of Ecotopian buildings are devoted to the heat-receptors for these devices, but since they greatly reduce the cost of operating a house and also eliminate the chief need for energy from a central source, Ecotopians regard this limitation with affection. They also like to point out that the system can be adapted to heating wash water and the distillation of seawater, which is useful in coastal communities where summer water supplies are uncertain.

No survey of Ecotopian energy developments would be complete without mention of an extremely daring project which will be truly revolutionary—if it works. The photosynthetic chemistry of a green growing plant, as is well known, enables the plant to capture solar energy and use it in the plant's own growth. Ecotopian scientists believe they have now worked out a process whereby, in specially bred plants, this process could be electrically tapped directly. Such an unbelievably elegant system would be nearly perfect from an Ecotopian point of view: your garden could then recycle your sewage and garbage, provide your food, and also light your house!

(June 1) Got back from the north this afternoon and found Marissa already at the Cove—sitting in "my" chair in the library, reading. It always surprises me how she fits into other scenes, without feeling like an interloper. Perhaps it is because Ecotopians have such strong ties to their own "family" turf, they feel secure everywhere? Or is it that the country is so small it is in some way all one huge extended family? At any rate she feels at home at the Cove.

We went up to my room arm in arm, very close and companionable. It's marvelous to be wanted by her: she's direct and solid and passionate, and it makes everything possible. I don't quite know what's different in making love with her. She uses her body in a direct and intimate way that enables me to do the same, somehow. She is in tune with herself, *her own biological being, and through some contagion I find myself doing the same. I feel stronger with her than I usually have—I like my own body better too, have more trust in its functioning. I don't worry about it getting cold, or sick, or tired, or not performing well sexually; I almost don't "think" about it at all, the way I have in the past. And the sexual contact between us goes on getting better and better. We are perfectly open and loose and trusting; sometimes we lose ourselves, our selfconsciousness, in tremendous bursts of shared feeling—closeness and orgasms that are really different from anything in my life before. Yet we never speak of it; it just happens. And not that it's weird—strange positions or anything. We sometimes fool around with oral sex in one way or another, and it's pleasant for fun and games or preliminaries, but for the real contact we both like intercourse, the old standby. (Odd, because Ecotopians are supposed to be so liberated about sex, I had imagined them doing almost everything* but *straight fucking!) We seem to do it for hours, it just goes on, rising and falling in intensity, changing tone or emotional color, like a leisurely walk up a lovely mountain, in no hurry to reach the top. But then finally we reach it, sometimes without realizing we were near, and the view is splendid and the air is clear and I feel like I am really living at last—*

Can it go on this way? At any rate it seems I can never get enough of her—I watch for the chance to drag her to bed, I'm almost shamefully focused on having her, on having more of this extraordinary kind of experience. . . . She is sleeping now, and I study her as she lies stretched out under my quilt. There is so much intensity in her—it brings out all of mine. When I am with her I feel more solid—heavier, almost literally, as if my feet are planted more firmly on the earth.

I realize the relation with Marissa is changing my whole idea of what men and women are like together. Things I used to take for granted with Francine now begin to seem bizarre to me. Men never snap their heads around to look at Marissa, the way they do with Francine—whose bright blonde hair is like a beacon. Marissa wears no make-up at all, never, and now that the fashion cycle with us has come round again to heavy lipstick and eye-shadow and so on, I first found her a little pale-looking, too reticent about herself. And yet what intensity there is in her eyes, the way she moves her mouth, the liveliness of her body! It is as if Francine possesses the signs or signals that are supposed to mean sexuality and vitality; Marissa just has *sexuality and vitality, so she doesn't need the signals. . . .*

I used to particularly enjoy going into a fancy restaurant or a cocktail party with Francine. It was like displaying a prize won in some contest. And she makes the most of it—breasts always seeming about to burst her dress; that special ambiguous look from me to the others, inviting competition and comparisons and flirtations. With Marissa, coming into a place is just coming into the place. We will relate to the people there individually or together, intimately or not at all, as it happens to go. Most people find Marissa attractive—she grows on you, subtly—but she never presents herself as an object to be struggled over, and she never pretends to feelings she doesn't have. And yet she expects a great emotional commitment from me—we have had terrible scenes because she felt I was not living up to our relationship.

Yet sometimes I miss Francine: her frivolousness, her lightheartedness, her sense of social style and repartee—Marissa's awfully serious, and sometimes I get angry that she won't indulge in game-playing. Francine is game for anything, I suppose because to her nothing much matters. Is her appeal that with her I can be irresponsible, loll about on those enormous tits, be childish?

(So why should it be hard for me to be grown up?)

Here I am, 36 years old, involved with one gorgeous, playful woman at one end of the continent, and with one passionate, serious woman at the other.

Marissa would hate everything about New York, and Francine would hate everything about Ecotopia. Lucky ladies, to have such a famous schizophrenic for a lover. . . . But how can I bear being so split?

Maybe I should have been a poet after all, as I used to think when I was a teenager. Maybe it's only artists who can really handle their personal contradictions—by putting them into their work?

Under Marissa's questioning (patient but unrelenting!) I have also been thinking back to my marriage with Pat. I don't see, when I look at Ecotopian love relationships, or marriages, that awful sense of constriction that we felt, the impact of a rigid stereotyped set of expectations—that this was the way we were going to relate to each other forever, that we had *to, in order to somehow survive in a hostile universe. Ecotopians' marriages shade off more gradually into extended family connections, into friendships with both sexes. Individuals don't perhaps stand out as sharply as we do; they don't present themselves as problems or gifts to each other, more as companions. Nobody is as essential (or as expendable) here as with us. It is all fearfully complex and dense to me, yet I can see that it's that very density that sustains them—there are always good, solid alternatives to any relationship, however intense. Thus they don't have our terrible agonizing worries when a relationship is rocky. This saddens me somehow—it seems terribly unromantic. It's their usual goddamned realism: they are taking care of themselves, of each other. Yet I can see too that it's that very realism that allows them to be silly and irresponsible sometimes, because they know they can afford it; mistakes are never irreparable, they are never never going to be cast out alone, no matter what they do. . . . And perhaps this even makes marriages last better—they have lower expectations than we do, in some ways. A marriage is a less central fact of a person's life, and therefore it is not so crucial that it be altogether satisfying (as if anything or anybody was ever altogether satisfying.) Though people* do *split up in ways that are clearly very painful for them. But not the wrenching feeling of failure that both Pat and I had when we broke up—the feeling that utter disaster had overtaken us, especially her of course, but also me, really: or the feeling of fault, that we had somehow not done it* right, *the way we were supposed to, that I had not given her what women were supposed to expect to be given (rather than finding for themselves or in themsedves) and therefore I and we had failed, and had to suffer for it. No Ecotopian seems to carry this kind of guilt. And even though it seems to dilute something intense and precious in life, I am beginning to envy them a little, and also to see that their joint way of protecting themselves is stronger and more fruitful than the individual defensive way I have tried by keeping my relationship with Francine light and tentative and limited . . .*

COMMUNICATIONS IN ECOTOPIA: PRESS, TELEVISION AND PUBLISHING

San Francisco, June 2. As a working newspaperman, I am naturally curious about the press of other countries, and I have spent a good deal of time with Ecotopian editors, writers, and television newsmen and women. The conditions they work under would be intolerable for me or most of my colleagues. Nonetheless, I have gained a healthy respect for their integrity, hard work, and devotion to the public welfare as they see it.

The basic situation of the Ecotopian media is that, in the political confusion after Independence, laws were passed which effectively broke up the existing media corporations. Friends in the legislatures who had previously protected the publishing and broadcasting industries were no longer in power. Thus the fundamental Ecotopian press law forbade multiple ownerships under any circumstances: that is, the corporations that owned magazines, newspapers, TV and radio stations were required to divest themselves of all but one operation in each city. Generally (and mistakenly, as it turned out) they decided to keep their chief TV stations.

But a series of further confiscatory laws followed, narrowly regulating the types and amounts of advertising that were permitted, requiring augmented quotas of "public service" broadcasting, and so on. These laws worked out to give unfair advantages to small, independent entrepreneurial groups, who came forth in staggering numbers. In place of the one daily newspaper San Francisco formerly enjoyed, there are now six—representing every shade of opinion—plus numerous weeklies, monthlies, and special-interest newsletters. These service a wider area than the San Francisco paper covered earlier, for the capital city's media have now, to a certain extent, become national in circulation. Still, papers are thriving in other cities as well: Seattle has four, Portland three, and even Sacramento has three. There has been an equal proliferation in the magazine field. This fragmentation does not seem to be as hard on the individual reporters and writers as might be expected. They do not yearn for the security of our big media corporations, but seem to enjoy the thrill of doing their freewheeling best for a small operation even though its days may be visibly numbered.

Television has been similarly decentralized and broken up. Each existing station was early forced into a great deal of local programming—though centralized news services were allowed. The government itself acquired several channels to be used for political programs—both local and national government affairs (as I reported in an earlier column) are more or less continually visible on TV: hearings, committee meetings, debates.

In such circumstances entertainment obviously was forced into a back seat. It consisted mainly of old films and a plethora of amateurish shows: rock music concerts, comedians, endless technical arguments about ecological problems. It is hard to imagine any large number of Americans watching such programs, which make little attempt at showmanship and are further dulled by the absence of the surrealist commercials we have.

How good is the news coverage in Ecotopia? Spot comparisons with our press from the months just before my trip reveal that Ecotopian coverage is surprisingly competent in those areas of the world it chooses to deal with. Because of the lack of diplomatic relations, of course, no Ecotopian correspondents can be stationed in the U.S., so information on U.S. events is skimpy and derived mainly from European press services. World news on the other hand seems to be excellent: for instance, the Ecotopian papers had run accounts of the latest American air strikes in Brazil more than a week before our newspapers had...

Although the general picture of the Ecotopian media is one of almost anarchic decentralization, a jungle in which only the hardiest survive, here too we find paradoxes. For the newspapers, which are even smaller than our tabloids, are actually sold through electronic print-out terminals in the street kiosks, in libraries, and at other points; and these terminals are connected to central computer banks, whose facilities are "rented" by the publications. Two print-out inks are available, by the way: one lasts indefinitely, the other fades away in a few weeks so the paper can be immediately re-used.

This system is integrated with book publishing as well. Although many popular books are printed normally, and sold in kiosks and bookstores, more specialized titles must be obtained through a special printout connection. You look the book's number up in a catalogue, punch the number on a juke-box-like keyboard, study the blurb, sample paragraphs, and price displayed on a videoscreen, and deposit the proper number of coins if you wish to buy a copy. In a few minutes a print-out of the volume appears in a slot. These terminals, I am told, are not much used by city dwellers, who prefer the more readable printed books; but they exist in every corner of the country and can thus be used by citizens in rural areas to procure copies of both currently popular and specialized books. All of the 60,000-odd books published in Ecotopia since Independence are available, and about 50,000 earlier volumes. It is planned to increase this gradually to about 150,000. Special orders may also be placed, at higher costs, to scan and transmit any volume in the enormous national library at Berkeley.

This system is made possible by the same fact that enables Ecotopian book publication to be so much more rapid than ours: authors retype their edited final drafts on an electric typewriter that also makes a magnetic tape. This tape can be turned into printing plates in a few minutes, and it can simultaneously be fed into the central storage computer, so it is immediately available to the print-out terminals.

Aside from this "professional" publishing, Ecotopia also supports a sizable "amateur" industry. Authors, artists, political groups, and specialized organizations have easy and cheap access to print because Ecotopia early developed portable, fool-proof, easily repairable offset printing presses, and deployed them everywhere—in schools, offices, factories and so on. Ecotopian children of eight know how to operate them with satisfactory results.

The variety of materials printed in this way is staggering: cookbooks (many Ecotopians are devoted to fine eating, no doubt one of their cultural links to the

French), political tracts, scientific papers, comic books (these have a wide and weird development, being the chosen medium of some excellent artists), experimental literature, poetry, how-to-do-it manuals for crafts or skills, and so on. These range in style from the tawdrily home-made to the superbly personal and creative.

The Ecotopian fondness for a craft, guild, almost medieval approach to things also surfaces in their publishing, despite its modern technology. Each newspaper, magazine, or book bears a colophon—a listing of who edited the manuscript, typed it for the tape, ran the press, handled the binding, etc. When I said this seemed rather immodest in the modern world, I was told that vanity had nothing to do with it—the main consideration was to fix responsibility, which the Ecotopians try to decentralize and personalize wherever possible.

(June 3) Sitting around the fire at the Cove last night, swapping old newspaper stories, drinking mulled wine. Every once in a while somebody would stomp in out of the chilly evening and join us to warm up. But they still like to tease me. After a while Bert began it: "Come on, Will, tell us what's the biggest story the Times *ever suppressed." "What do you mean by the biggest?" I parried. "Well, whatever* you *think was biggest. Bay of Pigs was pretty big, I guess, but that was a long time ago and anyway they did decide to run it, even if it took three days to get around to it."*

"I would have opposed holding up on that," I said, frowning. "They ran it, as I understand, when they realized other papers would break the story. Even then the old man felt he was betraying the President." A burst of unkind laughter greeted this remark, which didn't surprise me, of course—you don't find much sympathy for U.S. government policies or figures

among Ecotopians. "After that the paper printed everything, as far as I heard. Do you know about the Pentagon Papers?"

"Yeah, they were okay on that one," Tom agreed, "even if it was *stale news."*

"Look, Will," Bert said, leaning back with that intent expression he gets when he's getting down to serious business. "What are you going to write about the Helicopter War? We think that *was the most serious suppressed story since Independence. I know you were only 19 or 20 at the time: so was I. But there wasn't a line about it in any of your major papers. Your underground papers had some stuff, but they never get anything straight—it all sounded like third-hand paranoiac raving."*

Dead silence, all eyes on me. I took some deep slow breaths. I know, even though I was just a reporter on a student paper at the time, that rumors had circulated back in 1982 about trouble on the Ecotopian borders. A couple of young hotshot friends, a few years older than I, wanted to go out and track them down. But the wire service had a good man in Reno, and of course a whole bureau in Los Angeles. The editors thought that if anything important happened, they'd know about it all right. Soon after, the army had put through unusual rush orders for large numbers of replacement helicopters, but these were explained as part of the Latin American build-up that was beginning then. Besides, by 1982 the shock of the secession had largely spent itself, and readers were tired of Ecotopia. Public attention was mostly on the chronic economic crisis. The public opinion polls showed that while nobody was happy about Ecotopia, nobody was too unhappy about it either. The likelihood that our government would risk a secret invasion seemed remote; I certainly hadn't lost any sleep over it.

"Are you putting me on?" I said. "What Helicopter War?" "Oh, come on, *" said Bert angrily. "Are you giv-*

ing us the old no se nada?" "*We heard a few rumors,*" *I admitted.* "*Our people must have looked into it. What happened, some skirmishes on the border?*" "*It was a fucking* war, *man! There were thousands killed on both sides!*"

Red, who must be about 50, spoke up from the sidelines. He's less talkative than most Ecotopians, so his words tend to carry extra weight. "*I was in it,*" *he said simply.* "*Tomorrow morning I could take you down and show you something that might convince you.*" *But he wouldn't tell me what it was.*

We talked on through the evening. Their stories seem to agree too closely to be merely fabrications. Amount to something like this: a minor war took place in the spring of 1982. It lasted only a few days, but they claim it was a major turning point in maintaining the new nation. Ecotopians knew, of course, that Washington was full of hawks favoring an immediate and if necessary genocidal "solution" to the secession. Ecotopians also knew that the hawkish views had so far never won out—partly because of the economic problems that reannexing Ecotopia would have presented by then, partly because it had been feared since secession that New York, Chicago, Washington, and maybe other cities had been mined with atomic weapons.

Red's story is that immediately after Independence, the Ecotopians realized that anti-helicopter devices were a high priority, and several rather novel ones were produced in very large numbers. One, taken over by the Ecotopians from the U.S. Army upon secession and then manufactured by the former missile plants near Sacramento and San Francisco, was a radar-guided rocket carried by a single man (or woman). After its bazooka-like shell was fired, however, the firer continued to point the weapon at the moving target, and the radar beam actually steered the rocket till it hit the target. Another type was based on a French and Russian device, and used infrared hom-

ing to guide a missile toward the exhaust of a flying target; these were especially useful at night. Another, much cheaper, used a very simple rocket that trailed long wires, which tangled with the copter's rotors and caused them to lose control and crash. These weapons were, apparently, distributed throughout the country. "You mean to all army units?" I asked. "To all army units and all households and living groups too," Red smiled. "They were everywhere, hundreds of thousands of 'em, believe it or not."

What he says happened was that the U.S. Army and Air Force launched a major secret attack: from bases in Southern California, Colorado and Montana, and from several carriers offshore, huge squadrons of helicopters roared over the Ecotopian frontiers, escorted by fighter-bombers. This may not have been too much of a surprise: the Ecotopians claim an excellent intelligence operation. Much destruction was of course caused by the jets, which attempted to "soften up" landing sites in the approved Vietnam technique. An alarming number of jets, however, were shot down. Worse still, when the copters came in, they encountered heavy ground fire from the borders and coastline all the way to their touch-down points.

"We just shot them all down," said Red calmly.

"What do you mean, shot them all down? That's impossible!"

"You might think so," he replied. "But we had many times more rockets than they had helicopters. We just finished them off as fast as they came in. They might have got some on the ground if they had concentrated them all *on some open area out in the Valley. But they were overconfident and they had it all carefully programmed to lay down men all over the country. Well, we got something like seven thousand in three days. A lot near the borders, but all over the place too. When they counted up their losses,*

and still didn't have any men on the ground, they stopped."

"That's incredible," I said. "They soon would've realized what was going on and changed their strategy." "Maybe their computer wasn't set up for that," said Bert drily. "Also we messed up their communication channels a little bit. I've heard that half the time when they thought they were talking to each other they were actually talking to our guys. Who gave them, um, a lot of wrong information and got them into some nasty wrong places. What really stopped them, though, was probably that we finally told them we would detonate the mines in American cities if the attack went on another day. It was that close."

This fratricidal vision stunned me, though I know what civil wars are like. "What did you do with prisoners of war?" I asked. "There weren't too many," said Red. "You don't usually survive the crash of an exploding copter. We hung onto the pilots for a couple of months, until we were pretty sure it was over. (Your people were getting busy in Brazil along about then, too.) The other guys we talked to for a while and then shipped them down to L.A. Some of them, I've heard, later came back out here to live."

We talked long into the night. "Well, what are you going to do, Will?" Bert finally asked. What the hell did he expect me to say? "More checking, first of all," I replied. "And then I'd have to find a way to handle it that wouldn't be inflammatory. I don't want another war any more than you do."

"Lucky you have broad shoulders so you can carry the world around on them so easily!" Bert laughed. And everybody seemed disappointed by my reply. But I'm not some irresponsible nut who can write whatever comes into his head.

ECOTOPIAN EDUCATION'S SURPRISES

San Francisco, June 4. Schools are perhaps the most antiquated aspect of Ecotopian society. Our computer-controlled individual home instruction has no parallels here. Pupils are still assembled physically all day for their lessons. (Indeed few electronic teaching aids are used at all, in the belief that simply being in the presence of teachers and fellow pupils has an educational effect.) In fact if Crick School, which I visited, is any example, Ecotopian schools look more like farms than anything else. An Ecotopian teacher replied to this observation, "Well, that's because we've crossed over into the age of biology. Your school system is still physics-dominated. That's the reason for all the prison atmosphere. You can't allow things to *grow* there."

Crick School is situated on the outskirts of the minicity of Reliez and its 125 students trudge *out* to the country every day. (About a dozen such schools ring the city.) The school owns eight acres, including a woodlot and a creek. The name is in honor of Francis Crick, co-discoverer of the structure of DNA. There is not a single permanent building of any significance; instead, classes take place either outdoors or in small, temporary-seeming wood buildings barely big enough to hold a teacher and 10 pupils, which are scattered here and there on the school grounds. I was unable to locate the school office, and when I inquired, I was told the school has none—its records consist of a single drawer-full of cards! With only a half dozen teachers, my informants said, the coordination and decision-making for the school is simply part of everyday life. Since class periods fluctuate wildly (there are no hour bells) the teachers can always get together if they feel like it, and they also eat supper together once a week for more extended discussions.

Incredibly enough, the children spend only an hour or so a day in actual class work. When I asked how they are kept from destroying the school during the times they are not under teacher control, I was told that they are usually busy attending to their "projects." I could see evidence of such projects on every hand, so perhaps the explanation, optimistic though it may seem to us, is accurate.

The woodlot is a main focus of activity, especially for the boys, who tend to gang up into tribal units of six or eight. They build tree houses and underground hide-outs, make bows and arrows, attempt to trap the gophers that permeate the hillside, and generally carry on like happy savages—though I notice their conversation is laced with biological terminology and they seem to have an astonishing scientific sophistication. (One six-year-old, examining a creepy-looking bug: "Oh, yes, that's the larval stage.") There are some projects, such as a large garden and a weaving shed, which seem to be dominated by girl children, though some of the girls are members of chiefly male gangs. Most of the children's study and work time, however, is spent in mixed groups.

By "work," I mean that children in Ecotopian schools literally spend at least two hours a day actually *working*. The school gardens count in this, since they supply food for the midday meals. But apparently most schools also have small factories. In the Crick workshop I found about 20 boys and girls busily making two kinds of small wooden articles—which turned out to be birdhouses and flats for seedlings. (The flats, mercifully, are uniform in dimensions and style. The birdhouses assume fanciful shapes and many different sizes. This double standard is not by accident.) The system is intended to teach children that work is a normal part of every person's life, and to inculcate Ecotopian ideas about how work places are controlled: there are no "bosses" in the shop, and the children seem to discuss and agree among themselves about how the work is to be done. The shop contains a lot of other projects in one stage or another of development. In working these out together, as I watched them do for a half hour of so, the children need to use concepts in geometry and physics, do complex calculations, and bring to bear considerable skills in carpentry. They marshal the necessary information with a verve that is altogether different from the way our children absorb prepackaged formal learning. The children also, I am told, dispose of the workshop profits as they please. Though some of the money seems to be distributed (equally) among the individual children, some is used to buy things for the school: I was shown a particularly fine archery set that was recently bought in this way.

It was sunny during my visit, but Crick School must be appallingly muddy in the rainy winters. To provide some protection, and also to give a place for meetings, parties, films and video shows, the school possesses a giant teepee-like tent. The white canvas covering is no longer new and carries many charming decorative patches. Usually the lower rim of fabric is rolled up to head height, making the teepee into a kind of pavilion. Here the children sometimes play when it is raining heavily. (They are never forbidden to go out in the wet, and learn to take care of drying themselves off.) A large pit in the center is the site of occasional barbecues, when a deer (or one of the school pigs) is roasted and eaten; and a kitchen at one side of the teepee is often used by groups of children making themselves lunches or treats.

Does this extremely unregulated atmosphere lead to wild conduct among the children? So far as I could tell, not at all; in fact, the school is curiously quiet. Small bands of children roam here and there on mysterious but obviously engrossing errands. A few groups play ball games, but the school as a whole has little of that hectic, noisy quality we associate with our schoolgrounds. Indeed at first I could not believe that more than 30 or 40 children were present, considering the lack of babble. The tribal play groups, incidentally, are not all of an age; each contains some older kids who exercise leadership but do not seem to be tyrannical. This is perhaps encouraged by the teachers, or at least not discouraged, for they work with groups at one general level of development but do not object if an older or younger child wishes to join in or just watch one of the class sessions.

Some of the teachers, especially those occupied mainly with the younger children, apparently teach everything. But other teachers specialize to some extent—one teaches music, another math, another "mechanics"—by which he means not only that branch of physics, but also the construction, design and repair of physical objects. In this way they feel free to indulge their own interests, which they assume will have an educational effect on the children. Certainly it seems to keep their own minds lively. All the teachers teach a lot of biology, of course. The emphases and teaching loads are flexible, and set by discussion among the teachers themselves.

This, like the general operation of the school, is possible because of the most remarkable fact of all about Ecotopian schools: they are private enterprises. Or rather, just as most factories and shops in Ecotopia are owned by the people who work in them, so the schools are enterprises collectively but personally owned by the teachers who run them. Crick School is legally a corporation; its teacher members own the land, buildings and reputation (such as it is) of their school. They are free to operate it however they wish, follow whatever educational philosophy they wish, and parents are free to send their children to Crick School or to another school as *they* wish.

The only controls on the schools, aside from a maximum-fee rule and matters of plumbing and safe buildings, stem from the national examinations which each child takes at ages 12 and 18. Apparently, although no direct administrative controls exist, the indirect pressure from parents to prepare children for these exams—as well as for life—is such that the schools make a strong effort to educate their students effectively. The exams are made up yearly by a prestigious committee, comprising some educators, some political figures, and some parents—a partly elected and partly appointed body whose members have tenure for seven years and are thus somewhat insulated, like our senators or judges, from short-term political pressures.

Indeed there seems to be a brisk competition among schools, and children switch around a good deal. On the secondary level the situation is apparently a little like ours; one school near San Francisco, which has produced a large number of scientists and political leaders, consequently has a long waiting list.

It is hard to tell how the children themselves react to the competitiveness that exists, on some levels, along with the laxity of Ecotopian life. I often saw older children helping younger ones with school work, and there seems to be an easy working recognition that some people know more than others and can aid them. But greater ability doesn't seem so invidious as with us, where it is really valued because it brings rewards of money and power; the Ecotopians seem to regard their abilities more as gifts which they share with each other. Certainly I never saw happen at Crick School what I have seen in my daughter's American school: one child calling another "stupid" because he did not grasp something as fast as the first child did. Ecotopians prize excellence, but they seem to have an intuitive feeling for the fact that people excel in different things, and that they can give to each other on many different levels.

Do Ecotopians accept the idea that poorer parents might not be willing or able, given the tuition costs, to send their children to school at all? In this crucial area, Ecotopians have not allowed their thinking to revert to that of harsher ages. Rather than a scholarship system, however, they give outright sliding grants to families with incomes below a certain level, and one component of these is marked for tuition. Thus the Ecotopian state, while not willing to lift the burden of education entirely off the parents' backs (thus perhaps encouraging larger families!) is still willing to force citizens to educate their children in *some* manner. The possibility of "kickback schools," such as arose in the U.S. when tuition vouchers were first tried, does not seem a great worry in Ecotopia, where the welfare of children is discussed constantly —and where the children themselves generally run school newspapers that are, if anything, ridiculously critical of their own schools, and would surely spot anything sneaky going on.

Judging by my brief visit, the fact that no formal curriculum prevails does not mean that Crick students miss the basics of reading, writing, and arithmetic, though they tend to learn them in concrete contexts. But they also learn a great deal of sideline information and skills. An Ecotopian 10-year-old, as I have observed, knows how to construct a shelter (odd though some of the boys' shacks looked); how to grow, catch, and cook food; how to make simple clothes; how hundreds of species of plants and animals live, both around their schools and in the areas they explore on backpacking expeditions. It might also be argued that Ecotopian children seem in better touch with each other than the children in our large, crowded, discipline-plagued schools; they evidently learn how to organize their lives in a reasonably orderly and self-propelled way. Chaotic and irregular though they appear at first, thus, the Ecotopian schools seem to be doing a good job of preparing their children for Ecotopian life.

(June 6) This morning Red and I went out to a hidden scrap yard south of San Francisco. There, piled in formidable heaps as we pile autos in our junkyards, were hundreds of wrecked U.S. Army helicopters, most of them badly damaged. Had been gone over by salvage crews—instruments, cables, motors, and so on were missing from most. But undeniably U.S. aircraft, vintage 1982. I phoned Marissa with this crushing piece of information. "Well, did you really *doubt it?" she asked. "Do you still think people would try to deceive you?" "I don't know what to think, anymore. Except about you." "And what's that?" "I'll tell you when I see you."*

(June 7) Just came from the War Ministry, where I tried to get the official Ecotopian view on the Helicopter War. The whole Ministry occupies only three floors of what used to be the Federal Building in San Francisco. No press information section at all. I was just taken into an office and introduced to a young man by his name, with no rank—discovered later that he's some kind of general. He confirmed outlines I'd been given earlier, and offered 7,679 as the precise number of copters shot down, "although some of the count had to be made from rather fragmentary pieces, you know."

What he really wanted to tell me about was the militia system Ecotopia adopted after Independence. Regarded it as a great social innovation, seemed not to be aware we had tried it in 1789 and couldn't make it work. (And if we tried it now the units would probably turn into gangs of armed looters!) Local ar-

senals; men "train" yearly, do work projects for a couple of weeks. Their organization sounds more like guerrilla bands than a real army, but they evidently have excellent radio communications and a very efficient national command system. Denied that heavy fortifications exist on the borders, though they are mostly mountainous and could be made virtually impenetrable. "Remember Dienbienphu!" he laughed. Would not disclose locations of armaments research, which is evidently highly decentralized. Citizenry said to be the source of many usable military ideas: "An ordinary person invented one of our cheapest anti-helicopter weapons—a simple rocket trailing wires. He was a bad shot, and his idea enables you to bring down a copter even if you miss the body of the thing."

Says they would like their military establishment to wither away further (it's now about the size and relative cost of Canada's) but can't trust the U.S. enough yet. Seemed a very smart and hard-working officer. Not a trace of the kind of bureaucratic featherbedding mentality that plagues our armed services, either. I bet they do have Washington mined.

(Later) Have finally decided not to file a story on the Helicopter War. Can't see any useful purpose being served, at this late date. Yes, the Times *was wrong not to pursue and print the story while it was happening. And I suppose, hard though it is for me to admit it, there may be other unknown chapters of similar enormity in our recent national history—things that were mistakes, or at any rate grave risks, and should have been exposed, attacked, debated. But I can see what would happen if I re-opened all those old sores now. (Assuming, of course, that Max would print the story if I sent it, which is, to say the least, uncertain.) I would be the agent of new rancor between our people and Ecotopia. I'd be attacked by our rightwingers as a turncoat, "giving*

away our secrets." And I confess this charge would hurt a little, silly as it seems. Whatever seeds of mutual understanding my series of reports may be generating would be killed. The resulting tension would be sure to make it impossible to have any kind of serious opening conversations with President Allwen—or even to remain in the country, for that matter! (Responses from her secretary are a little warmer these days—he even commented favorably on that column about the economy. Still, nothing definite about seeing her.)

"You shall know the truth, and the truth shall make you free." I remember the chill that motto used to be able to send down my back. Then I had to learn that truth was not some single easy thing you could "know" automatically, but an uneasy and always tentative compound of facts, inferences, balances—inherently hypothetical even when it seems altogether obvious: like science, I suppose. We go on refining it, through the years, but we never ever really reach it. (And so our freedom is conditional too?) Someday I will write the Helicopter War story. But it is not part of this assignment.

Now must go downstairs and face the goading from Bert and the rest. Lucky bastards.

LIVING IN PLASTIC TUBING

Santa Cruz, June 8. We extrude plastic sausage casings, wire, garden hose, aluminum shapes, and many other items, but the Ecotopians extrude whole rooms. They have devised machinery that produces oval-cross-section tubing, about 13 feet wide and 10 feet high; the walls are six inches thick, and there is a flat floor inside. The tubing can be made solid, or windows can be punched out along the sides. It can be bought with ends cut off square or on the diagonal. The resulting houses take many shapes—in fact I've never seen two that were alike—but you can get the general impression by imagining that jet airplane cabins could be bought by the yard and glued together into whatever shapes you had in mind.

Most Ecotopian buildings are wood, the material Ecotopians love best. But wood houses are complicated to build and thus expensive compared to these extruded houses, which are made of a plastic derived from cotton. The extruded houses also have the advantage of portability (a standard section about 12 feet long is light enough to be lifted by four men) and Ecotopians show great ingenuity in using them.

Cut off at one angle and glued together, they produce a square house; on a different angle, a hexagonal or octagonal house. You can glue sections together into an irregular zigzag shape, or make them into a long looping string, with branches or protrusions, enclosing a sort of compound—a common pattern for extended-family groups living in open country. You can build a central space out of wood or stone and attach extruded rooms onto the outer edge. You can cut doors or windows with a few minutes work. And not only can the sections be glued together by unskilled labor, their cost is very low—a room-size section costs less than a fifth of what a standard-construction room costs, including a couple of windows. This, I was told, is the astonishing result of producing housing on a truly industrial continuous-process basis, instead of by handwork.

I have just inspected one of the plants in which these extruded houses are produced. It resembles one of our car-washes. A large vat cooks the ingredients into a foam-type moldable plastic. The foam is then squirted under pressure through a huge oval slot, and hardens as it comes in contact with the air. After passing over some supporting rollers, it has window holes punched if desired, and is then sprayed inside and out with a hard-surface plastic. This has a strange neutral color and resembles a dried corn leaf—which is not surprising since it is derived from corn plants; it is washable, can be painted though few Ecotopians use paint, and modestly fits in with natural landscapes. Finally the tubing is cut off into different lengths and stored in a nearby field until needed.

The floor of the tube has troughs molded along the sides to accommodate wiring and water pipes, which are also available in standard section lengths and connect to outlets, toilets, and so on.

Ecotopians are always talking of "integrated systems," by which they mean devices that cater to several of their ecological fetishes at once. The extruded house system offers a number of examples. Probably the most startling is the bathroom. Ecotopians have put into practice an early notion of our architects, and produce entire bathrooms in one huge molded piece, proportioned to slide neatly into a section of extruded room. It contains all the usual bathroom components, including a space heater. A companion unit, a large plastic tank, is buried outside, and connected by two flexible hoses. This, it turns out, is a septic tank, which not only digests sewage but produces methane gas in the process, which in turn operates the heater! The effluent that runs out the other end is not at all repulsive, but clear and excellent for watering gardens, so that ordinarily the garden is placed adjacent to the bathroom. Sludge is removed from the tank every few years and used for fertilizer. This system may seem disgusting to some, but it has its advantages, especially in rural areas. And when you remember that gas and electric energy in Ecotopia are inordinately expensive (costing about three times what they cost us) it is clear why such an odd but thrifty idea has caught on widely. Another integrated system Ecotopians are proud of is the heat-pump solar heating device; these are especially effective with the extruded rooms, consume no fossil fuel or even water, and require only a small amount of electricity to operate their pumps.

Incidentally, one curious symptom of the high cost of energy in Ecotopia is that houses tend to be abominably ill-lit. They contain lamps of several kinds, used for reading and work purposes—though Ecotopians avoid flourescent tubes, claiming their discontinuous emission patterns and subliminal flicker do not suit the human eye. But for ordinary socializing their houses are lit by small bulbs and often even by candles (which they produce from animal fats as our ancestors did).

Such peculiarities aside, an extruded house has a comfortable feeling once you get used to it. The fact that walls and ceiling merge into one another can make for unease at first, yet it is snug and secure too. Ecotopians decorate houses in many different modes, but those who live in extruded houses tend to use even more rugs, coverlets, blankets, and other woven objects, presumably to soften the severe geometrical lines of the structure. Sheepskin and fur rugs are also common. Because of the extremely good insulation and air seal provided by the foam shell, extruded houses are easy to heat—in fact the windows are usually kept wide open—and their inhabitants thus tend to wear little clothing indoors. (Indeed some of them are totally unconcerned about nudity—I was once greeted at the door by an Ecotopian wearing nothing at all.)

One of the pleasantest houses I have yet visited had extruded rooms arranged like spokes of a wheel around a central stone core. This provided the living, cooking and eating area, which was octagonal in shape and had a translucent dome over it. An indoor tree, perhaps 15 feet high, stood in a miniature garden under the dome. One side of the main octagon opened out toward the river from which the house stones had come. The other sides had sliding doors opening into a series of tube rooms, five of which were bedroom-study-retreat rooms, one a spacious and luxurious bathroom complete with fireplace, and one a sort of work room with a small bathroom. Plants and woven fabrics were everywhere, forming beautiful contrasts with the pale, graceful extruded shapes. In one of the bedrooms, a soft, deep-pile rug continued up the walls to window level; aside from a low bed, there was no other furniture, though a bank of cabinets lined the far end of the room. These, I discovered, are available prefabricated, like other kinds of dividers for the extruded rooms; but often people devote great artistry to making their own, with fantastically beautiful woods and intricate detail work.

Extruded houses lack the many built-in appliances of our trailers, but they are probably much more durable; some have been lived in for 15 years now. They are easily patched by the occupants. Once, to demonstrate this, an Ecotopian who was showing off his house to me took an axe and chopped a gaping hole in it! Then the family gathered round, plugged up the hole with shreds of foam, and neatly glued on a piece of surface plastic. The whole process, accompanied by much laughter, took about 10 minutes.

Like all plastics manufactured in Ecotopia, the extruded houses can be broken up and thrown into biovats, digested by micro-organisms into fertilizer sludge, and thus recycled onto the fields from whence their materials came. Oddly, the one serious problem encountered when they were first used was that they tended to blow away in high winds. But instead of our heavy, excavated foundations, they now use large adjustable corkscrew devices which anchor each corner but leave the earth surface undisturbed.

Many Ecotopians are fond of these products of housing automation. But they are very unceremonious about them, and treat them with none of the almost religious respect they extend to wood structures. If a family member dies or leaves, his room may be sliced off and recycled. When a baby is born or a new person joins a group, a new room can be glued onto the existing constellation—a long room for an adult, a short one for a child. Any self-respecting architect would shiver at such a prospect, but it does make the houses a direct expression of the life inside them.

(June 9) Marissa and I apparently on a more flexible basis now—after doing the Helicopter War checking I went out to the camp for a bit of rest, and yesterday she went down with me to the extrusion plant. It turned out she had never been in an extruded house—must have put a lot of energy into avoiding them!—and concluded they were awful. Got furious when she saw I was fascinated and impressed. "I knew it! They're just a piece of your American junk!" She pounded on the slick surfaces, made terrible faces. For a moment I didn't take it too seriously, but then suddenly realized her reaction was intensely personal and concerned something much more important: she felt I was backsliding, losing whatever sense she and other Ecotopians have banged into my head since I've been here. Began to weep. "How can you love wood the way you say you do, and yet be sympathetic to this insane artificial crap? Just feel it, feel *it!" (I felt it. She's right: it's got a sort of pale, neutral, clammy feel, and no smell, and very little texture.) Wildly, and crying again: "I will never, never,* never *live in one of those things, never!"*

Suddenly I knew we are on the verge of new developments I don't understand, where everything has taken on a new and subterranean importance; there is some sense in which she is watching me, evaluating me, which is different from her playful cultural arm-wrestling at the beginning. Whatever it is in me that she cares about, she really *cares about. . . . We have also reached some new, more relaxed level of sexual relating. For weeks she accepted my sexual appetite for her as a kind of aberrant fact of nature that would pass, and it has—we are now in a much better balance, she pursues me as much as I pursue her. We look at each other with a lovely sense of mutual desire. —Strange, swelling, bursting sensation in chest when I think about it—as if I want to pour myself out to her, from the heart. "I always worry about being sentimental," I said last night, "but I'm going to say anyway that I love you." She looked at me intently. "What do you love about me?" "Your intensity and your freeness. And the way we are joyful together—not just in bed, other times too."*

"Well," she said, speaking carefully, "I have begun to love you too. I love your intelligence, your kindness. And you startle me with your strange viewpoints on things. And actually I'm more joyful with you than with other people. Maybe you liberate me in some way. You're the most powerful person in my life these days."

"What do you mean, powerful? That I have friends in Washington?"

She laughed. "My God, no! You just bring out a stronger kind of love than I have for anybody else."

"The kind of love you would have for a mate?"

We looked at each other gravely for a while. "I'm not sure," she said finally. "If you were an Ecotopian, I think it would be. But maybe it's because you aren't *an Ecotopian that it's so exciting to be around you. You're more of a cynic than we are, so I want to test everything against you! But you're so terribly rootless too—"*

At this, to my surprise, she began to cry. And to tell the truth I suddenly didn't feel so cheery myself. She's right: I am a homeless wanderer, and somehow this trip is bringing into new perspectives the things I thought were settled—the way Pat and I had worked things out with each other and the kids, my easy loose relationship with Francine. I'm beginning to see that to an Ecotopian, who always has a strong collective base to return to, a place and the people of that place, my existence must seem pathetically insecure. I have never cried about it. But maybe I should. . . .

SEPARATION OF FUNCTIONS: RESEARCH AND TEACHING IN ECOTOPIA

Berkeley, June 9. American universities are our major source of scientific innovations, and important for social policy formulation as well. But, in line with their penchant for small-scale organization, the Ecotopians have attempted to separate research functions from teaching functions. This has brought about a striking proliferation of small research institutes. These are usually located near universities and their staffs are partly permanent members and partly university professors on their year-off research rotation. These institutes seem to contain 30–100 members—scientists, technicians, machinists, and so on—it is hard to tell who is what, as their professional roles are not so well defined as with us. One such institute I have visited, near Monterey, was studying a variety of oceanographic and related biological problems. Another, south of San Francisco, concerned itself with astronomy, astrophysics, and so on. (The Mt. Hamilton telescopes, I am told, are once again usable due to the drop in air pollution and city illumination levels since Independence.) Scientific institute laboratories such as these appear to a layman to be well equipped, and Ecotopian scientists are often invited to international congresses where their work is highly respected for its originality, though of course it is not as broad in scope as ours, nor anywhere near as well financed.

The atmosphere of the research institutes, considering the great national responsibility they bear, is surprisingly playful. There is a great deal of sitting around with coffee or tea or marijuana, and many projects seem to make constant use of children's construction-set materials. The electronic equipment in many labs lends itself to games in which, I was told, a certain amount of fooling around turns out to generate surprising und useful ideas.

Ecotopia also manages to support a sizable number of utterly independent and very small research outfits, often two- or three-person labs. Many scientists think these tiny grouplets are the source of the most brilliant ideas in Ecotopian science—for reasons that are not well understood but are thought to involve the kind of solitary, independent minds attracted to such free circumstances.

Is it not clear how these small projects are financed, much less supervised, if indeed they are supervised. Evidently there are central government funds that are disbursed through an organization like our National Science Foundation, whose advisory committees are required to devote certain sums to high-risk projects, usually proposed by younger scientists. It is believed that if one in a hundred of these project results in an interesting discovery, the money can be considered well spent. The great example cited to me was the finding of a photochemical mechanism that could tap electrical energy directly from algae and other growing plants. This was the work of two 26-year-olds, reportedly rather antisocial types with somewhat odd interests that happened to contain an unusual combination of botany, plant physiology, and electronic miniaturization. (Although this achievement has not yet proved itself in practical power-generation, it did win them a Nobel Prize.)

My scientific background is not sufficient to evaluate some of the claims that have been made to me, but great stress has been laid on the fact that natural processes have been adapted to produce chemicals we obtain from coal and oil. Thus fermentation —which we use mainly to make liquor—turns grain, beet sugar, and other crops into alcohol which is widely used for heating and cooking, as well as for the production of other chemicals. The Ecotopians are extremely proud that they employ petroleum products solely for lubrication—and even there are making progress toward producing heavy, durable oils from vegetable sources. Plant breeding is highly developed, and plant care has attained a positively Japanese level of sophistication. Special types of oceanographic research are highly advanced; a seaborne unit, for instance, has been at work for some years in an attempt to decode the "speech" of dolphins and whales—specially equipped divers live among dolphins at sea for long periods, just as ethnographers would do if they wished to learn the language of an unknown tribe. Active research also continues on additional ways of harnessing solar, wind and tidal power.

Ecotopian scientists complain as ours do about lack of funding for particularly intriguing projects. There is some grumbling even now about the abandonment of expensive high-energy nuclear and fusion research soon after Independence. But money seems to be available for a great range of basic biological investigations, and the reorientation of national production technology which followed Independence was achieved only through massive scientific effort.

There is one striking lack in Ecotopian science, which reminds one how drastic have been the effects of secession in some areas. Neither in Ecotopian universities nor in research institutes can one find professors of several once flourishing disciplines: political science, sociology and psychology. Their practitioners evidently drifted off into other fields—philosophy, biology, and so on. Many books on the former subject matters of these fields continue to appear, but they are treated as part of general citizenly concern and are not considered to have "scientific" standing. History, on the other hand, is an academic discipline that has blossomed in Ecotopia, although a good deal of it is occupied with muck-raking in pre-Independence archives. (A branch little known among us, "industrial history," is devoted to the alleged crimes of American industrial leaders and corporations—whose records fell into the public domain at the time of secession.) Economics is also still an active field, though of course its direction would seem questionable to most of our economists, and anthropology is very active. Such curious imbalances in academic life may help explain the disorganized and chaotic nature of Ecotopian life generally.

Student unrest seems to be even more chronic in Ecotopian universities than in ours. While I was visiting Berkeley, a college dean was expelled through the combined votes of students and a few disaffected faculty in the college assembly—a sort of quarterly town meeting. In keeping with Ecotopian notions of decentralization, the universities were broken up after Independence into a number of separate colleges, each managing its own affairs without benefit of—or interference from!—a central administration. (In time, the universities are to spin off into totally non-governmental forms, like the schools.)

During the alternating years they are on campus—and they often reside in former office buildings which have been made into living quarters—the professors devote full energy to teaching. In each college there is a group of professors actually hired by the students, and paid directly from student fees. These "collegial" professors, who are often felt to be brilliant but erratic by their regular colleagues, are sometimes lured away from other universities for a year; sometimes they are eminent men of letters, or scientists, or politicians, or simply people who have had unusual life experiences that the students wish to hear about and discuss in detail.

Another surprise is that the student body, at most Ecotopian institutions of higher education, has shrunk considerably. People seem to attend university because they like the intellectual life there, not for practical or ulterior motives. Ecotopian society is oriented toward experience and activity rather than credentials, licenses, and requirements. The mere possession of a degree confers little status, and Ecotopia has none of our scrambling for Ph.D's. (There are, as far as I can tell, no jobs in Ecotopia for which a degree is an absolute prerequisite.) The respect given to people thus turns upon achievement; and creativity and inventiveness are highly prized, both as intriguing personal qualities and because they are useful to society.

This has meant much less emphasis on certifiable expertise and defined professional fields, often with severe consequences. Thus the magnificent departmental system at Berkeley was abolished, together with its elaborate curriculum of huge standardized lecture courses. These lectures were videotaped by the best professors, and made available on videodiscs to students; they were also broadcast regularly on television, which took on extensive educational functions after Independence. Education through residence at a college assumed a pronouncedly novel form, by contrast. The elective system, where every student could choose, cafeteria-style, among the offerings of the various departments, became a public institution through video; and any citizen may acquire an education in biology, engineering, musicology, or hundreds of other subjects by enrolling in video courses. Students on campus, however, are expected to develop the ability to participate in the whole range of intellectual and creative activities. Thus each student is supposed to develop competence in the mental processes proper to the humanities, the biological and physical sciences, and political thought.

Incredible as it may seem to us, this competence is thought to be objectively definable, and thus testable; achieving it is taken to be the joint responsibility of the students and the teachers, who operate in small tutorial groups of 20 students each. The testing is apparently very tough. Exams in the basic year-long courses are given at the end of the year only, and are planned and prepared by intercollege boards of professors. I have seen some of the test materials, and they assume that a "generally educated person" will be able to think clearly about both the tonal system of gamelan orchestras and the endocrine functions of the cat. Judging by some of the weird conversations I have had here, the system works appallingly well!

Some specialized courses are also given, and even the basic courses involve a great deal of specialized knowledge, but most of what we would call graduate instruction has been converted into apprenticeship programs that take place in research institutes, farms, factories, and other productive institutions of the society. Here students are subjected to the same standards as their "masters." The publication of a brilliant short paper counts for more than a number of dull long ones. "Inventions," whether abstract ideas, proposals for better production processes or creative works, are greatly respected and much discussed. And participation in the community, whether a college, a living group, or an academic association, is thought to be important for all. (Dissident loner types refer to this last as the "togetherness test.")

Thus the service-station and degree-mill concept of the university, which still tends to prevail with us, has been destroyed in Ecotopia. The services in research, weapons development, policy formulation, and the like, which universities rendered business and government before Independence, must be performed by entirely new organizations. Such a great departure was, of course, facilitated by the fact that at Independence the support of the federal government in Washington, which had been the mainstay of virtually all university research, was abruptly ended. What has taken its place may not be as grand as the old universities, with their exciting conduits to the White House and Wall Street.

On the other hand, the curious combination of intellectual rigor and lack of customary disciplinary boundaries may explain why so many Ecotopians are expert at arguing esoteric positions (sometimes merely to see if they can successfully defend them!); intellectual discussion is enjoyed almost for its own sake, as an art. And this hypothetical turn of mind, encouraged by the Ecotopian universities, may have facilitated the adoption of so many startling innovations so quickly and with so little relative disruption.

(June 10) Encouraging message from President Allwen's office: she has expressed interest in my columns, and will work me into her schedule soon. This clearly justifies an extension of another ten days here if necessary. Sent message to Max, asked him to tell Francine and Pat. Felt odd and a little guilty about both of them.

Worse still, Marissa upset because of my dumbly mentioning the forthcoming interview, and then going back to New York. Looked at me as if I was a candidate for a buzz-saw execution. "You lousy rotten son of a bitch!" she said, and gave me a clout. We wrestled fiercely for a moment, and then both began crying, tears pouring all over us, holding each other very tightly. Not saying anything, just crying for a long time, not being able to bear letting go. Then after a while she got up and headed home, still tearful.

This thing between us, which began so easily and naturally, begins to look as if it has gotten out of hand. Maybe it was out of control all along, and I just didn't see it. Maybe I didn't want *it under control, for that matter? But how can it end, without terrible pain all around? Is that what love is, just a crazy lure and prelude to pain?*

I sit here, drained, exhausted, tight behind the eyes, watching the first summer tongue of fog creep past Alcatraz, heading up the Bay toward the great hot interior valley. The foghorn out at Land's End has begun moaning even though it's only midday. . . .

ECOTOPIAN MUSIC, DANCE, OTHER ARTS

San Francisco, June 10. Just as Ecotopians blur the difference between professional and amateur in science, there is almost no distinction between amateurs and professionals in the arts. People of all levels of skill and creativity put themselves forward unabashedly. There is hardly a young person in the whole country who doesn't either play an instrument, dance, act, sing, write, sculpt, paint, make videofilms, or indulge in some original artistic activity. However, few of these gain the recognition—and sales—to sustain themselves entirely through their work.

And competition is harsh in other ways too. Not only do audiences treat bad performances rudely, with whistling, booing, and taunts, but even successful artists cannot turn to foundations for the grants that are so desperately sought by our officially recognized artists. If they cannot make it with their art, young Ecotopian artists have only two alternatives: living on the minimum-guarantee level and continuing to strive for recognition, or taking a job and pursuing their art as a part-time activity.

Oddly enough, the avidity with which almost all Ecotopians pursue some kind of art work actually adds to the difficulty of achieving success as an artist, because it seems to diminish the respect for "name" artists. Even in music, people collect records by groups they like, but they don't seem to go terribly far out of their way to hear a visiting group if one of their own is playing. They collect paintings and sculpture, but mix them in with works given to them by friends, or which they've done themselves. Although international traveling art exhibitions come to Ecotopian museums, they do not generate the intense excitement we have in New York. Ecotopians spread their appreciation thin; they have a near provincial disregard for the very highest achievements, a kind of ultrademocratic shrinking of the scale of creative excellence. Apparently, if art is something everybody does, a Picasso or a Van Gogh no longer seem quite so special.

Nor do there seem to be big-name architects in Ecotopia. People themselves design and build structures for their living groups or enterprises with astonishing competence and imagination, often using modularized designs and standard materials that by now have taken on practically the quality of folk architecture. The community governments have design staffs for public buildings (and presumably to check plans before construction) but architecture is not at all the preserve of experts.

Among all the arts, music seems the most important to Ecotopians. Every farm, factory, or extended family has some kind of musical group, and those with professional status usually began in such places. There are several styles of new music being composed. Black bands play a music with roots in the jazz and blues we know from Chicago and New York, and in Caribbean music. Bands from Spanish backgrounds play with an obvious Latin American influence. White bands tend to play music that sounds to me something like Balinese gamelan orchestras—an intricate, cerebral, yet driving jazz, with many homemade drums and gongs prominent in it. (This is said to be derived from earlier rock styles.) There are also groups using classical instrumentation—violins, clarinets, flutes, and so on—who play an unearthly improvised music like nothing I have ever heard, and there are musicians who play instruments of a totally electronic, synthetic-sound type. The one dominant characteristic of all such music styles, however, is a strong dance beat. In fact you seldom see a band playing without some people in the vicinity dancing. Classical music, incidentally, is also heard widely, especially as played by street musicians.

It's difficult for my ear to catch the words of songs, and people dislike the idea of writing them down for me. Still, I was able to pick up the themes of several currently popular ones. They turned out to be largely romantic lamentations, not terribly different from our hillbilly music—complaints about being deserted, dirges for the unhappy end of true love, expressions of anger or despair. There is a resilient humor to some of these songs, but evidently the Ecotopian revolution, whatever else it may have accomplished, has not touched the basic miseries of the human condition.

The burning musical issue in Ecotopia at present concerns electrification. At the time of Independence, rock music was entirely electronic, and groups carried around with them a whole truckload of heavy amplifiers. They soon came under attack from "folkies," musicians who used only traditional instruments such as the recorder, banjo, guitar, piano, and antique types such as the lute or oriental types such as the sitar. Folkies argued that music could not be a truly people's art, accessible to all, if it depended on high-cost electronics; and they also maintained that music should not depend on the artificial aid of electricity. Their final argument was that amplified music was a biological offense because it damaged eardrums. The development of small, inexpensive amplifiers undermined their first point, and the last didn't seem to impress young Ecotopian musicians any more than it had our own. And so the debate rages on.

A number of Ecotopian artists have apparently gained some international status, with shows in Paris and Tokyo. However, the main focus of Ecotopian artistic activity is aggressively domestic. In fact one young artist went so far as to refuse even to give me his name, lest it be bruited about the world through my columns. "We're like the Balinese," he insisted. "We have no 'art,' we just do everything as well as we can." The effects of this attitude can be seen not only in the high level of beauty attained by craft products —pottery, weaving, jewelry, and so on—but also in the quality of Ecotopian furniture, utensils, and house decorations. Some of these last, like a stunning feather mandala given to me by an Ecotopian friend, are not exactly art and not exactly anything else either. But they certainly add to the aesthetic enjoyment the Ecotopians provide for each other.

(June 13) Must get this down straight before it gets furred over.

Got up yesterday morning and found the Cove all busy and excited about the War Games our team was to be in. Tom especially, but everybody *tuned in with it. Lorna, to my surprise, very militant. Even with me there, making an occasional crack, they had no shame about it, no hesitation—it's all real and accepted, they simply* like *it. After a bit I stopped saying much: felt like some nut who would ask, in a hot World Series game, "Why all the fuss? It's just a little old ball made of leather!"*

Breakfast more ceremonious than usual: melons and champagne. But people not too hungry. The excitement was contagious, I had to admit—it even got to me a little. People joking a lot, with a certain bravado. Somebody remarked on the warm weather, and Tom quoted the old plains Indian saying: "It is a good day to die."

About ten o'clock it was parade time. Some self-consciousness as the men got up, looked at each other. Hugs all around, glances at the door. Nina, Tom's friend, had come over and cried a little, which embarrassed him: "Don't cry, we're going to stomp them," he said. But she cried all the louder. I was to go along and observe it all. "It'll make a man of you," Bert jibed at me. They all picked up their spears and we jostled out the big door and into the street —the fighting band of about 15 men, and maybe 30 of the rest of us. The warriors began to chant as they set out, waving their spears, and the rest fell in behind them. A steamy hot day for San Francisco, humid and with little wind.

It was several miles to the place in a huge, wild park where the encounter was to be held. We headed there bravely, the men singing, the rest of us sometimes coming in on a refrain. People along the way watched us pass—if one of the men gestured with his spear or jumped around a little, they would cheer and smile. Couldn't help thinking of the highschool football games of my youth—and the rest of us were like the indulgent parents come to watch the pre-game rally. . . .

Very hot, and the champagne on so little breakfast got to me. Took off my sweater and gave it to one of the women—not sure if it was Brit or Lorna. The chanting grew stronger, and the spirit of the group changed. As we approached the park it was as if the voltage had suddenly been turned up. People were linking arms and looking at each other strangely; the rhythm of the walking was stronger, more like a march, more like a war-dance.

Then suddenly we were off the street and into the park, and there was the ritual cauldron, with barbaric cups hanging from the rim, gleaming in the sun. And off a few hundred yards, on the other side of a meadow, was the enemy, gathered around their cauldron. A thrill went down my back, taking me completely by surprise—I hated them! And my pride in our fighters was enormous, as they gathered around our cauldron. How beautiful they were, how courageous! One by one, they stripped off their street clothes and put on their war garments: leather jackets and shorts, decorated in gorgeous designs, some astrological, some totem-animal, some purely arabesque. Cups began passing around (nobody helped himself—you drank only from a cup given you by a brother) and the rest of us crowded in, yelling encouragement.

Can't recall exactly what happened next. Somebody—I think it was Bert—put a cup in my hand, closed my hand around it, clasped my arm. Yet I can't remember his face. Do remember feeling weak, as if my hand could not grip the cup, and expecting it to fall to the ground, ignominiously. Don't remember if I even made an effort to hold it. But I drank somehow, and there was a great shout, and hands were patting me on the back, and a fighting outfit was being pieced together for me, and another cup of the brew was in my hand. Out of the side vision of my eye I spotted a woman who looked like Marissa, and a pang went through me; turned to look, and couldn't see her anywhere. (My God, I thought, how much I love that woman.) My heart was beating strongly, with a terrible surge of energy, like what we call "second wind" but more so—all my muscles felt strangely powerful.

They banged the gong for the fight to begin. I had watched our men practice in the garden with their *spears, but the actual weapon seemed heavy and awkward. I was afraid my inexperience would endanger my brothers. But their eyes flashed companionably and we all rushed onward together, and began with our enemies the fearful dance I had dreaded and dreamed of. Their first charge horrified me. I had never seen such open looks of murderous malice in another man's eyes, and it was hard not to break and run and cry for mercy. But we rallied, regrouped, pushed back against their advance with a compact front of many spears; and they could see that if they pushed farther, one of them would be mortally exposed. Step by step then, not wishing to abandon an opportunity if we should falter, they began to retreat.*

At this, or so I seem to recall, I or someone near me uttered a bestial kind of triumphant growl, a truly blood-curdling noise. At any rate, I have never felt anything quite like that moment. The dread of their advance was replaced by an unutterable feeling of strength which we all shared, and knew we shared. Making feints and jabs with our spears, and threatening cries, we spread out and pushed them back, looking for weak spots, occasionally ganging up to single out one of their men and try to cut him off.

On one of these surges I must have gotten carried away by my enthusiasm and misjudged the distance. The balance of movement in these war games is more delicate than it seems, and the other side can seize an advantage in a fraction of a second. At any rate, I must have stepped a pace or two too far, or too much to the left or right. The enemy suddenly counterattacked in a way that isolated me on my left. Jerry, who was there, had to jump back for an instant until Tom leaped forward to give him added strength—and in that moment a spear pierced my side just above the waist.

Must have passed out immediately, though I dimly remember cries and shouting and hands helping me to lie down on bloody grass.

By asking people later, have found that I was then bandaged up by a doctor and taken to the small nearby hospital where I am making this diary entry. It is a messy wound, apparently, but did not affect anything crucial. It aches dully, but I can bear it. They took most of an hour to operate, cleaning up the wound and sewing me back together. I came to again just at dusk, and found I am assigned a rather beautiful nurse named Linda. "You were brave," she said, after explaining to me that I was emerging from the anesthetic fog. Did she mean the war games or the operation? I was too drowsy to ask. The hospital must be empty—she seems to have little to do except look after me. But this is very welcome, since I tend to hallucinate more fighting when I close my eyes, and I don't like the idea of going to sleep. . . .

(June 14) Last night after I finished diary entry I told Linda about the hallucinations. Figured she would get me a sleeping pill, but she just asked me to tell her about them. Then she began to massage my forehead and shoulders, which slowed my mind down very soothingly. After a while she just sat there, with a hand resting on my chest. Calmly, as if she would stay all night if necessary. I must have gone right to sleep, and this morning when I woke up she was sitting in the chair next to the bed. It turned out she did *stay all night (the couch in the corner of the room was rumpled and slept-in) and that, furthermore, this is standard practice in Ecotopian hospitals.*

Her long hair swung as she came over and sat on the bed. "How do you feel?" she asked. It was hard to say. I was tired, as if I could sleep for hours more. Yet the sun was appealing, it made me want to stretch. I became conscious of bandages, and of the fact that moving caused pain. I lay still and looked at her.

"Some of your friends will come visit in a bit," she said. "But maybe you'd like some breakfast?" "Yes, I'm very hungry." "The doctor'll be around in a little while. We can fortify you first. What would you like to eat?"

I thought a minute. "I'd like to have a farmer-style breakfast: steak, eggs, potatoes, pie, tomato juice, coffee, toast—" She smiled. "You do *want to get well, don't you? All right, I'll see what the cook can do for you." She pointed to a button at the head of the bed. "If you push that, it buzzes me here, no matter where I am or what I'm doing." She indicated a small radio receiver at her waist.*

As she went out, I felt something like you do when a slot machine pays off: you have trusted yourself to the fickle fingers of fate, and instead of the expected loss, you get bounty. I have survived, the sun is shining, and somebody has sent around this marvelous woman to take care of me. . . .

I gorged myself on the breakfast, though I wasn't quite as hungry as I'd thought. The doctor arrived. Not my favorite image of a physician—long of hair and loose of attire, and took a personal interest in my background and business which verged on prying, but he seemed competent enough. Probed and poked and listened, pronounced me well on the road to recovery. The antibiotics are evidently working: no signs of infection. Tomorrow, he said, I'll be able to move around. "Today, you'll have to content yourself with passive pleasures. I'll have Linda give you a bath this afternoon. And maybe a little massage for now."

I had been thinking of asking someone to phone Marissa for me, but Linda rather pointedly said she's already taken care of it, and to just relax and en-

joy the massage—which turned out to be a lovely sensual experience. Linda's aim seemed to be to make every muscle and nerve in my body warm and conscious of itself. She stroked and kneaded, with a soft, steady rhythm that put me into a dazed, dreamy state. As she worked I couldn't help sighing repeatedly with sheer joy and amazement, and this must have pleased her; at the end she sat down beside me, covered me up, gave me a hug, and said, "You're certainly appreciative!"

"Well, I've never been treated so well in hospital before. Our hospitals are—. Well, they're excellent medically of course, but they're impersonal. The nurses are all business, very overworked, and they're not so pretty." "I'm probably not so pretty as you think right now, either." "It doesn't matter, does it." "Not much." She sat back, and I closed my eyes happily. I must have dozed again. In a while I was wakened by voices, and there in the room was Marissa, full of a sardonic kind of sympathy, with some friends from the Cove. She appraised Linda with steely calm and efficiency; evidently decided she was all right. (But while Marissa was there she didn't let Linda near me, I noticed; and Linda took this in good grace, evidently feeling the patient would be back in her hands soon enough.) My guests had brought a picnic basket and a good deal of wine, which they proceeded to open. Linda pitched in too, as if such things were the normal way of life in a hospital room. They cranked up my bed so I could see the Bay, half hidden by trees, and opened the window; and before long the room was littered with bottles, little cloths spread out for the food, and laughing people.

Marissa's attitude toward me has somehow changed. Maybe it's my participating, even if sort of inadvertently, in the war games: she seems to feel I am a better person for it—more solid and real. (In a round-

about way I mentioned that I thought I had seen her in the park—could she have been there? She laughed and denied it.) And I am *proud of myself, after all. I will treasure my scar. Most of all, it feels good to be treated as less of a foreigner by her, even in jokes: "Anyway," she said, "now you have a little Ecotopian blood in your veins!" (because of the transfusion during my operation).*

What with the wine and the good company, it turned into rather a party. It was fine to be the center of attention, and I blurted out, "You know, I'm not used to being made happy when I'm supposed to be suffering!" This caused a burst of laughter. Linda looked at me protectively, as if I was a child who had just said something ridiculous but lovable, and everyone was beaming at me. It was some kind of magical moment. I became overwhelmingly certain that I was, indeed, going to get well. "You certainly have funny hospitals in Ecotopia," I said. "We try to stay out of ours, but yours are about the nicest places to be."

"That's the idea exactly," said Linda. "People recover best if they're happy. We don't separate medicine and life. So we do *try to make the hospitals the best places there are. That's why what you said about suffering seemed so crazy to us."*

"Don't patients just try to prolong their stays indefinitely, then?" I asked. "Why go home?"

"No, actually, they don't. They really truly recover, and want to get on with living. You'll see. In a couple of days. . . ." She smiled at me softly.

(Don't you see, I wanted to tell her, I am still needy of contact and affection and human directness, from Marissa and you and everyone, and I love you because you sat by my side during the long night when I was raw and wounded in body and soul, and because you somehow know what I need and simply give it to me, for this little while when I need it most, without my having to give anything in return—)

(June 15) "We believe in encouraging all your life forces," the doctor said when I expressed pleasure in Linda's massages. And then, as I half expected (is it Doctor's Orders or her own initiative?) in giving me a sponge bath she wryly stroked me into an erection and got me off. My ambitions leaped up, quite obliterating thoughts of sutures and bandages. Marissa has gone back to the camp, speaking stern words to Linda on leaving. Linda's hands and quiet smile fascinate me, but the pains I still have under the bandage keep me from moving my pelvis very much. Will I be considered well enough to leave just at the point I am well enough to really fuck her?

(Later) Cable sent over from Cove: "WHY DON'T YOU GET A GUITAR AND GO SING UNDER THE PRESIDENTIAL BALCONY? FAINT HEART NEVER WON FAIR INTERVIEW. THEN GET YOUR ASS BACK HERE WHERE IT'S SAFE. FRANCINE." *That damned woman could foul up my whole project yet. Hope the Ecotopian secret police have a sense of humor—and still understand our kind of women.*

HOSPITALS AND HEALTH CARE: THE ECOTOPIAN WAY

San Francisco, June 15. An unfortunate accident has given me the chance to observe Ecotopian hospital procedures first hand. I have been recuperating, the past few days, from a nasty gash. But I am mending well, and expect to be out of the hospital tomorrow, though I will have to take it a bit easy for a while.

The greatest difference between Ecotopian hospitals and ours is in scale. Though the medical care I have received seems to be at the highest level of sophistication, from the atmosphere here I might be in a tiny country hospital. There are only about 30 patients all together, and we are practically outnumbered by the nursing staff (who, by the way, work much longer hours than ours, but in compensation spend as much time on vacation as they do on the job). X-ray, surgery, anesthesia, and other services seem to be fully as competent as ours, though the physical appearance of the hospital might strike an American as a bit rustic: the walls are not tile, and I missed the smell of disinfectant which I've always associated with hospitals. On the other hand everything seems clean and well cared for, and the doctors, though clearly unfamiliar with the expectations of American patients, are alert and seem well trained.

In one respect the Ecotopians have taken a profoundly different direction than our modern hospitals. They do not employ electronic observation to enable a central nurses' station to observe many patients at once. The theory, as I have gathered it, is that the personal presence and care of the nurse is what is essential; and the only electronic gadget used is a small radio call set that can retrieve your nurse from anywhere on the hospital premises without bothering anybody else. The nurses are highly trained in a number of specialities unknown to ours, particularly massage, which they regard as important for stimulating the body's recuperative powers.

Ecotopians are covered by a type of cradle-to-the-grave medical insurance which has had drastic effects on the medical system. Instead of control by the profession itself, the clinics and hospitals are responsible to the communities—normally to the minicity units of about 10,000 people. Thus the power of the physician to set his own fees has evaporated, though a doctor can always bargain between the salary offers of one community and another, and in fact doctors are reputed to have among the highest incomes despite the fact that they are much more numerous than with us. Doctors perform many duties that nurses or technicians perform in our more specialized system; on the other hand, nurses and technicians also perform a good many of the services that our doctors reserve for themselves. I have noticed that conversations among doctors, staff, and patients are a good deal livelier than in our hospitals; evidently the moral and scientific authority of the doctor has been diluted. Conditions can't be too miserable for the doctors, however, or more of them would leave the country; as far as I can tell, only a few hundred left at the beginning (mostly very high-income specialists) and none at all have left in recent times. Ecotopia does not import foreign-trained doctors to staff its hospitals, as we are still forced to do, because its medical schools were almost doubled in capacity immediately after Independence.

My strength has not permitted me to do much investigating while hospitalized. However, the gravest problem of Ecotopian medicine would seem to be a dearth of really top-notch specialists. Specialists do exist, and are consulted on many occasions, but they are required to do general practice as well. This wasteful system is justified by the argument that it keeps them in touch with the medical needs of the people as a whole; but it clearly represents a serious reduction in the best utilization of specialist training and abilities. In fact some specialties have died out entirely. For instance, babies are usually delivered at home by nurse-midwives except in a few cases that present complications, and the hospitals have neither maternity wards nor obstetricians.

Intensive-care units are also not developed as highly as in our hospitals. This clearly involves a certain hard-heartedness toward terminally ill or very critically ill patients, who cannot be kept alive by the incredibly ingenious technology American hospitals have. This may be partly an economic necessity, but also Ecotopians have a curiously fatalistic attitude toward death. They prefer to die at home, and elderly

Ecotopians spend a good deal of time and energy preparing themselves for death. It is even said that, like American Indians, they can select the day of their death, and almost will themselves to die. At any rate, when they feel their time has come, they let it come, comforting themselves with their ecological religion: they too will now be recycled.

On the other hand, the Ecotopian medical system has a strong emphasis on preventive care. The many neighborhood clinics provide regular check-ups for all citizens, and are within easy reach for minor problems that might develop into major ones. No Ecotopian avoids getting medical care because of the expense or the inaccessibility of health facilities.

All Ecotopian doctors receive what we would call psychiatric training, though psychology and psychiatry no longer constitute separate fields. My doctor, thus, paid considerable attention to my psychic state as well as to my medical injuries. It is claimed that mental illness has shown a decline since Independence, but it would be extremely difficult to evaluate such claims because of the drastically altered circumstances. I can confirm, however, that Ecotopian streets are not enlivened by the numerous and obvious crazies we are familiar with in our cities. On the other hand, the security and confidence achieved by the Ecotopians with their dense, highly personalized style of neighborhood and extended-family living are bought at a substantial price in anonymity and freedom. Ecotopians have the feeling, I was told by one doctor, of "never being alone." The commonest psychiatric symptom for which people visit doctors, he told me, is having fantasies about solitude and about committing violent crimes. (It is a strange tribute to the ritual war games that it is mainly older people and women, who do not take part in the games, who are troubled by such violent impulses.) Some people find it helpful to take wilderness hiking trips by themselves, where they can be totally alone for weeks at a time. Still, it is doubtful if Ecotopians are happier than Americans. It seems likely that different ways of life always involve losses that balance the gains, and gains that balance the losses. Perhaps it is only that Ecotopians are happy, and miserable, in different ways from ourselves.

(June 15, later) Have just been given a message from the President's assistant: they hope I recover satisfactorily. I am to let them know when I am back in action. Good news!

The doors in the thick masonry walls have been opened, and I can chat with my neighbor—a woman of 45 who almost lost an arm in a fishing-trawler winch accident. Her nurse is a debonair man, maybe 30, good at telling stories, and probably at other things too. Gets her to laugh a lot, anyway, sometimes with pleased blushes. I am now allowed to take short walks along the hill outside. We see other patients, generally (though not always) with opposite-sex nurses. Remarked to Linda that their intimate methods of treatment could sometimes pose problems for the nurses. She was irritated by my attitude. "First," she said, "every treatment is unique. Second, there is something in every person to value and love" (here she smiled) "even in a dumb chauvinist ugly American bastard like you. Third, nurses are also persons, and we have control of what we do or don't do. Do you think I'm your slave or something?" She made a face, cuffed me on the shoulder, took me back inside. I'm afraid she was right. My culture has inflicted many handicaps along with its blessings.

Have been reading some Ecotopian novels. They exude a curious feeling of security, almost like 19th-century English novels: a sense, probably derived here from the stable-state notion, that the world is a decent and satisfactory place which will sustain us despite some difficulties. There are terrible dramatic incidents and psychologically harrowing events, of course, but none of the totally freaked out, nihilistic paranoia of our novels. At first the stories seemed puzzlingly vapid to me; I couldn't figure out why anybody would find them interesting. How come they didn't have that exciting nightmare quality? Some of them even have happy endings. . . . After a while, they seem more like life—okay to spend time with, reassuring. Come to think of it, Ecotopia itself is beginning to feel a good deal more reassuring: when I needed care, I was taken care of.

(June 16) Now my wound has been given a new bandage—very small. Linda and I have initiated it with a long, gentle session of love-making—with hardly any pain, just occasional small squeaking shoots of discomfort.

Linda, I'm beginning to realize, really isn't quite as pretty as I thought at first, and she is not perhaps the most piercingly intelligent person in the world either. But she is a born nurse: immensely kind, warm, sustaining, with an extraordinary accepting, loving, physical presence. Does she want me to leave, or stay longer? (I gather that an Ecotopian with friends or family in the vicinity would probably go home tomorrow.) But she won't discuss it. "There's nothing that can be said about that," she always replies, a little crossly. "When you are well enough, you will leave. You'll know when the time comes."

"And then you'll get another patient-lover?" "Idiot." But she knows I have not overcome my confusions on these things, so she comes over and hugs me. "When you go, I get a vacation, and I can go anywhere, on my railway pass. I'm planning to go hiking in the desert. And I'll think about you a lot. And you'll write about me in your diary." (She has discovered my notebook.)

"Yes," is all I can reply, and I hug her, and feel like crying. This country has certainly taught me to

cry, and for some reason it feels good, as if it is not only my tear ducts that have been opened up. . . .

(June 17) When I left the hospital this morning and headed out to see Marissa at the camp, I stopped at one of those fantastic camping-supply stores they have, and bought Linda a new sleeping bag—a super down-filled job that rolls into a tiny stuff sack and will keep her snug in the coldest desert night. Choice of dark green, brown, blue, or flaming orange. I picked orange. Feeling foolish, I wrote on the card, "Stay warm. Love." Had it delivered to the hospital so she would get it before her vacation begins.

Marissa delighted to see me. Asked wicked titillating questions about Linda's attentions, insisted on inspecting my scar, made fun of "pretty nursie taking care of poor wounded Willie." We laughed and horsed around gleefully—it really did feel sensational to be back with her.

Somehow, though, we got into this ferocious argument. Carried away, I mentioned my recurrent fantasy of taking her back to New York with me when my assignment here is over. She reacted instantly that it was an asinine idea, absurd: "What would I do *there? I'd be just an appendage to you. There's no way I could make a life for myself in that kind of society." I felt, to my surprise, terribly hurt at this: as if our love for each other could have no impact on the real world. I raged and moaned, accused her of not caring for me, of not wanting to continue being with me. She reassured me about loving me, but would not budge on the basic question. I broke out in a cold sweat, feeling horrible. I wanted desperately to make love to her, but my sexual feelings were somehow bottled up; nothing would happen.*

Eventually we took a long walk through the forests. Am beginning to understand how she feels about trees. We walked up the valley, taking it easy, then came back past the hollow tree where we had first made serious love. It was still a magical place. But this time we just sat down quietly inside the old trunk, watching the light fade into dusk, touching each other lightly. Despite the quarrel, I am happier than I have been in a long time, and dread it coming to an end. Will put off for one more day going back to the city, and the work which will soon be over.

(June 18) Was told this morning that Vera Allwen would see me today at four, though strictly off the record and informally. Have just returned from her office, and transcribe here the essentials of what happened.

The President is a very direct person. Despite being rather small and a trifle stout, gives off a strong air of authority. Clearly well used to exercising power. But not businesslike and cool about it, like many of our politicians, who are sometimes hard to tell from businessmen—heads full of impersonal calculations that happen to be power equations instead of money ones. She is powerful as a person, *not as a bureaucrat or the head of an institution. Difficult to express. (Have heard that some of the old-time communist leaders, Ho Chi Minh and Mao Tse-tung, had this quality too.) Gave me the feeling I've had in playing chess with people who turn out to be much better players—of being mysteriously outclassed. A truly remarkable woman. Found myself taking refuge in the feeling of being an emissary—I might not measure up to her myself, but at least I had a mission to carry out.*

I presented our President's case for normalization of relations, explaining the advantages, chiefly economic, that could ensue for Ecotopia. She is not against this—replied that Ecotopia already has a certain trade with many other countries, and in fact would welcome additional outlets for some surpluses (wine above all) and would buy a few things from us in return (though vague about what). Medium of exchange would have to be yen, but this could be concealed from our public.

Asked me why we are prepared to take risk of having Ecotopian consulates in our major cities, considering the unrest already generated by Ecotopian ideas among our youth. Not sure I handled this right—made light of danger, expressed confidence, etc. May have seemed ridiculously naive if their intelligence service is as good as I suppose. For all I know, they may be financing the secessionist movements we are beginning to notice in the Great Lakes region and the Southeast.

Main point: absolutely no hope for reunification, now or ever. Long, impassioned speech on this—that the notion shows the lack of contact with reality of our government, that on every major social index Ecotopia would lose by reunification (she ran down the list), the problem is how the United States can follow Ecotopia's lead, not vice versa, that all the large countries should break up into smaller ones, that even if her government wanted reunification her people would not stand for it, and so on. A wildly nationalistic, aggressively secessionist diatribe. Then she stopped short, fixed me with powerful eyes: "You cannot be serious."

"My government—" I began, but she interrupted: "You cannot be serious." Silence. Long silence. She waited, sat back, still glaring at me. Uncomfortable moment—to be sure, at that point I was no longer clear what would really be gained from steps toward reunification. For the U.S. or anybody, including myself.

She gave me a faintly ironic smile. "You know," she said, "I have now said everything I have to say as an official. Perhaps we could just talk as two human beings from now on?" She poured me a brandy (Ecotopian, I noticed, not French!) from a shelf next to her desk. She walked around, sat down nearer to me.

"It is Friday afternoon, the end of a long week. No more business—but I would like to hear what you really think of our country, what you have seen and done. We have, naturally, been reading your reports with care. To be frank, we have been pleasantly surprised at their growing fairness, and the unusual curiosity they reflect. Perhaps you have had a better time in Ecotopia than you expected?" Her eyes crinkled in an almost conspiratorial smile. Startled, I looked back rather blankly, then managed to say, "Well, yes, in fact that's true."

"You are not as personal in your columns as our journalists tend to be, so we have not been able to judge if you have had good experiences among us."

"I put down my personal experiences in a diary. Many of them have been very good, but they're not for publication. —You should understand that by our standards my columns have probably seemed rather too personal."

"Yes, I know. I also know that you have been doing in Ecotopia as the Ecotopians do, where that has been possible for you. We are grateful for the moderation you've expressed. But of course we want more of you still. We have more to give you, I suspect, and there are still things you haven't grasped." "But I have grasped correctly that I cannot give our President any real hope?"

"None whatever."

"And if our hawks prevail?"

"Your hawks were not insane enough to destroy the country in order to reunify it back in 1980, so we doubt if they will be now. —But that's enough of that. I'd like to know what you have been feeling while you've been with us. You can be frank; I have not reached this position by being a gossip, and nothing will go beyond these walls. I like you—you have done brave and good work. I am interested in everything that has happened to you here."

Rest of conversation uncomfortably personal, can-

not record. It was almost like a psychiatric interview. Kept getting the feeling that she was somehow, without ever even hinting at it, probing my loyalties, exploring the ambiguities of my feelings. I kept quoting what I have so gingerly written in the columns—to which she would always have some oblique reply, pretty much indicating that she saw how my mind had worked. Even seemed to know about Marissa—which I suppose should be no surprise. (In a small country ordinary conversation does the work that a secret service is required for in a big one?)

The talk left me feeling exhausted, depressed, as if a huge weight has settled on top of my head. This country is really too much. Even the President wants to mess with your soul. . . . What I had hoped would happen in the interview did not happen. Whatever she *was hoping for must not have happened either—got the feeling that she was disappointed, had expected more. As I left, I had the flash that she reminded me of my grandmother, whose disappointments were visited upon several generations of my family.*

Went back to the Cove, where everybody was dying to know what happened. Was surly to them, came upstairs to write down these notes. It has stayed cloudy the whole day today. Dismal auguries all around.

(June 18) Visit with the President has really gotten me down. Whole trip now seems like a waste of time. This place is lost for us—no question about it! Forever. Period. The journalists at the Cove keep hounding me to tell them what was discussed. I say nothing. Since they're not dummies, they know there may have been more than reportorial reasons for my visit out here. And they can see from my downcast state of mind that it didn't work, whatever it was. They are sympathetic but a certain distance between us has been apparent since the interview.

Have caught some sort of flu—headache, sore throat, a little temperature. (Thermometer is marked in Centigrade, so I don't quite know how serious, but only one notch above normal.) Couldn't sleep at all last night. I go down for a bite now and then, but everybody is always after me. Even Bert. Had to tell him plainly to stop it.

Must try and sort the whole experience out in my head in some new way. Find that I dread the idea of Marissa coming in and seeing me in such dismal shape. The "perspective" she said she loves in me seems to have dissolved utterly. Must phone her and tell her I'm sick so she won't come.

Was fantasizing a balance sheet headed "Ecotopia," and down in two long columns go all the pros and cons. The list gets grotesquely long and dim and blurry, and I hear Marissa laughing. Finally I just rip it up, and my head spins, and I despair.

ECOTOPIA: CHALLENGE OR ILLUSION?

San Francisco, June 19. Where is Ecotopia going in the future? After more than six weeks' intensive study of the country, I find it still hazardous to guess. There is no doubt, I have been forced to conclude, that the risky social experiments undertaken here have worked on a biological level. Ecotopian air and water are everywhere crystal clear. The land is well cared for and productive. Food is plentiful, wholesome, and recognizable. All life systems are operating on a stable-state basis, and can go on doing so indefinitely. The health and general well-being of the people are undeniable. While the extreme decentralization and emotional openness of the society seem alien to an American at first, they too have much to be said in their favor. In these respects, I believe, Ecotopia offers us a difficult challenge, and we have far to go to even approach their achievements.

On the other hand, these benefits have been bought at a heavy cost. Not only is the Ecotopian industrial capacity and standard of consumption markedly below ours, to a degree that would never be tolerated by Americans generally, but the Ecotopian political system rests on assumptions that I can only conclude are dangerous in the extreme. In my earlier columns I described the city-states that have already, in effect, themselves seceded within Ecotopia. There is talk currently of formalizing the Spanish-speaking and Japanese communities of San Francisco—the latter, of course, an economically sinister development because of the threat of Japanese capital taking over. Jewish, American Indian, and other minorities all contain militants who desire a greater autonomy for their peoples.

It is, admittedly, difficult for an American to criticize such trends when our own society, after the failure of the integrationist campaign of the sixties, has grown ever more segregated—though somewhat less unequal. However, it is still the American ideal that all men and women should obtain equal protection from the law and have equal status as citizens of one great and powerful nation. The Ecotopian principle of secession denies this hope and this faith. While seemingly idealistic, it is in fact profoundly pessimistic. And the consequences seem clear. The way propounded by Ecotopian ideologues leads away from the former greatness of America, unified in spirit "from sea to shining sea," toward a balkanized continent—a welter of small, second-class nations, each with its own petty cultural differentiations. Instead of continuing the long march toward one world of peace and freedom, to which America has dedicated itself on the battlefields of Korea, Vietnam, and Brazil (not to mention our own Civil War), the Ecotopians propose only separatism, quietism, a reversion toward the two-bit principalities of medieval Europe, or perhaps even the tribalism of the jungle.

Under Ecotopian ideas, the era of the great nation-states, with their promise of one ultimate world-state, would fade away. Despite our achievements of a worldwide communications network and jet travel, mankind would fly apart into small, culturally homogenous groupings. In the words of Yeats (an early 20th-century poet from Ireland—a very small and secessionist country) "The center cannot hold."

Ecotopians argue that such separatism is desirable on ecological as well as cultural grounds—that a small regional society can exploit its "niche" in the world biosystem more subtly and richly and efficiently (and of course less destructively) than have the superpowers. This seems to me, however, a dubiously fetishistic decentralism. It assumes that the immensely concentrated resources of the superpowers are innately impossible to use wisely. I would be the last to deny that the huge administrative machines of our governments and international corporations do not commit an occasional error, or miss an occasional opportunity. Nevertheless, to condemn them and eliminate them, in favor of small-scale innovations modeled on the Ecotopian experience, would seem to risk throwing the baby of civilization itself out with the polluted bathwater. If we wish to achieve better living conditions for ourselves and our descendants, surely the wiser utilization of the methods we know best is the only way to accomplish it.

(June 20) Blah, blah, blah. Can hardly bear to reread that last column. They'll probably love *it in New York. Real "objective" pseudo-think, trying to come to conclusions at any cost. . . . But have just about decided to cut and run, back to N Y. I'll probably come down with pneumonia if I stay here. Can't stand talking to Bert or the others, though they keep*

after me, and the attention does sometimes feel good, but I can't afford to give in to it, or I'll lose my bearings entirely. So I stick in my room, try to sleep, without much success. Alternate between desperate desire to see Marissa and horror at the thought. Nothing further to do here really. Could tidy up a few further columns—amusing details, a little expansion here and there. But I know everything I basically need to know.

Marissa said she wants to come to the Cove and cheer me up. Don't know if I could bear that, and then leaving—. Got out my suitcase and tossed a few things in it. Thought about the evening train to the Sierras and Reno. Or could drop down via Los Angeles and return that way. No goodbyes are the best goodbyes.

Last night, hardly slept at all. Disjointed flashes of interview with Allwen, bits of experiences keep floating through my mind. Times with Marissa when there is nothing particular to be said and we just look at each other, touching lightly. Walking through San Francisco in my snug serape in the fog. Receptor plates at the solar power station—soaking up the sun, patiently, silently; no movement, just a lark singing. And the way people here look at each other—and then in my fantasies they turn and look at me, expectantly, and I can't meet their eyes. Except Marissa's. Hope I'm not cracking up. Have got to get out of here.

(June 21) Notebook may be taken away from me, but I'll write this entry anyway. I've been kidnapped! Yesterday as I was packing, three men and a woman came into my room and told me to come along with them. "What the hell for?" I asked. I knew two of them—one, with huge bushy eyebrows that give him a demonic look, was a friend of Marissa's brother. (My first thought was that this must be the Ecotopian Mafia.) But he smiled as he came in, put his hand on

my shoulder for a moment. The other I recognized from parties and had also seen him around the Cove, talking to Bert. Some kind of scientist, and I remembered conversations as a little creepy, something about "vibrations." (You never know whether some of these people are creeps or geniuses.) The other two I hadn't seen before as far as I know. Girl is attractive but in a frizzy blonde way. They all appear to be good friends.

"Come on." They began to edge me toward the door, and one threw the rest of my clothes in the suitcase. Suddenly I was sure they must be secret police. I waited until we were downstairs in the hall, then shouted for help. Bert and seven or eight other Cove people appeared, and gathered round. I felt much relieved. My captors, however, didn't seem at all abashed. I began to think I'd have to ask somebody to call Washington. One of the group took several of my friends aside and spoke to them out of my hearing. There was some argument, with glances in my direction, but then apparently agreement. "Will," said Bert, "we think it's all right for you to go with them."

"What do you mean, all right?" I shouted. "I don't want to go. Is this a free country or is it not? Somebody please get on the phone. This is going to mean a big diplomatic mess, do you all understand? I want to get hold of the State Department, or the White House if necessary. This is ridiculous!"

Bert came over and took me aside. "Look, Will," he said, "we know you've been through a bad time since you saw Vera Allwen. Sitting up there in that room is not doing you any good at all. You could use a change for a few days. These people are friends, really. They want to take you to a really extraordinarily lovely place near here for a few days. I've been there myself when I've been in a difficult situation, and we all think it's a good idea. I'd go with you now if I could, but tomorrow's impossible. They've promised you can phone the Cove anytime you like, and I'll come down tomorrow evening and see you."

"What I could use right now is to get out of this fucking country!" I burst out. "And right now! Take me to the train station!"

"That's where they're taking you," said Bert. "But it would be a defeat if you left Ecotopia in your present state of mind. These people know that too. Go on, Will, take our word for it. They're not police, if that's what you're worried about. Somebody from the Cove could come with you if you feel that's essential."

This somehow relieved my mind. I was probably a lunatic to go, but I have learned to trust Bert, even about unusual things. Washington is a long way off, and I would *feel bad about just retreating. Besides, my "captors" had begun to seem less forbidding as they talked with the people at the Cove. The thought hit me that even if they weren't Ecotopian police, they might be from our C.I.A.: if our President really attaches importance to my mission, he might have made arrangements to ensure I stay here as long as needed to carry it out! God knows it was no secret at the Cove how depressed my Allwen visit had left me; and several people saw me get my suitcase from the hall closet. . . .*

They took me to the train and we sped off southward, but got off at the third stop. Then transferred to a minibus that headed east into the mountains. Soon it began winding along a small river, through country half forest and half grassland. We got out at the end of the route—in a spot that, as the sun sank lower, looked more like a resort than a community. A large low building with relaxed people strolling on its verandas lay to the right. Cabins with little porches were scattered all about, of a rough-board design.

"We'll eat after a bit," they told me, "but first we'll go down to the baths." Turns out this is a famous hot springs resort that has been rehabilitated by a Japanese commune. My captors seem to half-believe in its

alleged restorative powers. We put our luggage in one of the cabins and headed down the hill. Nobody had said much all along—a resentful silence on my side, and who knows what on theirs. I looked around to study escape possibilities. It was all open country around the resort. Once out of sight I'd have a good chance of making it. The problems would be in getting away to start with, and making the six or eight miles back to the station through open farmland, hard to hide in. I'd have to do it at night.

Baths housed in beautiful but simple buildings. Each has a changing and sweating room. You leave your clothes and go in, naked, to the bath room, which has a tub about 12 feet square and maybe four feet deep. You wash with soap under a shower, then lower yourself, inch by inch, into the steaming hot water. It doesn't smell foul, to my relief, though it does have a slightly unusual odor and a silky feel. We all sank into it gratefully, my captors smiling at me and making loud happy groans in the water. The tension dropped a bit. The tank is big enough that you can move around in it; has scratchy walls to rub your back against, and an underwater bench to sit on.

Besides us, there were a young couple, who sat in one corner with eyes closed, oblivious to us, and one old Japanese man, who ducked his head occasionally and then, coming up slowly, said "Aaaaahh." We stayed in about 15 minutes, then went out, wrapped ourselves in huge towels, and lay down to sweat. Sweating room has large windows through which I could see the dimming sky and trees moving gently. Made me doze a little. Even thought I might be able to sleep tonight.

The nonconversational behavior of my captors was still annoying, but I held to my resolve to let them start whatever they were going to start. My only request was to call the Cove, and this I was allowed to do right after supper. Bert, it turned out, couldn't come until the second day, but it was reassuring to talk to him anyway, and he said he had already let Marissa know where I was. Then we settled down in big chairs in the main lounge. It had gotten fairly cool, so there was a fire, which felt good. Somebody produced a bottle of brandy in another corner of the room. Glasses were sent for, and we all lifted our drinks to the giver. Chess and domino and go games were in progress. This was all pleasant enough for a while, but I found my nervousness returning. My companions just seemed to be patiently waiting for something—or someone? They are the most silent *Ecotopians I've yet met in this nation of blabbermouths.*

Finally went back on my resolve. "All right," I said, "let's get on with it. What do you want from me? What's this little game all about?"

"We don't want anything from you," said the devilish one who knew Ben. (His name is Ron.) "We're just giving you the chance for a few days of change. You can do with it what you will." "By whose authority?" I said. "Who are *you, anyway?" "We can't tell you that right now. But we're friends. We will do you no harm. We wish you would treat us as friends. You remember that's Marie, and this is Vince, and he's Allan."*

"It's not harm to keep me here against my will?" Nobody answered this; they just sat there and looked at me, a little uncomfortable perhaps, but unmoved. "Look," I said, "I don't know who you're working for, but this caper is going to cause somebody a lot of trouble."

"Why do you assume we're working for somebody?" asked Marie. "It's obvious," I replied. "You're committing an illegal act, for one thing. You're dealing with a quasi-official visitor to the country, for another, whose welfare can't be a matter of indifference to your government."

"That's true enough," she said. "Well, how about

telling us the current state of your welfare?" "I am sick of being held against my will. That's the only part of my welfare that concerns you." "No," said Ron, "you're wrong about that—it all concerns us." He sounded almost hurt; the others nodded. I folded my arms staunchly, and would say no more. In a few minutes we all went off to the cabin. Ron and Marie went to sleep; Vince and Allan are sitting up, watching me write this diary entry.

(June 22) Hardly slept at all again last night. Being watched by them adds to the strain. About three o'clock they woke Ron and Marie up, to change shifts I guess, seeing I wasn't going to sleep. By this time I was pretty jittery, so asked if I could go outside and walk around. Marie volunteered to accompany me. "We'll stay in shouting distance," she said.

We walked around a while. She seemed to be in a friendly mood, put her arm through mine. Surprisingly sexual feeling flooded over me at this, but I resisted the temptation to make some kind of pass. Then she spoiled it by beginning to pry, like some miserable amateur psychologist: "Why don't you open up and tell us what you're thinking? It's not human to try to keep it all inside!"

I pulled away. "Why should I talk to you? Give me one earthly reason." "Well, we're here with you." "I was aware of that. Now give me some good news."

We walked on in silence around the courtyard of the resort. She took my hand, and I suddenly realized this girl is probably only 20 or so. "All right," I said, "I'll tell you something. I want to go home, to get away from this country. Everything here upsets me. It isn't real, it just isn't real."

"It's real for us—you're not letting it be real for you." "Well, I've done my job here, as well as anybody could, but now it's time to go."

"Why do you think about it just as a job?" she asked. "It's also been an adventure, if that's what you

mean." "It's still an adventure. Even if we're the ones who're keeping it going." She grinned. We went back to the cabin. Ron greeted us with some curiosity, but I wouldn't respond and Marie wouldn't say much either. I must have dozed a couple of hours; it's six A.M. *now. I'll get through the day somehow. Quivery—don't dare drink any more coffee.*

(June 22, evening) We took the baths morning and afternoon, and did some walking. I don't know what they're up to. Seem genuinely interested and curious about what I think of Ecotopia, what happened to me here, what I'm going to do next. After we sweated out the morning bath I felt like talking to them about it a little. It's very hard, I find, to get my ideas and my feelings within range of each other, and I keep flying into a kind of flat, blind rage at the whole situation. I've gathered a lot of facts, many of them hard to accept rationally. I've gone through remarkable personal experiences. Does it all add up to good or evil? I honestly don't know.

Some aspects of the country strike me as downright entrancing—the beauty of it, even the cities, which make such a contrast with the hellish way we live. Some aspects of life here reach me emotionally in ways I wouldn't have believed just a few weeks ago—everything connected with Marissa, the horror of the ritual war games, the security of the hospital and the Cove. Other things are just mystifying, like their economic system. Over it all hangs a kind of feathery curtain of disbelief, which I keep wishing I could tear aside, or maybe duck under.

They listened to me talk, but don't seem to find much to respond to. At one point Ron interjected impatiently, "Well, you've told us all this stuff about what you think. It's interesting, but we really pretty much knew how you think. *What are you* feeling? *And what are you going to do?"*

"What do you mean? Go back to New York, of

course." But precisely as I said that a great twinge of pain throbbed through my head. "My God," I said, "I have this awful headache." I staggered over to the bed and lay down. Vince brought a cold cloth for my forehead. Paranoid fantasies: the baths must have screwed up my circulation or something! Never had anything like this happen before. They all seemed pretty worried. Vince went to the office and found a doctor who was staying at the resort. She came in, checked me over, gave me the names of some tests I should have made when I get back to the city, but said the chances were 99 to one that it was psychological. Certainly not due to the baths.

By that time it was midafternoon. The headache subsided. We went down to the baths again. Ron, as if thinking it might make me feel better, suggested I file by phone, at their expense, one of the briefer stories I've got stockpiled. So I polished one up a little. Not one of my favorites; but it felt good to be working again. Toyed with the idea of tacking on a message to Max about my kidnapping. But decided it might risk some kind of international confrontation, and I don't after all seem to be in any personal danger.

WORK AND PLAY AMONG THE ECOTOPIANS

Gilroy Hot Springs, June 22. The more I have discovered about Ecotopian work habits, the more amazed I am that their system functions at all. It is not only that they have adopted a 20-hour week; you can't even tell when an Ecotopian is working, and when he is at leisure. During an important discussion in a government office, suddenly everybody will decide to go to the sauna bath. It is true they have worked out informal arrangements whereby, as their phrase has it, they "cover" for each other—somebody stays behind to answer phones and handle visitors. And it is also true that even in the sauna our discussion continued, on a more personal level, which turned out to be quite delightful. But Ecotopian society offers so many opportunities for pleasures and distractions that it is hard to see how people maintain even their present levels of efficiency.

Things happen in their factories, warehouses, and stores which would be quite incredible to our managers and supervisors. I have seen a whole section close down without notice; somebody will bring out beer or marijuana, and a party will ensue, right there amid the crates and machines. Workers in Ecotopian enterprises do not have a normal worker's attitude at all. Perhaps because of their part ownership of them, they seem to regard the plants as home, or at least as their own terrain. They must be intolerable to supervise: the slightest change in work plans is the occasion for a group discussion in which the supervisors (who are elected and thus in a weak position anyway) are given a good deal of sarcastic questioning, and in which their original plans are seldom accepted without change. The supervisors try to take this with good grace, of course, even claiming that the workers often come up with better ideas than they do; and they believe that Ecotopian output per person hour is remarkably high. It may be.

Incidentally, many rather intellectual people seem to be members of the ordinary factory and farm work force. Partly this seems to be due to the relative lack of opportunity for class differentiation in Ecotopia; partly it is due to a deliberate policy which requires students to alternate a year of work with each year of study. This is perhaps one of the most startling arrangements in the whole Ecotopian economy—for not only is the students' education prolonged, but their ideological influence is responsible for many of the new policies that prevail in Ecotopian enterprises. (I was told, for example, that it was students who were originally behind the whole movement toward workers' control.)

Ecotopians are adept at turning practically any situation toward pleasure, amusement, and often intimacy. At first I was surprised by the ease with which they strike up very personal conversations with casual strangers. I have now gotten used to this, indeed I usually enjoy it, especially where the lovely Ecotopian women are concerned. But I am still disconcerted when, after speaking with someone on the street in a loose and utterly unpressured way for perhaps ten minutes, he mentions that he is working and trots off. The distinction between work and non-work seems to be eroding away in Ecotopia, along with our whole concept of jobs as something separate from "real life." Ecotopians, incredibly enough, *enjoy* their work.

Unemployment does not seem to worry Ecotopians in the slightest. There were many unemployed just before Independence, but the switch to a 20-hour week almost doubled the number of jobs—although some were eliminated because of ecological shutdowns and simplifications, and of course the average real income of most families dropped somewhat. Apparently in the transition period when an entirely new concept of living standards was evolving, the country's money policy had to be managed with great flexibility to balance sudden inflationary or deflationary tendencies. But the result now seems to be that, while enterprises are not seriously short of member-workers, there is also no significant number of people involuntarily unemployed. In any case, because of the minimal-guaranteed income system and the core stores, periods of unemployment are not considered disasters or threats by individuals; they are usually put to use, and sometimes deliberately extended, for some kind of creative, educational or recreational purposes. Thus in Ecotopia friends who are unemployed (usually through the collapse of their previous enterprise) often band together and undertake studies that lead them into another enterprise of their own.

If it is sometimes hard to tell whether Ecotopians are working or playing, they are surprisingly generous with their time. I was told, for instance, that many workers in factories put in extra hours to fix machines that have broken down. They evidently regard the 20-hour week quota as applying to productive time only, and take the repair of machinery almost as a sideline responsibility. Or perhaps it is just that they enjoy tinkering: despite the de-emphasis of goods in Ecotopia, people seem to love fixing things. If a bicycle loses a chain or has a flat tire, its rider is soon surrounded by five people volunteering to help fix it. As they do during many casual social encounters, someone will bring out a marijuana cigarette and pass it around; people joke, touch each other, and take turns helping with the work.

The propensity of Ecotopians to touch one another is remarkable. To most Americans, it is offensive to be touched familiarly by a stranger, except under special circumstances, and even friends do not have a great deal of physical contact, which is reserved for lovers and children. The Ecotopians seem to have abandoned such proprieties, and are virtually indiscriminate in their contacts. Adults will pat children approvingly as they go by. Acquaintances routinely shake hands whenever they meet, even if they have seen each other a few hours before, with a novel arm-to-arm clasp. When people sit down to talk, they snuggle up to each other or interlace arms or legs quite intimately. And I have even seen a man in the street walk up to an attractive woman, say something to her with a smile, give her a hug or a stroke on the shoulder, and walk on; the woman continued on her way, with a friendly glance back.

To us, such behavior is a forbidden fantasy. The Ecotopians act out such fantasies all the time. They bathe and take steam baths together freely. Both men and women, not to mention children, stroll public streets arm in arm. Old friends who have not seen each other for some time customarily give each other a warm and extended embrace, and occasionally they even excuse themselves and go off to a private place, evidently for sexual purposes. Naked massage is a common group amusement.

Such looseness in personal contact may be a result of widespread marijuana usage; certainly it is associated with it. One of the riskiest experiments of the new government was to deliberately make marijuana a common weed. Not only were legal prohibitions ended, but free top-quality seeds were distributed, in a campaign aimed at providing "do-it-yourself highs." The result is that every house and apartment can have its own garden or windowbox where the hemp is grown. It is as if, among us, we had a third tap in the kitchen which provided free beer. But most Ecotopians seem to smoke marijuana with considerable discretion, and it is likely that the worst feature of the policy is that it deprives the government of a large source of tax revenue.

(June 23) Last night I made my move. Nerves must have woken me about two o'clock; suddenly felt overwhelmingly anxious to get out of here. Looked around cautiously, surprised they would all be asleep at once; they've grown lax about watching me. Marie, I noticed with a tic of envy, had crawled in with Ron: damn. I felt around for my clothes, wormed into them under the covers. Picked up my shoes, slid softly to the door, and got out. Quiet outside, no wind stirring. Went barefoot for a while; it felt good. Headed away from the concentration of buildings, uphill—once over the brow of the hill I'd

be in the clear. There was a half moon, so I could pick my way all right.

Coming to a clearing on top of a rise, found a small square structure raised on posts, a kind of pavilion with a roof but no walls. Fascinated for some reason, I crept up the ladder for a quick look around. It appeared my route was well chosen. In the moonlight the scene had an unearthly beauty. Saw a huge owl coasting along silently, and realized I could hear the creek, even though it was 50 yards away.

Suddenly there was a rustle and thump directly below the floor of the pavilion, and then a heart-stopping scream. I froze utterly, against one of the posts that supported the roof—not daring to look down through the ladder hole. Dogs instantly began barking in the resort, and in a moment I saw a large tan shape loping off toward the woods—a mountain lion, carrying the rabbit it had seized under the pavilion! By the time I grasped what had happened, and my blood had unfrozen a little, it was too late —two large dogs appeared, barking and sniffing, and a few yards behind them was Vince. I wasn't sure if he had spotted me, but clearly my absence had been noticed; the game was up. I crawled down, rather shakily. "Lion killed a rabbit right under the platform," I said. "That set the dogs barking."

"Scary, isn't it?" Vince said. "Nice night though. How do you like the moon-viewing porch?" "So that's what it is. Actually I was sitting on it, viewing the moon, when that damned monster struck."

He eyed me quietly. "Out for a little walk, huh? Nasty scare number two." "For me, anyway," I said.

"For all of us." We walked back to the cabin. Evidently the others were out searching for me too, but after a bit they came back. Nobody accused me of anything, but a kind of disappointment hung in the air. I felt depressed and confused. For the rest of the night somebody sat guard, reading a paperback

in the corner. Marie went back to her own bed.

After breakfast, finally decided I must face the fact I will stay depressed for a while, and could use some company—so I phoned Marissa. She isn't at all worried my captors are up to anything sinister; didn't exactly make light of my anxieties, but seemed to imply they were pretty excessive. She is doing heavy tree-cutting today, but will come down late tonight or tomorrow. I must get myself together a little, somehow.

(June 25) Dream: I am at home in New York, in my apartment. It must be night, and I am working on a column. I get a tremendous urge to talk to Marissa. I pick up the phone. I give the international operator the instructions, and there is a pause. "I'm sorry, sir, but we cannot complete that call." "Why not?" "We are not allowed to carry traffic to San Francisco at this time." We argue about a possible Vancouver routing, me feeling increasingly frustrated and desperate, the operator driving me crazy with her mindless, "I'm sorry you feel that way, sir." Is something wrong? Has war broken out? All she will say is that she is doing her job. I wake up, furious, thinking of that maniac Jerry in the San Francisco wire office, who used to piss me off because he'd never *just do his job. Jerry would have given me a hard time, maybe, but he would have worked out some clever way to get my call through, even if it had to go via Timbuctu, because he could tell it mattered.*

After that dream, lay awake for a while. Looked around the cabin; my captors were, surprisingly, all asleep again. Maybe they no longer cared. In my imagination I saw myself getting up, sneaking off, hiking to the train, probably making it across the border near Los Angeles by the time they woke up. Could be back in New York by dinner time! Max would still be at the office. I could get hold of Francine, we could hit the town, celebrate my safe return.

Why didn't it sound more inviting? I goaded my imagination on a little, toward the end of the evening with Francine, and the delicious new tricks she was always coming up with. Nothing. All I felt was the warmth of my blankets, the slight chill of country air on my face, and an enormous inclination to just lie there, snug, waiting for dawn, waiting for whatever would happen next.

Marie's eyes opened and she looked over and saw I was awake. "You look better," she whispered. "Go back to sleep!" Then the silly kid blew me a kiss. Next thing I knew it was morning.

Everyone else went down to the baths early, but I didn't feel like it—afraid of my flu coming back or something. Ron stayed with me, sitting in the corner, reading some poetry. I decided to kill a little time by putting my clothes in order. Shook out my New York clothes, laid everything out neatly. Then, just fooling around, thought I'd put on my regular shirt, see how I look—it's been seven weeks since I last wore it, and I had the feeling I've lost some weight out here. It felt sort of comfortable slipping into my cool drip-dry shirt, and I tucked it into the snug pants —first time in weeks that I have had a shirt tucked in. Belt a little loose, but not too bad—one extra notch. Figured what the hell, might as well put on a tie too, just to see what it looks like. I walked over to the mirror, putting the tie around my neck and absently beginning to tie it.

Suddenly I caught sight of myself in the mirror. The hair stood up on the back of my neck. I looked awful, I didn't look human! *My image was tight, stiff. I sat down, stunned. Then, curious, I finished tying the tie, and put on the jacket besides, and went over to the mirror again. This time the ugly American me was almost sickening—I really thought I might have to throw up. I was filled with the desire to get into the hot water of the baths. My body longed to get out of those terrible clothes and sink into the lovely supporting water, and just float there. I pulled the clothes off, threw on a robe, and told Ron (who had watched my clothes experiment without comment) that I wanted to go down to the baths now.*

We took the baths for a long time—I couldn't bear to get out, and sat neck-deep, staring at the water splashing from the pipe, listening to the complicated sounds it made. My body floated weightlessly in the warm, comforting water, feeling only the slightest of sensations. I closed my eyes and sank deeper, with practically nothing but my nose above the water. I lost all sense of horizon, of place—all sense of everything except the steady gurgling of the water coming to me from deep inside the warm earth. I have no idea how long I remained in that state, but suddenly I heard my own voice saying, "I am going to stay in Ecotopia!"—startlingly loud and clear. All at once my head felt light again—and I realized I must have been fighting off saying that for weeks. I stood, rising up out of the water, dripping and smiling and quivering. The quiet of the room was split by shrieks of joy from Marie, and we all staggered up the steps, everybody patting me on the back and hugging me: five grown people, naked, prancing around and laughing and yelling.

We went out into the sweating room, getting curious smiles from people dozing there. Then Vince threw on his big towel like a poncho and dashed out, returning in a minute with Marissa—it seems she had come down late the day before, but they had told her they thought I was about to "break through," as they put it, and she had decided she didn't want to influence the process by her presence, no matter how badly she wanted to see me. She looked splendidly radiant. We hugged and cried a lot, the tears feeling liberating and warming, and the others held onto us, obviously very pleased with themselves. Then we got up, threw on our clothes, and went out-

side. There was a spot nearby with an accumulation of soft dry pine needles, and we began dancing around, kicking them in the air and sliding on them and leaping, Marissa and I doing a sort of courtship dance in the middle, and then walking off together past the moon-viewing porch, up the hill to the foot of a large oak tree, where the spring grass had remained thick and green. We made love slowly, solemnly, feeling the earth heavy and solid beneath us, resting our beings on it, smelling its richness and fertility. When I am with Marissa I feel like all the lusts of the universe are focused through me and onto her; it is supremely intimate and yet almost impersonal at the same time. Afterward she smiled lazily. "Good place to conceive a child," she said, glancing around at the oak. But she wouldn't tell me whether she was in her fertile period, or whether she still had her loop in. "It's my *body," was all she would say. Knowing the kind of commitment she feels to family and the continuity of generations, the idea was profoundly scary—yet I seem to be ready for it.*

After a while we went down the hill, found the others, and went into the baths for a last quick time. Then we headed back to the city, and went to the Cove. Somehow a great party had already been prepared. (Ecotopians are good at impromptu celebrations!) Much to my surprise, Marissa's brother Ben was in the forefront of everything, and played chief host with enthusiasm as great as his earlier bitterness: huge bearhugs and backslapping.

When I decided to publicly thank my mysterious captors for taking me to the hot springs when I was in such bad shape, they insisted Ben share in the honors. "Well," he said, "I will now divulge a state secret. You know, Will, I got so mad I went to Vera Allwen to try and get you thrown out of the country. She wouldn't have any of that. But she thought the hot springs might do you some good, help you get through it all."

I was dumbfounded: that weird old woman must have seen what was going on in my mind when I didn't know it myself. "After all," Ron whispered to me, "Ben did *manage to protect his sister!" It was too much. I began crying openly, happily, amid those shining faces.*

As I write this all down, it is early the next morning. Marissa is still sleeping, black hair a tangle on the pillow. I begin to see that I have fallen in love with her country as much as with Marissa. A new self has been coming to life within me here, thanks to both her and her people. This new me is a stranger, an Ecotopian, and his advent fills me with terror, excitement, and strength. . . . But I am ready for it at last. I don't know what it will all mean, how we will live, or even where. But all the possibilities seem natural and inviting. I want to stay at the forest camp for a while—have never lived in such close touch with natural surroundings, and would like to know what it's like to work with my hands. There are painful breaks ahead with Francine and Pat. I have decided, though, to ask Pat to send the kids out for the summer. If it takes a diplomatic passport, well, the President owes me a favor! And I want to try out some different kinds of writing. There are a lot more things about Ecotopia that the rest of the world needs badly to know. Maybe I can help in that.

EDITORS' EPILOGUE

The foregoing text has been printed from the notebook and news stories written by William Weston during his trip to Ecotopia. Despite the questionable or controversial nature of some of the notebook entries, we have respected Weston's wishes in keeping the text just as he wrote it. Readers may also be interested in the following note, which was enclosed with the notebook when it arrived at the TIMES-POST offices, addressed to the editor-in-chief:

Dear Max—

You told me to go ahead and write the whole story, but I realized, once I had gotten into it, that I couldn't really do that. So I am sending you my notebook, even though I'm not sure what, if anything, you can do with it. As far as I'm concerned, you can pass it around the office, put it in the archives, or print it. (Intact or not at all, please.) I've decided not to come back, Max. You'll understand why from the notebook. But thank you for sending me on this assignment, when neither you nor I knew where it might lead. It led me home.

—WILL

ABOUT THE AUTHOR

ERNEST CALLENBACH lives in Berkeley, California, where he is editor of *Film Quarterly*. He is also the author of *Living Poor with Style*, a pocket encyclopedia of modest and ecologically less damaging life styles. Mr. Callenbach spends a considerable amount of time speaking and promoting his books and his ideas.